"Do we just forget that kiss ever happened?"

"No." Keith's ego hoped that, like him, Treble would find it unforgettable, even if she had made the first move.

"Good. Because, if I'm not mistaken, you were thinking about kissing me, too."

"Thinking isn't the same as doing, Treble."

She gave him a scathing look. "Tell me about it."

He blinked, feeling as though the tables had been turned with no warning. "Now you make it sound like I should apologize. For what? Exercising self-control?"

Self-control? Yeah, sure. Right up until the moment he'd seen it coming, thought *hell, yes* and bent into the kiss like a man rushing to his doom....

Dear Reader,

I have always been fascinated with coming-home stories, perhaps because as an army brat, we moved around too much to have a true "hometown." (However, I *was* born in Tennessee, just like my heroine Treble James. But while I may have got into a smidge of trouble here and there, I was nothing like the hellion Treble was growing up. Honest.) In *Trouble in Tennessee*, Treble agrees to visit her pregnant sister, a nervous first-time mommy, even though the visit will take Treble back to Joyous, Tennessee, and face-to-face with her bad-girl past.

The trip also brings her face-to-face with handsome town newcomer Dr. Keith Caldwell. The last thing Keith needs is a dead-end fling with a woman who will probably be sprinting out of town the second her niece is born, and the last thing Treble needs is yet one more person in her life judging her. However, the more Treble and Keith get to know each other, the more they find in common, including past loss and an attraction that just might have a future.

If you enjoy Treble and Keith's story, please drop me a note at t.michaels@earthlink.net. You can also check my Web site, www.tanyamichaels.com, for news about my next Harlequin American Romance novel set in the fictional town of Joyous, due out in 2008.

Best wishes,

Tanya

Trouble in Tennessee
TANYA MICHAELS

HARLEQUIN®

TORONTO • NEW YORK • LONDON
AMSTERDAM • PARIS • SYDNEY • HAMBURG
STOCKHOLM • ATHENS • TOKYO • MILAN • MADRID
PRAGUE • WARSAW • BUDAPEST • AUCKLAND

ISBN-13: 978-0-373-75174-7
ISBN-10:   0-373-75174-5

TROUBLE IN TENNESSEE

www.eHarlequin.com

Printed in U.S.A.

ABOUT THE AUTHOR

Tanya Michaels started telling stories almost as soon as she could talk…and started stealing her mom's Harlequin romances less than a decade later. In 2003 Tanya was thrilled to have her first book, a romantic comedy, published by Harlequin Books. Since then, Tanya has sold nearly twenty books and is a two-time recipient of the Booksellers' Best Award as well as a finalist for a Holt Medallion, National Readers' Choice Award and Romance Writers of America's prestigious RITA® Award. Tanya lives in Georgia with her husband, two preschoolers and an unpredictable cat, but you can visit Tanya online at www.tanyamichaels.com.

Books by Tanya Michaels

HARLEQUIN TEMPTATION
968—HERS FOR THE WEEKEND
986—SHEER DECADENCE
1008—GOING ALL THE WAY

HARLEQUIN NEXT
DATING THE MRS. SMITHS
THE GOOD KIND OF CRAZY
MOTHERHOOD WITHOUT PAROLE

For Jen, with five years' worth of gratitude. Thank you for everything you've taught me, for laughing at my jokes, for helping me find the right home for this story and for your uncanny ability to always pick the perfect restaurant.

Chapter One

"Please?" The word was simple and dignified. As if it hadn't been preceded by twenty minutes of cajoling.

Even though they were on the phone, Treble James could picture the earnest expression in her half sister's big blue eyes. "Charity, you know I'll make time to visit after the baby is born, but—"

"How would I know that? You've been back home to Joyous all of, let me think, *once* in the past decade."

Maybe that was because Joyous, Tennessee, had never quite lived up to its name for Treble. *Stifling, Tennessee.* That *would have been appropriate.*

"I was there for your wedding," Treble pointed out, keeping a wary eye on the digital clock atop her bedroom nightstand. "You don't think I'd make the trip for you again?"

"Then make it now," her sister begged. It was unlike Charity to request favors, particularly those that inconvenienced other people. "I'm scared. The books say placenta previa isn't all that uncommon, and my OB says mine isn't a severe case and that panicking is no good for me or the baby…but I'm a first-time mommy. Having my big sister here would make me feel better. Besides, being on bed rest is driving me nuts! Come tell me dirty jokes or something, keep me from killing my poor husband."

Charity doing harm to *any* living creature was laughable, but to Bill Sumner? They'd been smitten with each other since high school, as evidenced by their marrying shortly after Charity's graduation. It blew Treble's mind that her sister, at twenty-two, was expecting a child and had already been married four years. She hadn't even been old enough to drink champagne at her own wedding! Treble had taken it upon herself to imbibe enough for both of them.

It had been the best way to cope with being in Joyous two weeks after a bad breakup with the boyfriend who was supposed to have been her date. Twenty-nine-year-old Treble's relationship record—in contrast to Bill and Charity's seven years together—was about six months.

"Charity, I don't want to cut you off, but I need to leave for work, so—"

"You know what being pregnant makes you think about? Motherhood. I'm about to have my own little girl, and I wish Mom… Even though you've never been pregnant, you're my closest female relative. It would mean the world to me if you were here right now. *Mom* would have wanted that, her two girls together."

Treble did a double take, actually staring at the receiver. "I thought you were the good sister. Since when do you use emotional blackmail?"

"Is it working?"

Yes. "I really do have to leave for the station." Charity's soft-spoken barb had found its mark, though. Despite Treble's cynical shell, she retained weak spots for her late mother and younger sister.

"All right." Charity sighed. "I'm sorry to dump this on you. I know you have a career, a life in Georgia beyond all of us, but I miss you, Treb. And I love you."

"Love you, too, brat." The epithet had become a term of endearment over the years, but this evening it seemed particularly applicable. Didn't her sister *know* what she was asking? To go to Tennessee early and just wait around for Charity's due date in July…

Few citizens of Joyous would welcome Treble with open

arms. *More like the sign of the cross.* She'd been a somewhat, ah, spirited youth, and folks in small towns had long memories.

Treble hung up, catching sight of herself in the oval mirror on the wall. "Don't give me that look," she chastised her reflection. "You don't want to go back any more than I do."

Talking to herself? Never a good sign. But Treble, a weeknight DJ for an Atlanta pop station, was used to addressing an audience. An audience she'd be late for if she didn't get moving.

Although she would be in-studio tonight and not doing a remote broadcast at one of the clubs she occasionally visited, she stopped long enough to run a brush through the dark ringlets that spilled past her shoulder blades and to apply her favorite dark red lip gloss. Even if her listeners couldn't see her, it helped her get into character for "Trouble J," one of the most popular noncommuting show hosts in the city. While the best airtime was in the mornings and afternoons, when most of the working crowd was stuck in gridlock on I-75, I-85 or the 285 loop around Atlanta, Treble held damn good ratings for her period and liked the late hours that allowed her to sleep in on weekdays and leave her weekend free for a social life. Not, she reflected as she headed toward the parking garage, that she'd had much of one lately.

The last guy to ask her out had been a producer on one of the station's other shows, and she wasn't interested in merging her professional life with her personal life. The producer aside, she'd been subtly discouraging men for several months. She had been busy booking extra personal appearances for her off-hours, making the most of her minor celebrity status. The additional funds deposited into her savings account were the start of a down payment. Maybe it was the almost-thirty part of her, but when spring had bloomed, she'd actually been sorry she didn't have a real house to subject to seasonal cleaning, and a yard to enjoy instead of a railed-in concrete balcony.

It was time she found a home of her own—a paradoxically domestic wish for a woman who would be on the air from seven-thirty to midnight playing rock songs interspersed with risqué commentary. Well, risqué within proper FCC guidelines, of course. No matter how grown up she was or where she moved, there was always *someone* who'd disapprove of her.

And in Joyous, Tennessee? Possibly hundreds of someones.

So what? Outside of ratings, she never cared what strangers thought. Witness "Trusty," the eyesore of a car parked among other residents' vehicles. If cars were status symbols, what did the hatchback say about her? *That you take risks.* It had been used when she purchased it during college, and couldn't possibly have much life left in it. Still, now that it was paid off, she wanted to get her financing approved for a house before taking on new monthly bills.

But her rebellious attitude and antistatus-symbol car aside, opinions in Joyous would carry more weight than most. Maybe she was sensitive because some of the criticism from the town's citizens would be deserved. After all, she had been something of a hellion, sneaking out to meet Rich Danner her sophomore year, trying to use a fake ID to get into Duke's bar and "borrowing" her stepfather's car to attend a rock concert two counties over after Harrison had refused to let her go with friends. The fall of her junior year, there had also been that period of indiscriminate and outrageous flirting. Everyone had heard about Rich dumping her before he left for college. She'd tried to hide her broken heart with drawled comments and suggestive smiles directed at any boy in range—even a cute chemistry teacher.

Despite the exaggerated gossip, she hadn't meant to cause breakups between other classmates or steal anyone's boyfriend. She *certainly* hadn't planned for anything to ever happen with the chemistry teacher, no matter what the nervous guidance counselor had told Harrison in a meeting about Treble's "acting out" for attention. The memory of Harrison Breckfield's icy condemnation as he'd walked Treble to his car was enough to make her shiver even now. Harrison didn't believe his wife's death was any excuse for misbehavior. He'd pointed out savagely that *Charity* had lost a mother, too, yet continued to be a perfectly respectable daughter. Even if Treble had known how to articulate her unspoken insecurities, pride probably would have kept her from asking if Harrison had ever loved Treble, the born troublemaker, as he did his own child.

He had been the adult in the situation. Couldn't he have reached out to his stepdaughter just once and assured her of her place in his home? Still, were bitter memories of Harrison not being there for Treble a valid reason not to be there for Charity now?

ON SATURDAY, Treble's only scheduled appearance was at a mall grand opening midafternoon. *Let's just hope I don't blow the small stipend I'm getting on cute shoes before I even leave the premises.* Ah, retail therapy. Thank God for clearance sales and outlet stores.

A coworker from the station had recently invited her to do some outlet shopping near the Georgia-Tennessee border— Treble's enjoyment over her finds had been marred by the guilt of being less than an hour and a half from the pregnant sister she hadn't seen in four years. Treble knew she'd been a disappointment as a daughter, but did that mean she was doomed to be a bad sister, too?

Stop it. She refused to spend a sunny June morning cooped up in her apartment, agonizing over Charity's recent request. At the very least, Treble could agonize by the pool.

After loading this morning's juice cup and cereal bowl into the dishwasher, Treble changed into a fuchsia-striped bikini.

"You're so lucky," Charity had said back when she'd been selecting bridesmaid dresses. "You can pull off *any* color. I have to stay within three main hues or look so washed out I scare people."

Untrue. Charity looked like an angel, a beautifully blond vision of their mother. Petite, fine-boned with flawless porcelain skin. Treble took after her biological father, the first of many men who'd been unable to commit to her. When she'd tracked him down after leaving Joyous, she'd been surprised at how handsome he still was. But the dimpled persona and rich drawl were just superficial niceties.

Treble had inherited his height, dark hair, bold features and almond eyes. *And his tendency to run away?* No, her leaving Joyous had been best for everyone, not an act of cowardice. Trouble J was audacious and unafraid.

She packed a tote bag bearing the station's call letters with a towel, SPF protection, a black pen and a Sudoku book—one of the assistants at the station got her hooked on the puzzles—then hurried toward the front door. Fresh air would do her a world of good.

Outside, the warmth embraced her. Though the sun would be punishing in large doses, she looked forward to stretching out for a little while like a relaxed feline basking in the rays. Treble had barely situated herself in a poolside lounge chair when she heard her name called. She peered over the top of her sunglasses at the smiling Latina woman in a one-piece suit coming through the gate.

"Hey, Alana." Treble waved, then waited for her friend to come closer so that they weren't yelling over the commotion of kids splashing in the pool.

Alana Torres was a fellow tenant and friend. Sometimes Treble got the woman passes into clubs where Treble was broadcasting. Both of them were fans of high-octane action films, and they went to a lot of movies together when they were mutually between boyfriends. The curvy bank teller, however, had been seeing an airline pilot since February.

"Haven't seen much of you lately," Treble said as her friend dragged a chair closer across the concrete. "But seeing you now, you look incredible. *Muy caliente.*"

The woman lowered her dark eyes but smiled proudly. "Thanks. I haven't entirely adjusted to the new haircut." Since they'd known each other, Alana had worn her thick black hair long, but had had about six inches taken off recently.

"It's sophisticated." Treble put her hands behind her and lifted her own hair off her neck. "And probably a lot cooler."

"My high school reunion is this month. I know it's shallow, but I'm determined to look hot. Chubby girl's prerogative."

"I doubt you were ever as chubby as you felt, and you've already lost—what, fifteen pounds?"

"Twelve."

"Promise me you won't drop so much that you turn bony, okay?"

Alana laughed as she opened her sunblock. The citrus scent was strong, but preferable to the chlorine from the water. "Yeah, *that's* likely to happen, given the way I'm addicted to the bakery across the street from the bank. Whoever invented soup in a loaf of bread was a diabolical genius."

To Alana, baked goods equaled what cute shoes were to Treble—an irresistible vice.

Glancing around, Alana lowered her voice. "Thank goodness Greg has such stamina and creativity when it comes to helping me burn calories."

"You mean his suggestions are more fun than jogging?" Treble grinned. "No, seriously, I'm asking. It's been so long that I barely remember what it's like to…burn calories."

Alana returned her smile. "Your listeners would never believe you. I heard some of the advice you gave your callers last night and, girl, where *do* you get those naughty ideas?"

"Repressed sexual energy. It leads to a rich fantasy life."

"You had a great show. I know you tease that your main concern is boosting the ratings, but I think you enjoy helping people. You're a generous soul."

Yeah, so generous she wasn't even bothering to examine her schedule for the possibility of lending physical and moral support to her only sibling. Treble heaved a sigh.

"Don't tell me work's not going well?" Alana asked, misinterpreting her friend's brief frown.

"It's not the radio thing, it's… You know the expression 'you can't go home again'? Let's just say I always clung to that as kind of a guarantee."

"Okay. And…?"

"Someone I really care about wants me to take a few weeks out of my life and go home. I think I'd rather have my show canceled."

Alana winced. "*That* awful?"

"Hard to say. I've managed to avoid finding out for the past four years and was tipsy for part of my last long weekend there." Her behavior had fuelled the fires of gossip.

While she wasn't proud that she'd had too much to drink at Charity's wedding, she didn't feel she should have to apologize, either. The person with the real right to be annoyed was the bride, who had been so starry-eyed over Bill anyway, she wouldn't have noticed if Treble had set herself on fire at the rehearsal dinner. In fact, one of the underaged bridesmaids had downed four glasses of champagne at the reception and thrown up in a topiary, garnering nothing but an off-color joke and some pitying "Guess she learned the hard way" comments. Treble, on the other hand, had been a legally drinking adult who neither table-danced nor drove anywhere while under the influence. Couldn't a girl nurse a broken heart with a few festive libations without, the next day, her stepfather acting as though an intervention was in order? It was as if he held her to a high standard of behavior, then watched her, waiting for her to screw up.

Harrison had financed the open bar in the first place! Why was it no one minded when weathered, old farmhand Bobby Charles Picoult got buzzed on draft beer and started loudly guffawing at the same anecdotes he'd been telling since Treble first moved to Joyous as a girl? *Because Bobby Charles is local color. You're an outsider.* Even though Treble had moved to Joyous right before kindergarten, by the time she'd left, she'd felt completely out of place. She doubted anyone besides her sister had been sorry to see her go. Even poor Charity had probably been relieved at the decrease in tension at home.

"A few weeks is a long time," Alana pointed out loyally. "Do you have that much vacation? Whoever asked should completely understand if you say no."

"Charity would understand. It's not in her to whine or hold a grudge." The thought made denying the request even more difficult somehow.

Well, Alana's right, a few weeks is *a substantial chunk of time.* Weren't first babies often overdue? There'd been a woman at the station who'd seemed pregnant for, like, a year; by the end of it, she'd been miserable, the size of a house and threatening violent death to anyone stupid enough to ask, "Still haven't had that kid?" Treble couldn't imagine sitting around her sister's house waiting for an unknown date.

"I know what you mean about not wanting to go back," Alana said. "I skipped my five-year reunion. I told myself it was because I was busy that weekend and most of the people I cared to keep in touch with, I already was. But that was just rationalizing. At the time, I'd been interning for a company, making less than minimum wage and sharing a closet-sized apartment with three other girls, but that job was supposed to lead to a great full-time position. Until the corporation declared bankruptcy and cut their losses, me included."

Treble shot her friend a sympathetic look. Interning had been crucial to getting Treble's foot in the door at the station, and she would have been devastated if no job had materialized. She loved having her own show, loved her listeners and the relative freedom of sharing her opinion over the airwaves.

"In high school," Alana continued, "I was one of those socially acceptable nerds. Chubby and awkward, never with an actual date to a dance, but smart enough that I had my own niche with the other straight-A geeks. So when the reunion rolled around and I was minus a job and plus the college 'freshman fifteen' I never lost… It's frustrating how the least healthy food is usually the cheapest. I felt like a total failure."

"You're not! Corporate America has many problems, none of them a reflection on your abilities. Also, you're gorgeous."

"Now, maybe. And it's sickening how much I want other people to see that. I've asked myself a dozen times why I even care what they think."

"Ever come up with an answer?" Treble's comparatively small graduating class held an annual reunion in conjunction with the town's July festival. She'd never once been tempted to attend.

"I don't know." Alana shifted on her lounger. "I think for most of us, adolescence is when we were the most insecure and vulnerable. Maybe when we're around the people who knew us then, we think they can see those insecurities. Or maybe their presence brings back all our vulnerabilities the way catching an old song on the radio can lead to visceral déjà vu."

Tell me about it. When Treble had helped deejay parties in college, there were one or two songs with such negative personal connotations that she tried never to play them. Then there was music that to this day made her feel good all over. Particularly the U2 song that had been on the radio her junior year at university when Brady McCall had…

"Something funny?" Alana asked. "You sure are grinning."

"Um, it's nothing."

"Liar."

"Ask me about it next time you invite me over for peach daiquiris."

"It's a date." Alana scowled. "I'm going to hate it when you finally find your dream home and move out of the complex."

"Hey, I'm looking in the metro area! Aren't you spending half your time at Greg's place anyway?"

"More like three quarters. So I guess I'm being a tad hypocritical about hating to see you leave. How *is* the house hunt going?"

"It's on hiatus until I've saved up more. Nothing I saw was quite right anyway. Even the ones that didn't need so many repairs felt…off. During a walk-through, I told the agent it's like the perfect pair of shoes—occasionally I see some that are adorable, match an outfit I have exactly, but when I slide them on, they're not comfortable. They're just not me."

"Maybe homes are something you have to break in, like boots?"

"Maybe. But when it's worth the blisters, you know. No sense in my shelling out my life savings for something that's wrong. I want a place that's *mine,* one where I belong." Although the only place where she'd truly felt that sense of belonging was at the station, her employers would frown on her sleeping in the studio, but, at least there, they liked Trouble.

Some of the people in her past would never like her, never approve of her, but avoiding them wouldn't change that. What if visiting Joyous was not only a chance to help Charity but an opportunity for Treble to return on her own terms? She wasn't expecting citizens to be thrilled to see her or her stepfather to applaud her job as a titillating radio host, but perhaps once she looked them all in the eyes and knew for sure that their opinion didn't matter, memories of the past would lose their mythical power over her. She'd be free to visit her bouncing baby niece without dreading the homecoming.

On her next birthday, Treble would be thirty. Wasn't that grown up enough to stop letting Joyous be some geographical boogeyman in her life? Maybe once she'd slayed the demons of her one-time home, she could return to Atlanta and start building a home that was truly hers.

Chapter Two

"Trusty, you move your chassis now," Treble instructed the car, "or I swear I'm renaming you!" *Traitorous Pile of Junk* had a nice ring to it.

As warnings went, hers lacked oomph, but she didn't want to threaten dismantling in case that invited even worse vehicular karma. The air conditioner had sputtered and died before she cleared north Georgia, blowing only warm air until she gave up and rolled down the windows. Then the fuel light had come on, alarming her. She should have had a full tank of gas…unless there was a leak? Not even wanting to contemplate that, she'd been thrilled when the light turned off by itself. Maybe the gas had just been sloshing around as she drove through mountainous territory and temporarily confused the monitoring mechanism.

Most recently, the "check engine" light had begun flashing. Concerned, she'd pulled onto a wide shoulder alongside fenced meadows to give Trusty a chance to cool down. After all, Treble rarely drove for this long at a stretch; the car might simply be overworked. Treble's sensible plan had backfired, however, now that the hatchback wouldn't start again. Turning the key only produced a grating sound that made Treble want to get out and kick something.

"This is the thanks I get for assuring Charity you're roadworthy?" she asked the vehicle in exasperation.

Her sister had been *ecstatic* when Treble called Monday afternoon to say she was making the trip to Joyous. Treble had accumulated some vacation time at the station and almost never called in sick. All she'd had to do was explain to her manager that her pregnant younger sister was experiencing complications, and the father of four had been happy to help her schedule some replacement talent.

"It's a nice way for up-and-comers to get experience and start building a name," he'd reminded her. "We can also do a week of 'best of' clips where we replay interviews of favorite guests or phone segments. You go take care of your sister—just don't get too 'down-home' on us. We need you full of sass and attitude when you get back."

"Don't worry," she'd assured him. "I am all attitude."

"I can't believe you're really coming!" Charity had squealed when she heard the news.

Neither can I, Treble had thought. "I should be in Wednesday afternoon. Or evening. I'm not what you call an early riser."

"We'll be watching for you. What are you driving these days?"

"Same car as always."

There had been a brief pause before Charity said, "Maybe you should look into flights."

Ridiculous. The nearest airport to Joyous was in Chattanooga. By the time Treble drove to Hartsfield—two hours early to allow for security and long check-in lines—caught her plane in Atlanta, deboarded in Chattanooga and met Charity's husband for the ride to Joyous, it would have been just as quick to drive straight there. Besides, while Treble had talked herself into making this journey, keeping a getaway car at her disposal was mandatory.

"So much for being a reliable escape plan," she growled at her motionless hatchback. She hadn't expected a triumphant return, but she would have preferred something less embarrassing than being dragged into town limits by a tow truck.

Picking up her cell phone, she said a quick prayer that she could get a decent signal out here. She exhaled a whoosh of relief when the call to her sister's house went through.

"Hello?"

"Hey, Charity. It's Treble. I don't suppose Bill's there?" Bill worked in the office of a milk plant for Breckfield Dairy Farms and Creamery, but he'd been keeping sporadic hours to look after his wife. *One of the perks of the CEO being your father-in-law.* "I have a car question for him."

"He and Dad went to look at some heifers one county over, but they'll be back by dinner. Just how urgent is this question?"

Treble wondered how long it would be before any other drivers came down the two-lane road. "Oh…fairly urgent."

"I knew it!" Charity's voice took on a breathless, panicked rhythm. "That darn car. It's crapped out on you, hasn't it?"

As much as she would have liked to assure her sister otherwise, there was no escaping the reality of the situation. "Pretty much. But maybe we can save the I-told-you-so's until after we've rounded up a mechanic?"

"Well, that would be Ronnie over at Carter and Sons, but Carter closes for a late lunch every day from two to three. How far away are you?" Charity listened, did some mental calculations, then decided, "I could have Doc Caldwell come get you. Ronnie can go back with the tow truck later, but there's no sense in you just waiting on the side of the road."

"Who is Doc Caldwell, and what makes you think he's available smack-dab in the middle of the day on Wednesday?"

"A friend and sometimes fishing buddy of Dad's. He's Doc Monaghan's replacement, moved to town right after Bill and I found out I was pregnant."

Doc Monaghan had been the general practitioner in Joyous who'd told Treble's mom that she was pregnant with Charity and later diagnosed Treble's tonsillitis. He had to have been nearing seventy by the time Charity got married, so it was about time the town brought in someone else. Hopefully this Doc Caldwell still had a few good years left in him before retirement.

"As far as his schedule," Charity continued, "he told Bill he didn't have many appointments and could check in on me. I keep promising these men I won't do anything more strenuous than get up to pee, but apparently they don't believe me. I'd just as soon sic the doctor on you as have company show up when I'd rather be napping. Afternoons hit me hardest."

Treble laughed. "If asking him to come get me will gain you a little peace, I suppose you should do it."

Ten minutes later, Charity called back to say the man was on his way.

"Sorry I didn't have any distinctive landmarks to give him," Treble said, looking around at a whole lot of nothing. Wildflowers dotted the roadside, and bales of hay had been spaced across the meadow for unseen cows. Some people might find the pastoral scene beneath the blue sky and cotton-ball clouds soothing, but the charm had worn off, leaving Treble antsy for air-conditioning and antihistamine.

"Don't worry," Charity said. "He knows that if he sees Peggy's Pancake House he's gone too far. How many brunettes stranded inside old hatchbacks do you think he's going to pass between here and there?"

"Good point." So Treble settled into her car, which she was thinking of having compressed into a doorstop, and waited. She considered turning on the radio to help kill time, but taxing the battery was probably a bad idea.

To keep from screaming in boredom or thinking much about the inevitable moment she saw her stepfather tonight, she pulled out her omnipresent Sudoku book, but she couldn't concentrate. Instead, she grabbed a small manicure kit from her duffel bag. Her fingernails were looking ragged and could use some attention.

She'd finished applying a second coat of metallic blue polish when a pickup truck rounded a bend up ahead and came toward her in the opposite lane. The scuffed white Chevy veered onto the grassy shoulder across the road and parked. From her position, Treble could tell it was a man driving, but between distance, dusty windows and the billed cap he wore, any other details were obscured.

Wondering if this was her stepfather's buddy or just a random soul stopping to offer assistance, Treble watched with unabashed curiosity. The truck door opened and a pair of long, denim-encased legs unfolded. In addition to the jeans, the stranger wore a green polo shirt, the short sleeves loosely molding nice shoulders and revealing equally nice forearms. She climbed out of her car, experiencing a tingle of prurient appreciation over the man's chiseled profile as he looked both ways for nonexistent traffic. The cautious habit made her grin, and she was still smiling as he reached her. As he got closer, she realized he was taller than her five foot ten by at least three inches.

Hellooo, Good-Looking Samaritan.

Beneath the Tennessee Vols cap he wore, he had thick brown hair and a fantastic face. Not blandly attractive in the urbane "metrosexual" way as some of her guy friends back in Atlanta, but rugged. Though he couldn't be much older than Treble, there was a lot of character in the intriguing planes and angles of his face, the slashes bracketing sensual lips where dimples might appear when he smiled, the deep, deep blue eyes.

Charity had sky-blue eyes, nearly pastel. This man's were dark like the ocean with serious potential for undercurrents that could suck a girl in without her realizing. Or protesting.

"Treble?"

Her body warmed when he said her name, making her feel silly. "You know me?" Had they gone to school together in Joyous? With her somewhat public antics, there were plenty of people who might recognize her before she recognized them, but she imagined this guy would have left an impression even as a teen.

"No, I haven't had the pleasure." He shoved the cap back on

his head, that blue gaze sliding over her in assessment. "Keith Caldwell. Charity sent me."

Treble was dimly aware of gaping. This broad-shouldered man with the piercing gaze and large hands, currently resting with thumbs hooked in his front pockets, was Doc Caldwell? Women in Joyous must be forming lines down Main Street just to get their temperatures checked—though a fever in the good doctor's presence seemed a foregone conclusion.

HIS BRAIN ON autopilot, Keith extended a hand toward the woman in front of him. "Nice to meet you."

There was a framed wedding picture on Charity and Bill's mantel that included Treble, but the flesh-and-blood version looked less like the satin-clad demure brunette in the back row of a bridal party and more like the wild-child stories he'd heard since moving to Joyous. He'd never asked Harrison or Charity to expound on the gossip about the "ungrateful stepdaughter" and her unlawful habits of shoplifting and grand theft auto. Keith knew what it was like not to want to discuss a painful family past or self-destructive siblings.

"I'd shake your hand," Treble drawled, "but I just painted my nails." She waggled her fingers near her face long enough for him to notice the flash of blue, a color choice that made him think momentarily of frostbite.

He almost laughed at the irony since everything else about this woman said *hot*.

She wore a cropped black T-shirt, with sleeves so short it was almost a tank top, and denim shorts. While her outfit wasn't unduly revealing for June, she definitely showed a tantalizing amount of supple skin. There was even a light sheen of sweat across her rosy cheeks. Whether she'd wanted her hair off her neck because it was cooler or she just customarily wore it up, she'd pulled the wavy mass into a haphazard topknot with a sparkly black barrette. Several strands fell free, however, giving her a look that was arrestingly bold when combined with her full lips, high forehead and the tiny cleft in her chin. Each detail from the almost indefinably exotic shape of her dark eyes to the sliver of bared skin at her midriff suggested she was a girl who liked to color outside the lines.

Or was he projecting based on speculation?

"You about done looking?" Treble asked, her tone amused.

Keith's face warmed. He felt as awkward as a teenager caught ogling a hot substitute teacher. "Sorry. Guess I was surprised. For sisters, you and Charity don't look alike."

Treble's eyes narrowed. "Half sisters. I'm sure as a doctor you understand how having different fathers leads to very different genetic makeup."

Which part was she touchy about, Charity or the father situation? Harrison certainly looked tense whenever someone made mention of his stepdaughter. The last thing the older man needed right now was more tension, although that was something the family would have to sort out themselves.

For now, best to change the subject to something that didn't make her glare daggers. "What all do we need to grab out of your car before we lock it up and go?"

"I have a couple of suitcases in the trunk." She turned on her heel and headed toward the back of the vehicle.

Keith wished he could realistically offer to help get the car started, but his specialty was fixing people, not automobiles. He'd leave the mechanical maintenance to the professionals. Treble hefted two bright red suitcases, and he reached to take them from her.

She frowned, not letting go. "I'm able-bodied, Dr. Caldwell."

"And so gracious," he said mildly. "Why do I feel like we got off to a bad start?"

Silently, she handed over the cases, then ran a hand through her hair as if she'd forgotten it was pulled back, further dislodging ringlets that fell into her face. "Sorry. It's been a stressful day."

"Well, don't worry. Ronnie will take care of your car, for sure."

Treble laughed dryly. She followed him to the truck, strangely rigid for a woman with blue fingernails and carefree curls. There was more on her mind than automotive problems, but he didn't pry. She didn't owe him explanations in return for the ride. In fact, Keith frequently sought out chances to do favors for Harrison Breckfield and Charity.

Keith had first seen moving to Joyous as an escape—from the double loss he'd suffered in Savannah, from the chaos of working in an Atlanta E.R.—but it had become more than that. With the endorsement of the town's leading citizen, Keith had gradually become a true part of the community. He had a brand-new life and was aware of how much he owed to Harrison's support. When you were replacing a town institution like Doc Monaghan, people didn't warm to you right away. Some old-timers didn't cotton to the idea of progress and had repeatedly stressed the way Monaghan had done things. Meanwhile, husbands and fathers expressed discomfort—and occasional outrage—at the thought of Keith examining their wives and adolescent daughters. A few people had actually chosen to drive to the GP in nearby Devlin rather than visit "that young newcomer."

Harrison Breckfield, however, had been propelled into the downtown clinic five months ago when he'd experienced chest pains. After a brief subsequent stay at the county hospital, Harrison had taken Keith under his wing. He'd invited the younger man to dinner, given him a tour of the original Breckfield Dairy—part of a Southeastern empire with its own line of milk, yogurts, cottage cheese and desserts—and made it clear to the townspeople the new doctor was to be trusted and accepted. Following that first dinner at Harrison's gigantic house, office appointments had doubled and other invitations had gradually trickled in. Keith loved this town, its slow rhythm and the way he'd been accepted here. Though it would be crass to think of them as replacements for the sister who drowned or the father who later died, Harrison, Charity and her husband were the closest thing to family Keith had found since his mom remarried while he was away at college. If only Keith could pay back the older man's generosity by getting Harrison to take his heart problems more seriously….

Temporarily lost in thought, Keith hadn't realized how quiet it was in the cab of the truck.

"Um, Keith? Is it cool with you if I turn on the radio?"

"Of course. Sorry, I'm usually more companionable than this, I was just thinking about…a patient."

"Stumped by a medical mystery?" she asked. "I occasionally tape episodes of *House.*"

He laughed. "Nothing that dramatic. And only a really talented actor can pull off that bedside manner. The people of Joyous expect someone more traditional."

"You got that right," she muttered, a scowl darkening her face. But then she forced a smile and reached for the radio dials. A twangy ballad about a redneck Romeo seeking his honky-tonk Juliet spilled from the speakers.

"Yeesh." She punched the buttons quickly.

"Not a fan of country music?" he asked. There were a few other options in this neck of the woods, but not many.

"My view on music mirrors my philosophy on men," she told him with a mischievous glance. "I don't have just one type, but I am selective. That song was bad on many levels. Ah. This is more like it." She'd landed on a classic rock station for the opening chords of a late-seventies hit.

Keith smiled as he turned up the volume. "This one's a little before your time, isn't it?"

"Baby, I'm *timeless.*" She flashed him a grin that nearly had him skidding off the road.

It occurred to him that, since moving to Joyous, he'd been subjected to a much different male-female dynamic than he'd known in his twenties. Lately, potential romances involved aging couples with single daughters inviting him to Sunday dinner or available women bringing him frozen casseroles and gelatin molds. Treble hadn't meant anything by her throwaway comment, but there was a lot to be said for a brazen smile and baby-doll T-shirt over a strawberry gelatin salad.

Not that Keith would ever do more than appreciate from a cautious distance the smile that belonged to the notorious prodigal stepdaughter of Harrison Breckfield. As appealing as she might be, the woman had *trouble* written all over her, and that was the last thing Keith needed in his new life.

Chapter Three

By the time they'd rolled into town on picturesque streets flanked by storefronts and pink flowering crepe myrtles, Treble was so tense she felt as if her neck muscles might actually shatter. If Keith had noticed, he hadn't commented. About all he'd done was occasionally bob his head in an endearing manner along to guitar riffs and drum solos. Maybe he was oblivious to her stress, but weren't doctors trained to be observant? She'd *flinched* when they'd passed the town limits sign.

Technically it read Welcome To Joyous, Home of Famous Breckfield Ice Cream, but judging from her suddenly clammy palms and the unpleasant way her stomach had flipped, it might as well have proclaimed, Abandon Hope All Ye Who Enter Here. *Get a grip, girlfriend. Nothing scares you, remember?* Well, except low ratings and spiders. She was only human.

A fan had asked her once if she ever worried about losing her train of thought or not knowing just the right comeback. Treble could say she truly wasn't too worried about that. Saying something that got her called into the boss's office the next morning was possible, but speechlessness? Unlike her. In fact, in times of nervous crisis, she usually talked *more,* relying on her radio persona until she felt balanced again.

She relied on chatting now. "Will you be taking me straight to my sister's or are we going to the garage first?"

"Your call."

"I do like an accommodating man."

He shot her a quick look with those too-dark blue eyes. A shiver—the good kind—rippled through her.

"Penny for your thoughts," she said.

The corner of his mouth quirked. "Doctors make decent money, even out here. I can afford to keep this to myself."

"Spoilsport. Do you need to rush back to the practice?" she asked. "I missed lunch and owe you for the ride. I could buy us some barbecue."

"Not necessary. This was a favor for Charity. But if you're hungry, I'll stop and eat with you."

A favor for Charity. There'd been a protective note in his voice. If her sister weren't so happily married, Treble might have entertained a twinge of envy. As it was, she found herself curious.

"So…you're pretty good friends with my family?"

"Yes, ma'am."

She waited for him to elaborate before realizing he'd completed the thought and showed no signs of voicing another. Treble was nothing if not hardheaded, a trait her mother had remarked upon often. "How did you meet them?"

"In a town this size? I've met most everyone."

She already knew he wasn't as talkative by nature as she was, but now she got the distinct impression he was actually stonewalling her. Did he not want to discuss her family? It wasn't as if she were a stranger nosing around for Breckfield secret recipes, for crying out loud. She was making small talk. Okay, and prying a little, too, but they were *her* family.

Maybe she should tackle his instead. "Do you have relatives in the area?"

"No." His jaw tightened in punctuation.

Well, she was just batting a thousand. By the time they parked in front of Adam's Ribs, her appetite was no longer her top concern. What had Keith heard about her? Charity wouldn't have said anything bad, not purposefully, but the doctor was a friend of Harrison's. Had her stepfather disparaged her? Was he glad she'd done the sisterly thing by coming home, or did he wish she was still in another state? Treble told herself she didn't personally care, she just didn't want any latent tension or awkward moments upsetting Charity this late in a complicated pregnancy.

Whatever bad karma was responsible for her defunct car apparently hadn't finished toying with her. Feeling borderline apprehensive already, the *last* person she needed to see the second she stepped into the smoke-scented restaurant was Rich Danner. *Now you know that's not true, Treb. It could have been Mitchell Reyes…* But her mind immediately shied away from that memory and the pain associated with it. Rich Danner was bad enough.

He'd been a high school senior, two years older than her, the year her mother had been killed by a drunk driver. Treble had desperately needed solace and felt outside the circle of grief Harrison Breckfield shared with his younger natural daughter. Blindly adoring, Treble had turned to Rich.

More than a decade later and he was still good-looking, she noted dispassionately. Was there no justice in the world? Ex-boyfriends who casually took your virginity, then moved on to college and older girls, were supposed to go bald and develop a paunch. It should be a law of physics. Rich's black hair was close-cropped, but showed no signs of male pattern baldness. His body was as lean as ever.

Rich had been enjoying a plate of the best spareribs in the state, but looked up as if he'd felt her watching. For a second he was frozen with surprise. Then his lips curved into a slow, meaningful grin. As if he was remembering the "good times" they'd shared.

Good times that had ended one muggy August night. "It wouldn't be fair of me to ask you to wait until we can be together again," he'd cooed with persuasive and patently false caring. "I'm moving on, and you'll be here with football games and high school dances you shouldn't be cheated out of. There will be plenty of guys your age who want to go out with you." Yeah, especially after Rich shot off his mouth about how willing she'd been in the backseat of his dad's Cadillac.

Looking away from Rich, she whirled around so quickly she almost collided with Keith, Treble conjured a bright smile and equally bright tone. "It's been forever since I ate here. What do you recommend?"

"I'm fond of the pulled pork sandwich." He raised an eyebrow. "I would have you pegged as a woman who liked to decide her own order without advice."

Pouting prettily, she wagged a finger at him. "Shame on you, judging so quickly. Wouldn't it be more fun to get to know me? I don't bite. Well, rarely."

He studied her, looking unimpressed. "Are you always so… flirtatious with virtual strangers?"

Embarrassment warmed her cheeks, but she refused to get defensive. "That was just joking around, Doc. If I decide to flirt with you, trust me, you'll know." Irritating man. She hadn't been coming on to him. She'd been anxious after his responses—make that *non*responses—about her family, and seeing Rich had been the toxic icing on the cake. Would it have killed Keith to smile back at her? Surely a guy who looked like this had some experience bantering with women.

"If you decide to flirt," he said blandly, "give me a heads up so I can be elsewhere. I prefer genuine to calculated feminine wiles."

No wonder the man was good friends with Harrison. Two like-minded judgmental sticks-in-the-mud.

A gangly teenager with minor acne and major amounts of musky aftershave cleared his throat, making it clear Keith and Treble were blocking the entrance. The doctor mumbled an apology and steered her away with his hand on her elbow. His touch was gentle but seared her skin nonetheless.

She jerked her arm away, then sighed inwardly. Now she probably looked petulant on top of everything else. What if she approached the situation as she would a caller she had inadvertently offended? Debate and sassy comebacks were good for the show, but there was a line she didn't cross when it came to antagonizing listeners. Why not just try the direct approach?

"Sorry if I was snippy there for a moment." Unwilling to discuss the family part of how difficult coming home was, particularly when she had a feeling Keith was already prejudiced on the subject, she gave him the other half of the truth. "There's an ex-boyfriend of mine in here."

She gave Keith credit for not turning to scope the ex in question, which Alana would have done immediately. Then again, Alana was a friend with a vested interest in Treble; Keith most likely didn't care.

"Bad breakup?" he guessed.

With aching, unwanted clarity, she remembered crying all night over the one-two punch of losing her mother, then her first love. She'd gone behind Harrison's back and against his wishes to see Rich; learning that her stepfather had been correct in his assessment had only made her angrier. How could Harrison be so perceptive when it came to a teenage boy he barely knew yet remain so blind about how much Treble needed him?

She swallowed. "Bad enough. I wasn't trying to use you to make him jealous or anything. I haven't even thought about him in years. It was just disorienting, walking through the door and… Sometimes we're not prepared to come face-to-face with our past, you know?"

"Yeah." He glanced away, but not before she saw the sudden intensity in his eyes.

Her earlier annoyance faded into curiosity. She knew what *her* issues were. What lurked in Dr. Caldwell's past that he'd rather not face?

LUNCH WITH Treble reminded Keith of his first-year labs in med school. Part of him had enjoyed the challenge while the rest of him was edgy because he'd sometimes second-guessed whether he knew what the hell he was doing.

Treble's earlier moment of vulnerability had startled him, leaving him to wonder if he'd imagined it as she effortlessly dazzled the young man working the register. By the time they left the counter with their food, Keith concluded that his companion was as unpredictable as she was gorgeous, which was saying something. The more moods he watched play across that expressive face, the more the full impact of her beauty hit him. Did she know men were watching her as she sauntered across the room?

Of course she does. She paints her fingernails blue and carries bright red luggage. This is not a woman who hides from attention. And yet she'd seemed sincerely nervous about running into some long-ago flame. From her reaction, Keith guessed the guy must have dumped her. Had this ex been the jealous type and didn't like others checking out Treble? Or maybe he'd been intimidated by her. Or—

"Well, well, well. Looks like Trouble's back in town." A man stopped next to Treble's chair. "Time's been good to you, darlin'."

"Certainly better than you ever were," she returned sweetly.

Or maybe the guy who dumped her was just a jerk, Keith concluded. He didn't know Rich Danner very well except that the land-scaper had moved back to Joyous about two months ago, apparently licking his wounds from a divorce. He'd remarked to Keith that they were the most eligible bachelors in town. *"Us and Jason McDeere, but he's raising a toddler, which puts us ahead in desirability. 'Course there's plenty of fillies to go around for all three of us."*

Now, Rich was turning green eyes full of apology toward the "filly" he'd let get away. "Don't be like that, Treb. I was a kid. Teenagers make bad romantic decisions."

She reached for her sandwich. "I couldn't agree more."

Keith grinned at her implication, but the diss had obviously sailed over Rich's head.

"I knew you'd understand. How about I join you, and we can reminisce about what good times we had before I screwed up?"

"Actually," Keith interjected, his impulsive words surprising him, "I kind of wanted Treble all to myself for another few minutes before we have to leave. She was fascinating me with stories about her job as a DJ in Atlanta."

Treble's eyebrows shot up, but she played along. Truthfully, they'd never once discussed what she did for a living, but Charity had mentioned it. Whereas Harrison rarely spoke of his step-daughter, Charity was effusively proud of her older sister, her naked affection almost masking her disappointment when Treble missed yet another holiday or birthday at home.

"Sure, buddy." Rich held his hands in front of him and gave a quick nod of male understanding. "I get it. But, Treble, we'll have to catch up some other time."

When they were alone again, Treble said, "Thank you. I don't *need* a man to rescue me, but I'm not gonna look a gift horse in the mouth, either."

"Does everyone born in Tennessee compare people to live-stock?"

"What?" Lines of confusion furrowed her brow.

"Never mind. And you're welcome," he added. "That guy can get on my nerves."

She nodded, taking a big bite of her sandwich and letting out a moan of pleasure. "God, I forgot how great Tennessee barbecue is. I mean, I knew I loved it, but this… This is better than sex."

He squeezed his own sandwich and barbecue sauce ran down his fingers.

If she'd noticed, he would have been embarrassed, but she seemed oblivious, lost in enjoyment of her food. Some of the women in town would have fainted—blushed, at the very least—at having the word *sex* tossed casually into meal conversation, but Treble clearly thought nothing of it.

She washed down her food with a swallow of soda. "Earlier, you said people 'born in Tennessee.' So you're not a native?"

"Nope. Charity first mentioned you when she heard I'd moved

here from Atlanta. I went to med school and interned there. Grew up in Savannah."

A city steeped in rich tradition and history, Savannah seemed like a good place for ghosts. He preferred to leave his there. In the E.R. of a major Atlanta hospital, he'd found himself dealing with too many reminders, too much trauma. He'd become a doctor because he wanted to save people, but if he'd stayed where he was, he was the one who'd wind up needing saving. So he'd found salvation in the relatively peaceful town of Joyous. He had the practice, real friends. Of course, Charity tutted that he'd be even happier once he found a girlfriend.

"It's not as if there aren't willing women," she'd teased, threatening to count the number of foil-covered casseroles in his freezer.

He'd considered deflecting her interest in setting him up by suggesting she encourage her dad to date instead—Harrison needed something in his life besides control of the dairy business and grueling workweeks. But even though it had been a long time since Charity's mother died, Keith didn't push the idea of a replacement romance. Losing family was hard, and Charity had mentioned how much she'd been missing her mom lately.

"I suppose you think it's pitiful that I called my sister and begged her to come be with me?" Charity had asked.

"Of course not." The only thing Keith hadn't understood was why Bill and Harrison had been so shocked Treble agreed. If Keith's older sister were still alive, there wasn't anything he wouldn't do for her.

"Keith." Treble's voice was soft, but persistently inquisitive. "Are you okay?"

He met her eyes, not sure what to make of the woman. Her gaze was filled with what seemed like empathy, hardly the selfish person she'd been painted as in unflattering gossip. He understood better than most the value of a fresh start. Maybe Treble had changed, maybe she'd returned not only to help her sister but to earn her stepfather's forgiveness for whatever youthful transgressions were in her past.

"I'm fine," he assured her, "but a lousy lunch date, huh?"

"Well, you won't be winning any awards for witty conversation, but you're easy on the eyes, so it balances out." Leaning forward, she lowered her voice conspiratorially. "You *do* know there's a blonde in the corner who's been checking you out, don't you?"

His gaze darted in the direction she'd subtly indicated, and he spotted elementary school receptionist Dinah Perkins having lunch with two other women. When Dinah caught him noticing, she smiled and offered a small finger wave. Moments later, she and her girlfriends huddled into hushed conversation. Either they wanted to know who the stranger was sitting with Dr. Caldwell, or they already knew and, like Rich Danner, were intrigued by Trouble—er, Treble's—return to Tennessee.

"Friend of yours?" Treble asked Keith.

"Just a friend," he stressed.

How long had it been since he'd had a girlfriend? Med school and his stint at the hospital had been hectic, and since moving here he'd been…cautious. There'd been a few dates and a nice weekend when a female friend had come to visit, but if his love life hadn't completely flatlined, its prognosis wasn't rosy, either. Eventually, he wanted to find the right woman to make his fresh start complete, but now that he was fitting in, he didn't want to jeopardize that with social missteps. Citizens gathered round their own, and if Keith broke up with a local girl, he risked becoming an outsider again. Maybe he was overanalyzing, but he hadn't felt at home anywhere in a long time.

It wasn't something he was willing to lose.

"About done?" he asked Treble.

She nodded. "I've taken up enough of your day. If you can swing me by the garage so I can give the mechanic my keys, you'll be rid of me soon."

Standing, she leaned over to grab a couple of napkins and clean off the table. He found himself looking straight into a tempting view of her cleavage. *Stop ogling Harrison's daughter!* But forcing himself to turn away was damn difficult.

In one short afternoon, Treble had had more of an effect on him physically than any of the women he'd met in town. Maybe it helped that she had a body that was sinfully perfect, making him think of fallen angels, but he was a doctor. He'd seen lots of bodies, many of them undressed.

The sooner he delivered her to Charity's, the better.

With the "downtown" area covering only a half-dozen blocks, it didn't take them long to reach Carter and Sons. Keith had just pulled up to the garage when a mechanic in dusty blue coveralls emerged from one of the open bay doors.

"That's Ronnie," he told Treble. "She'll have your car working better than when you drove it away from the dealership."

"She?"

There was no need for him to answer since Ronnie was removing her cap. Sleek red-gold hair fell to her shoulders.

"Huh," Treble grunted. "You know, before you came to get me, I was expecting 'Doc Caldwell' to be a good bit older. And Ronnie's *definitely* not what I anticipated. Lots of surprises for such a sleepy little town."

Sleepy? A twinge of foreboding rippled through him as he regarded the woman seated in his truck. He'd watched her varied reactions to Joyous—apprehension over arriving, sassy rebuffs to an ex-boyfriend, nearly sensual enjoyment of good barbecue—but now he wondered how the town would react to her. Treble James looked like a wake-up call waiting to happen.

Chapter Four

Treble stepped down from the truck, shaking her head. She'd always teased Charity over her affection for routine. "Don't you ever want to mix things up a little?" she'd asked her younger sister.

"Nope," Charity had maintained. "Predictability suits me just fine."

At the moment, Treble could use a few less surprises herself. "You're the mechanic?"

The woman nodded. She was shorter than Treble, their height difference exaggerated by the mechanic's flat-soled sneakers. Her clear jade eyes were lovely, but Treble wondered if men looked past the freckles bridging her nose and the shapeless, grease-stained overalls to notice.

"Ronnie Carter." The redhead extended a hand, noticed some black smudges near her fingertips and winced, dropping her arm to her side. "Technically, Veronica. No one calls me that. My brothers use 'Red,' but only to make me crazy."

Keith came around the side of the truck to stand with Treble. At his renewed nearness, her body hummed—it was like static electricity she couldn't control. *Try harder.* The good doctor probably wouldn't appreciate it if she drifted closer and stuck to his clothes.

"Afternoon, Ronnie," he said. "Treble had some car trouble outside town, and I assured her you were the best in the state at taking care of the problem."

"Flatterer." Ronnie grinned at him, but then her eyes widened and she swung her gaze back to Treble. "Good Lord. You're Treble Breckfield, aren't you?"

"James. Treble James." The distance she put between herself and her stepfather's name was automatic, although at least Harrison Breckfield attempted to stand by his responsibilities. More than she could say for her biological father. "I'm Charity Breckfield's sister. Er, Charity Sumner's."

"Wow. My brother Devin was crazy in love with you in high school." Ronnie nodded thoughtfully. "I can see why."

Treble couldn't remember Devin but hoped she wasn't awful to him.

"Daniel warned him that a guy two years younger didn't have a shot." Ronnie's tone was matter-of-fact, not vengeful on her brother's behalf. Good thing. A mechanic wielding a grudge was not someone you wanted tinkering with your engine.

Treble searched her memory for Carter brothers and finally landed on a name, though she couldn't put a face with it. "Are you related to William Carter? He was in my grade. Salutatorian, I think?" Her high school graduation ceremony was a blur, mostly occupied by plans to leave that summer. Despite the times she'd been sent to the principal's office for behavior problems, she'd kept her grades up and aced her SATs—college had represented her ticket out of town.

"Yeah, Will was the bookish one," Ronnie confirmed. "Though you wouldn't know it to look at him—he's as hulking as the other two. He went to university in North Carolina and settled there. The rest of us stayed," she said wistfully. Gifted mechanic or not, Ronnie didn't sound one hundred percent satisfied with her life.

Well, who is? Treble ignored the impulse to draw out the conversation and brainstorm solutions; this wasn't a radio broadcast. "So, Ronnie, are you as good with cars as I keep hearing?"

"No. Better." The woman's confident smile completely endeared her to Treble.

They chatted for a few minutes about where Trusty was parked, what the escalating symptoms had been before the vehicle died altogether, and where Treble could be reached.

"I'll call you this evening at your sister's," Ronnie said after she'd filled out some paperwork and taken Treble's keys. "I doubt I'll have fixed anything yet, but I should at least have an idea of the problem."

Moments later, Treble and Keith were back in the truck and en route to Charity's house. Charity had issued several invitations to visit over the years, and Treble might have been quicker to accept any of them if her sister had moved more than four miles away from the Breckfield family manor. Treble wondered if she could ever step inside the ancestral home—built on profits of the century-old dairy—without immediately thinking that it seemed cold. She'd been four the first time she'd visited, once her mother and Harrison were seeing each other, and it had seemed large and drafty. Like the haunted houses in scary stories. It hadn't improved her opinion that the place was full of antiques and Breckfield heirlooms that she was admonished not to touch.

At least Mom warmed it for a while. With her gone, the place had become positively glacial, full of long, mournful silence and, as Treble grew more rebellious in her teenage years, even colder arguments and chilly words.

"Hey." Keith's voice was amused. "I've seen people in hospital waiting rooms less nervous than you. Your car's in great hands with Ronnie."

"Hmm?" Treble followed his sidelong gaze to where she'd been drumming her fingers on the passenger side windowsill. "Oh, no, I…" On second thought, it suited her fine if he attributed her apprehension to vehicular woes and not her dubious homecoming.

"You what?" Keith prompted.

"I'm sure Ronnie's terrific. I guess I'm anxious because I know the car's on its last legs. Or tires, as the case may be. I need it to hold out until I find a house, get approved for financing and close." The goal warmed her from the inside, and she smiled at the plans she couldn't wait to start making. Decorating, furnishing, even landscaping. "My apartment's become a bit claustrophobic over the past year."

Keith nodded. "For me, the city got claustrophobic. A mentor of mine knew Doc Monaghan and let me know he was looking for a replacement. I'd never even heard of this place, but as soon as I moved… It's like I could finally breathe again."

She chuckled wryly.

"Guess that was corny," he said, sounding more guarded.

"No. No, I was laughing at the irony. I feel free in Atlanta, whereas here I would suffocate." Under expectations, the watchful eyes of nosy neighbors, the weight of the past.

"To each his own, right?"

"Exactly. To each her own." Because her natural inclination was to fill dead air, when it became clear conversation had lagged, she turned back toward him. "So, did you always know you wanted to be a doctor?"

He stiffened, so imperceptibly she wouldn't have noticed if her body weren't bizarrely attuned to his. "It…seemed right for me."

She hadn't expected his profession to be a sore subject. Yikes, she'd promised her boss she wouldn't lose her edge out here in the sticks, yet only a few hours in, she was already floundering her way through awkward chats.

"What about you?" Keith returned. "You always know you wanted to be a radio host? Charity makes it sound fascinating."

Treble smiled self-consciously. "It probably seems more glamorous than it is because she's lived in the same place her whole life and works for her dad." The girl should have been named *Patience;* Treble would have snapped by now.

"You mean she's easily impressed because she's a local yokel?" Keith's tone was deceptively mild, his delivery belying the disapproval of his words.

"I didn't mean it quite like that. I adore Charity."

He slanted her a look. "Yeah. I could tell you two are close."

Was he being sincere? Had Charity painted a rosy picture of their sibling relationship? *Which would be like her.* Or was he being sarcastic, passively condemning Treble for not being a better big sister? He didn't have that right.

I swear I'm better with people than this.

Well, not all people. Definitely not her stepfather. Or her actual father. Sometimes not even with her sister. But, normally, she was very popular with people who didn't know her well.

It was being back in this town that was messing with her head. By the time she'd left here, she'd been full of misery and anger, feeling unloved and paradoxically going out of her way to be unlovable. She hoped for all their sakes that Charity had that baby on time and not a single day late.

"Just about there," Keith said, apparently seeing—and misreading—her impatience.

She nodded, the cloudless sky outside her window vast. "I recognized this particular spot of nothing."

Joyous had undoubtedly grown some over the years, but the town moved at a slower pace than the rest of the world, still relatively untouched by urban sprawl. Pastures and trees that had been there since before she was born existed today, and even though there were few landmarks on this last stretch before they turned onto the dirt road that would lead to Breckfield property, she could have found her way from here blindfolded. Having not been home in so long, the familiarity was unexpected. There were some blocks in Atlanta where new gyms grew overnight as if having sprung from magic seeds and, if you blinked, the restaurant you were used to driving past could be replaced entirely by a shopping center without you ever noticing the construction crews.

As promised, they reached Charity and Bill's place a few seconds later. Keith took a left on Willy Wooten Drive—a mud strip probably no more than twenty feet long, named for a guy who'd once built a house there—and quickly encountered a paved fork. One finger of asphalt snaked its way up the hill and led to her stepfather's house. Another jogged a shorter distance to a well-kept yard and honest-to-God white picket fence. Treble didn't need to see the cheery *Sumner* stenciled on the mailbox to know this must be where Charity lived.

If Harrison Breckfield had ever run for mayor, he would have won by a landslide. So many townspeople were employed by or in some way affiliated with the dairy that the Breckfield family held a prominent position in the community. Yet Treble couldn't help wondering why Harrison had never proposed that the town pave Willy Wooten or even offered to have it done himself—especially now that his pregnant daughter had to drive over it in all manner of weather conditions. His own vehicles must have jostled over the years as he plowed through puddles and potholes, but something about that very specific concrete, starting precisely at the Breckfield property and not one inch sooner, personified the man. He had clear boundaries. He stayed unswervingly within them and expected others to do the same.

There were both a garage and carport to the side, but Keith parked more casually in the curve of the circular driveway, right out front. The house was predominantly brick, although it had a cottage-style facade bordered by a railed-in wooden porch. Treble imagined Bill and Charity sitting in the double swing, discussing baby names and drinking cold lemonade. Of course, she could just as easily imagine Charity in the picturesque little house, singing as woodland animals helped her clean and making seven beds for seven little men.

Treble hadn't finished climbing down from the passenger side of the truck when the screen door clattered and her sister appeared on the front porch. In deference to her current medical condition, Charity didn't try to navigate the stairs and greet them in the yard. Still, her enthusiasm was evident even from several yards away.

"You made it!" she called to Treble.

"Thanks to your friend Dr. Caldwell." Treble really was

grateful to the man for riding to her rescue, even if their short time together had been…charged.

"Well, come in, come in. I have some iced tea freshly brewed," Charity told both of them. She placed a hand over her distended belly. "Decaf, of course."

Treble turned to collect her luggage, only to find that Keith had grabbed both suitcases and slung her duffel bag over his shoulder.

"You should at least let me get one of them," she chided.

He half shrugged as he passed, repeating her words from their first meeting. "I'm able-bodied."

I'll say. Her gaze slid down from where his thick hair lay rumpled against his collar to his jeans.

She followed him up the stairs. Charity had stepped aside to make room for Keith and the baggage he carried, but as soon as Treble cleared the top step, the blonde swooped in for a hug. The sideways angle, not to mention the bulk of Treble's unborn niece, made the embrace a little awkward but it was appreciated nonetheless. Treble couldn't quite hook her arm around her sister so settled for patting her on the arm in greeting.

"Thank you for coming," Charity said softly, still not letting go. "Thank you, thank you, thank you."

"You're welcome," Treble said. "In triplicate. But, about my needing to breathe?"

Charity laughed, stepped back. "Guess I always was the hugger in the family."

Well, it sure as hell hadn't been Treble or the aloof Harrison Breckfield. "Like Mom. You have a lot in common with her." As soon as tears began welling in Charity's eyes, Treble wished she'd said something else. She struggled to lighten the moment. "Although, now that I think about it, that bone-crushing grip might have come from Harrison. Imagine the tackles you could have made if you'd played football!"

Harrison had been a college linebacker for the Tennessee Vols. At six foot three with steel-gray eyes, he was as formidable off the field as he'd reputedly been on it. Maybe Treble should have been smarter than to try making end runs around him, but she'd been sixteen. In theory, she was older and wiser now, but she was also a grown-up no longer seeking her stepdad's approval. She was who she was, and she refused to make apologies to him if she liked her music loud and her heels high.

"Where'd I lose you ladies to?" Keith asked, sticking his head out onto the porch. He'd obviously set the bags down somewhere inside.

Charity sniffled. "Sorry. Just exchanging sisterly greetings."

Keith glanced at the woman's obviously teary expression, then shot Treble a look that bordered on accusatory. *Two minutes and you already made her cry?*

"We're coming," Treble said brightly. As soon as he retreated, she told Charity, "I hope I didn't upset you. You warned me you were thinking about Mom a lot, and I didn't mean to say anything that made you miss her more. I know I'm a poor substitute for her being here right now."

Charity squeezed her hand. "It's wonderful that you're here. And I'm touched that you think I'm like her. Don't worry about the waterworks. It's the hormones. Honestly, all I do these days is cry—and eat Breckfield banana ice cream. Sometimes I cry *while* I'm eating the ice cream."

Treble laughed, glad they were on less sentimental ground as they joined Keith in the cool, aromatic house. Charity's air-conditioning bill must be a fortune, but the low temperature felt heavenly after driving in the heat for much of the day. Equally divine was the scent of spices and meat cooking. Treble had never been all that proficient in the kitchen, but she thought she smelled thyme and rosemary, underscored by sautéed onions. A little garlic? As her eyes adjusted to the comparative dimness of the living room, she stood still, breathing in the tantalizing scent. An archway at the far end led into a modest kitchen. Treble saw maroon laminate flooring and gold appliances.

"You." Keith took Charity by the hand, steering her toward a rose-and-cream sofa. A rocker upholstered in matching fabric sat by the large picture window in the room, a wicker basket full of knitting supplies and remote controls tucked next to the chair. "Off your feet. Then explain to me how you whip up one of your gourmet dinners while adhering to your OB's advice. Don't make me call Dr. Whalen because you know she will kick your butt. Metaphorically speaking."

Much as Treble wasn't ordinarily a fan of men chastising grown women over their choices, she had to admit this was no time for Charity to be rolling out the welcome wagon. "He's right. Well, I wouldn't know about the doctor, but definitely the dinner part. Don't you dare try to cook just because I'm visiting. You and this baby are what's important."

Leaning back against the couch, Charity shook her head, her honey-blond ponytail swishing. "Boy, you guys impress easily. I promise I wasn't slaving over a stove. I gave Bill some basic instructions for what to throw in the Crock-Pot, then stood long enough to season it myself. Honestly, the most strenuous thing I've done today was lift a pepper grinder. I spent hours in the rocking chair with my feet up, watching television, dozing and talking briefly on the cordless phone to both of you. Those are all approved activities, aren't they?" The impish grin she shot Keith made her look so young it was hard to believe she was going to be a parent soon.

He sat on the couch next to her. "If I overreacted, I did it because I care."

"I know," Charity said fondly. "You're a good friend. You will join us for dinner, won't you?"

"Um…" Keith darted a look toward Treble, who shifted her weight from foot to foot and tried to ignore feeling out of place. "I should check in at the clinic."

Charity laughed. "Well, I wasn't planning on eating dinner in the middle of the afternoon. Come back tonight. Bill and Dad said they'd be back by six, so I'll have dinner on the table around six thirty."

Treble cleared her throat. "You'll do no such thing."

"All right," Charity amended. "*Someone* will have dinner on the table around six thirty."

"Won't I be intruding on a family get-together?" Keith asked.

"Don't be ridiculous." Charity swatted him on the arm with all the force of a two-pound kitten batting string. She'd always been diminutive in height and build and, in some ways, her protruding beach ball of a stomach highlighted that; it was comically disproportional in comparison to the rest of her. "You're like family. The more the merrier! Right, Treb?"

"Right. Sure." Merry? Not the word Treble would have used to describe an evening with her stepfather, but rumor had it Keith actually enjoyed the man's company.

It probably helped that when *Keith* spent time with Harrison, the conversation wasn't laced with disapproval and derision over his dating life and career choice.

"I GOTTA SAY, Keith, I'm disappointed that you won't find enough time in your schedule to at least *go* on a date." Charity put her hands on her hips, but given her reclining position, it wasn't as effective a stance as it could have been.

When he'd returned this evening, Keith had turned the sofa that served as a divider between the two rooms so that it faced the kitchen. It was a more comfortable choice than the four chairs at the small oval table—besides, the spindly-legged seats didn't look sturdy enough for a woman in her final weeks of pregnancy. Tonight they'd eat in the dining room. For now, Treble was tearing and washing lettuce leaves while Keith sliced vegetables for the salad.

She was glad *she* wasn't the one wielding the knife or her occasional glances at Keith, who was standing a foot away by the kitchen counter, could have been disastrous. He'd obviously showered before changing into a starched white button-down shirt and dark jeans, because the ends of his hair had still been damp when he'd arrived, filling the small room with the scent of soap and sandalwood cologne. *And I thought the beef stew smelled delicious.*

Keith could definitely make a girl's mouth water. In fact, according to Charity, that's exactly what he did. Girls throughout town were lusting after him, although Charity had put it more discreetly as the two sisters chatted over tea this afternoon.

"If I thought he was happy as a single bachelor, I wouldn't nag him about finding someone," Charity had said. "But, honestly, I'm not convinced he's happy. We're friends, but there's a lot he still doesn't tell me."

"Not for a lack of your asking, I'm sure," Treble had teased.

"I think he's lonely."

Since Keith had ignored Charity's previous statement, his only response being a rhythmic *chop chop chop,* she pressed on. "I know your occupation is important to you, to the town, but do you really want your career to be the be-all and end-all of your existence?"

Treble stole another covert glance at the dark-haired doctor. He could have his pick of women in Joyous. Was he simply a loner by choice? The way he'd chatted with Charity earlier made that seem unlikely. Though he couldn't discuss any medical cases, he still had lots of funny anecdotes about patients and their families, especially kids. His genuine smile when he spoke about them, compounded with his willingly coming here tonight to have dinner with a pregnant woman and her family, made him seem like a people person.

"Enough," Keith warned his hostess, brandishing a carrot menacingly in her direction. "You have to at least feed me before interrogating me."

"I thought I might be able to wear you down easier on an empty stomach," Charity said. "You know, weaker state and all that. But now that you mention food…if Dad and Bill aren't ready to eat soon, we're digging in without them. I'm famished."

Treble grinned at her sister's newfound appetite, thinking about the snacks Charity had downed earlier. Healthy snacks granted, but plentiful.

Charity cocked her head, listening. "I don't hear the water running anymore, so maybe Bill's done with his shower. That just leaves Dad." Bill had come through the kitchen door shortly after Keith arrived. He'd spared a nod for the doctor before smiling in Treble's direction.

"I'd hug you, but I smell like cow." Then he'd sent his wife a glance of such sheer adoration that it had almost been too intimate to watch. "Hey, gorgeous. How are you and that daughter of ours?"

Beaming back at him, Charity had assured him she and the baby were doing great. "But clean up fast," she'd warned. "This kid is getting hungry again."

By the time Treble was scooping all the salad ingredients into a large pottery bowl and Keith had his head stuck in the refrigerator to find Charity's homemade dressing, Bill padded into the living room clean and nicely dressed, but barefoot beneath his khaki slacks. A man with calloused hands but a soft smile, he was solid, short and just the right height for Charity. He kissed his wife, giving her the greeting he'd postponed when he was gritty and malodorous. He rested his forehead against hers, his sandy hair a few shades darker than her blond. They were a well-matched couple.

Treble hoped that the listeners who periodically called her show, wistful for this kind of love, found what they were looking for, but she suspected it was more elusive than movie producers and greeting card companies would have the public believe.

As Bill entered the kitchen to see what he could do to help, Treble noticed his soapy, fresh scent was similar to the way Keith had smelled when he walked in the door. Recalling her visceral overreaction to the doctor, she mentally smacked herself in the forehead. So the man bathed—it took more than basic hygiene to impress her.

"Treble?" Keith's voice directly behind her made her jump. "What are you doing?"

Trying not to imagine you in the shower. "Um, tossing salad?"

He peered over her shoulder at the nearly mangled lettuce. "Interesting technique you have there."

Her face warmed. "Would you believe I learned it on one of those Food Network cooking shows?"

He laughed, the sound as rich as dark chocolate and just as addictive. "No, but you get points for creativity."

"Yeah, I always did have an imagination." She turned slightly as she said it, and their gazes collided. It wouldn't have mattered except that he was just so close. Not crowding her or being overly familiar, just there, his body near enough for her to melt with its heat, his indigo eyes—

"I take it Harrison hasn't called?" Bill's voice broke the spell, and Treble seized the opportunity to scoot away from Keith while she had the good sense to do so. Her brother-in-law was staring down at the wristwatch Treble knew had been an engraved anniversary present from Charity. "He said he'd be here by six thirty."

"It's just that now," Charity said. "Let's set the table, and the timing will probably work out perfectly."

They did, but it didn't.

Bill sat on the edge of the couch. "We should go ahead and get you fed, sweetheart. Treble, you wouldn't recognize her when she gets hungry. The woman turns mean."

Keith scoffed. "Mean? Charity? You must have her confused with some other tiny blonde who has a Napoleon complex."

"I do not," Charity protested, glaring up at him with twinkling eyes.

"You're a bossy nag," Keith retorted with a grin. "If I'd known the dinner invitation was just another excuse to needle me about dating…"

Treble took a seat at the kitchen table, a safe distance from the doctor, and smirked at her sister. "He's right, you know. She used to play 'school' with all her adorable stuffed animals and collectible dolls, and she was very strict. She's the only person I know who's ever given detention to a teddy bear."

The men laughed, but Charity sniffed daintily. "Well, I wanted the best for Mr. Snuggles and he was never going to get anywhere in life if he didn't do his homework." She wagged her finger at Keith. "I only want what's best for you, too."

"So, what did we decide about waiting for Harrison?" Treble interjected. Funny how much she wanted to help Keith avoid the subject of his love life. Normally, she made a living off of commenting on people's love lives or asking them to do so.

Charity frowned. "I'm sure he wouldn't mind us starting without him, but…this is a special occasion. Bill, if you'll please freshen up my tea, I can wait a few more minutes to eat." She extended her empty glass.

As Bill pressed the automatic ice maker, the refrigerator performed noisy variations of a churning grind, the sounds mirroring Treble's stomach. She knew why Charity was so intent on this dinner, it would be the first time since the weekend Charity was married that the two sisters and Harrison had sat down for a meal together. But the night hadn't truly started and already the déjà vu had her insides in knots. After her mother's car accident, Harrison dove into work. In retrospect, she understood that had probably been his coping mechanism, but that didn't excuse him for being late to meals or letting the girls eat with the housekeeper, Joan, while he had a sandwich in his study. Treble couldn't truly say whether her initial stunts—shoplifting cosmetics, stealing Harrison's car—were because she was trying to get his attention or because she was just so angry.

Charity, living up to her name, had always been more understanding, the family peacemaker. She'd been content with the moments of absent affection her father managed to give, the pats on the head in passing even if he wasn't sitting down and asking about their day the way their mother had. Maybe if he'd looked at Treble the way he did his own daughter, *she* would have been content, too. What she usually got, though, were reminders not to talk back to her teachers and admonishments to change into shirts that weren't so revealing.

Not that I'm bitter, Treble thought with a wry smile. Well, she was, but at least she had a sense of humor about it.

Charity sipped her sweet tea. "Oh, I almost forgot! Treble, I had Bill pick up a bottle of wine for you at the store. Could I get one of you strapping men to open it for us?" She glanced to Treble, her expression apologetic. "You usually drink white, don't you? The selection in Joyous isn't all that sophisticated, but—"

"I'm sure whatever Bill found will be fine," Treble said. She would have been okay without a glass, but refusing seemed inhospitable. Bill was more a beer man than wine drinker, and it was a sure bet Charity didn't plan to have any; Treble couldn't let it go to waste. Of course, she didn't intend to drink a whole bottle, either, so hopefully her stepfather and Keith would have some. Bill disappeared into the dining room, hunting through the china cabinet while Charity called out likely locations for the corkscrew they obviously never used.

Treble caught Keith's gaze. "Join me for a drink?"

He took longer than necessary to answer, and she wondered what he'd been thinking. "Sure." Turning, he opened a cabinet and reached for the wineglasses on the top shelf. It wasn't the first time he'd known without asking where something was kept. He seemed at home here.

Home. During the afternoon, Treble had had ample opportunity to study her surroundings, not so much the floor plan and the furniture as the personal touches that made the place uniquely Bill and Charity's. This was what Treble wanted for herself, this…sanctuary.

Because Bill was out of the room and Keith was wiping the

infrequently used wineglasses with a paper towel, Treble was the only one whose hands were free when a quick knock sounded against the kitchen door.

"That must be Dad!" Charity looked giddy. "Treb, will you answer the door?"

"Of course." Taking a deep breath and reminding herself this night was important to her little sister, Treble twisted the knob.

In the glow of the back porch light, Harrison Breckfield looked down on her. "Hello, Treble."

"Harrison." She swung the door wide and stepped out of the way.

"I understand you had some difficulty with the trip?" he asked as he entered the kitchen. His once black hair was now as gray as his eyes, yet that only made him look distinguished. It was something else—indefinable in his face, in his carriage—that made him look as though he'd aged.

"Nothing insurmountable," she said. Come to think of it, she hadn't heard from Ronnie the mechanic yet. Was no news good news...or silent foreshadowing that expensive parts needed to be specially ordered?

Harrison nodded absently. "It was good of Dr. Caldwell to leave his practice for the afternoon and bail you out."

Would it have killed him to say "help you out"? It wasn't as though she'd called from the county jail. One could argue that it was just an expression, but Harrison never *just* said anything. "Yes, I'm very grateful to the doctor."

Harrison stopped to greet Keith, and the younger man clapped him on the shoulder and leaned in to say something the rest of them couldn't overhear. Then Harrison shook hands with his son-in-law, who'd successfully found the corkscrew and opened a chilled chardonnay, before crossing to his daughter.

"Smells wonderful in here. I hope you haven't been waiting on me?"

"Not at all," Charity lied. "We were just enjoying some cocktails before dinner."

Harrison glanced over his shoulder in time to see Treble accept a glass of wine. He frowned at her, no doubt thinking of Charity's wedding.

Looking him dead in the eye, she tilted her glass and took a hefty swallow. He shook his head in disgust.

Truthfully, Treble might have been annoyed if she allowed herself to dwell on the moment. What was it about the man's low expectations that goaded her into wanting to say stuff like, "Could you all excuse me for a minute—I think I left my bong in Keith's truck?"

You know the answer to that. Maybe they'd never had the warm fuzzy step-bond that would earn them a biopic on the Hallmark Channel, but deep down, she'd at least respected the way Harrison lived up to his responsibilities. He might not love her, but he'd tried to do right by her. Until spring break of her senior year, when he'd walked in on Treble and dairy worker Mitchell Reyes. Instead of asking what had been going on or even acknowledging the uncharacteristically grateful way Treble flew to his side, Harrison had simply concluded that his flirtatious, rule-breaking stepdaughter had once again caused trouble that reflected badly on the family. But that was a long time ago.

Right now, Treble's only concern was getting through this dinner.

Chapter Five

Bill and Harrison, seated opposite each other at the antique walnut table, talked at length about the day they'd had and their decision to add another large-animal vet to the dairy farm's permanent staff. Even though it was the kind of conversation Treble had grown up around, she couldn't intelligently contribute. Then again, with home-cooked food of this caliber, keeping quiet and enjoying the meal wasn't a hardship.

Her well-meaning sister, however, had other ideas. She cleared her throat gently and, judging from Bill's slight double take, Treble wouldn't be surprised if Charity had poked him in the thigh, too. "All this talk about work, and what I really want to hear about is Treble's job! I know you were already involved in radio last time you were here, but to have your own show? We're all so proud of you!"

Seated as the dubious guest of honor at the head of the table, Treble smiled. "Thanks, Charity. It was very gratifying to get my own slot. The station manager displays a lot of trust in me, and that means as much as the callers who check in and let me know they like what I'm doing."

"Reaching all those people. It's very impressive." Charity turned to her father, adopting the reproachful tone she'd used when Mr. Snuggles hadn't lived up to his potential in stuffed animal class. "Isn't it, Daddy?"

With a sigh, Harrison leaned forward so that he could better see Treble around Keith. "What exactly do you do on this show? Mainly play records or is it more like talk radio?"

Keith chuckled. "Harrison, I think there are only about ten people left in the country who still own 'records.' One day I'll introduce you to this modern marvel called a compact disc."

"Fine, disrespect your elders. I'll have you know all that walking to school uphill both ways in the snow made me the determined, successful man I am today."

Treble froze, stunned by the exchange and the genuine humor in her stepfather's eyes. The man adored and indulged Charity, but even with her, he'd rarely joked. Had he mellowed with age? Four years was a long time. Maybe he wasn't exactly the person she remembered.

"Actually, it's a little of both," she explained. "I play music and take requests for songs, but do a lot of interaction with the audience, too. A lot of nights, we'll form a theme. I'll try to find songs that match up somehow with the topic we're discussing."

"What kind of topics?" Charity asked, looking both genuinely interested and pleased by the way things were going.

"It varies, but my trademark has become relationship stuff. Dating advice, commiserating, popular—"

"*You* give dating advice?" her stepfather asked incredulously.

"I…" Treble trailed off, aware that all eyes were on her. This conversation would have been easier if she were in a booth somewhere with her familiar headset. "I've never made false claims to be an expert in the field. My listeners understand that I'm more like a moderator. People call in to share their experiences and perspectives, and I keep things moving, provide food for thought, color commentary. Last week, this woman called in complaining that her boyfriend—" *Uh-oh.* Probably not the best example for this group.

Harrison raised his eyebrows, waiting.

There was a pause while Treble tried to think of a less risqué anecdote. She hated the uncertainty churning inside her. Her job was terrific; she worked hard and received steady e-mails from grateful listeners who enjoyed her show.

She squared her shoulders. "Well, they were having a problem in their love life and some of my other listeners were able to offer constructive solutions for not only the woman who called, but also anyone else out there experiencing the same problem, who might have been too shy to seek advice."

Harrison's ruddy complexion had turned blotchy. "By love life, you mean their sexual relationship?"

"Yes, I do."

Out of the corner of her eye, Treble saw Charity open her mouth, no doubt to rescue them. But her stepfather was already speaking again before anyone had a chance to diffuse the tension rolling in like a low-pressure front.

"This is what you've chosen to do with a college degree? Make your living by discussing sex with the entire city of Atlanta?"

"It's not like I'm *having* sex with them," she snapped.

There was a squeak from Charity's end of the table, and the sound helped dispel some of Treble's temper. In spite of herself, she found the humor in her stepfather's words. If the entire population of Atlanta actually tuned in to her show, her station manager would name all his future children after her. And possibly rename the first four.

She focused on sounding calm rather than defensive. "Male-female relationships aren't something to be ashamed of. Most healthy adults have a sex drive. Isn't that a medical fact, Doctor?"

Keith whipped his head toward her. Though she wouldn't classify his strained expression as outright hostile, he clearly didn't appreciate being dragged into the discussion. Was he going to back her up or agree with Harrison that her job was distasteful?

Charity seized the opportunity created by Keith's hesitation. "Did everyone leave room for dessert?"

Obligingly, Bill sprung out of his seat. "I could go for a bowl of ice cream. Keith?"

The man pushed his chair away from the table. "I'll help you scoop."

Charity glanced between her father and sister, her baby-blue gaze equal parts crestfallen and beseeching. "I have three flavors of Breckfield ice cream and some store-bought chocolate chip cookies."

That they could no doubt wash down with a nice cold glass of Breckfield milk. Possibly the only way Treble could be *more* of a misfit in this family was if, on top of everything else, she were lactose intolerant, too.

KEITH KEPT HIS GAZE lowered as he finished his dessert. No offense to the man seated next to him or the many hundreds of employees who made the ice cream possible, but Keith barely tasted the Neapolitan he'd selected from Charity's freezer. Normally, whenever Charity asked him to dinner, he accepted her offer automatically. His fondness of the family aside, her food beat the hell out of whatever he microwaved at home. After tonight, however, he might think twice about future invitations.

Previous experience had braced him for Charity's habitual hassling about his lack of a romantic life, but he hadn't been sufficiently prepared for working with Treble in that warm, cramped kitchen.

They'd spent a fair amount of time in his truck this afternoon, but that had been static. This evening, they'd bumped into each other more than once or simultaneously reached for the same drawer. She'd changed from her travel clothes into faded jeans and a bright pink shirt with a satiny collar. Whenever she brushed by him, he caught a whiff of something appealingly spicy. Almost cinnamon, but not quite. It didn't smell like perfume, but maybe a body lotion? It somehow made him think of baked apples and sex, *not* a normal combination for him.

But he had a feeling Treble James and "normal" rarely co-existed. Look what had happened to tonight's dinner. Usually Bill and Harrison talked business for a few minutes until Charity complained, then redirected conversation with either plans for the baby or mild local gossip. The men would praise her on another wonderful meal and the evening would conclude peacefully. Tonight had been so tense Keith had the urge to whip out a blood pressure cuff and make sure Harrison's readings were still in a safe range.

With his bowl empty, Keith glanced up to make his farewells. "Charity, thank you for having me, but I should head on. No need for you to get up, I can show myself out. Wait—Treble, walk me to my truck? Couldn't hurt to double-check and make sure you didn't forget anything. Wallet, sunglasses, whatever."

Her amber eyes narrowed. He pretended not to notice as he bid Harrison and Bill goodbye.

As already evidenced, Treble didn't have a problem speaking her mind. The second they hit the front porch, she turned to him in the dark. "So, why did you really want me to come with you?"

He sighed, formulating his words as he preceded her down the stairs.

"You're not denying an ulterior motive," she observed when they reached the yard. "So I was right?"

"You are. I'm just trying to figure out a way to say this without getting my head taken off."

Her face was inscrutable, the light shining from the house windows and the moon not enough to illuminate her expression. "If it makes you feel any better, I haven't decapitated anyone in days. Practically weeks."

"Maybe we could just drop the wordplay and get to it?" He'd unconsciously adopted the stern, authoritative tone he took when giving patients advice he knew they weren't going to like. "While I don't want to exaggerate your sister's condition, I'm sure you can understand why it's not a good idea to upset a pregnant woman, especially one this close to term."

"This is about dinner tonight," she said. It wasn't a question

"And the rest of your visit. You and Harrison seem to…agitate each other."

Her voice fell surprisingly quiet, nearly inaudible beneath the buzz of summer insects. "Yet I don't see *him* out here getting this little reprimand."

Keith leaned against his truck. "Don't you think you should cut him some slack?"

"I'm sorry, were we at the same dinner?"

"Try to see it from his perspective." Keith didn't object to what Treble did for a living—although for his own sanity, he preferred not to think about her discussing sex in that throaty drawl of hers. Understandably, Harrison held more old-fashioned views. "What dad wants to think of his daughter as sexually active, much less giving other people instructions on how to do it?"

"It's not…*he's* not…many of my shows have nothing to do with that. And I've given reminders about abstinence, not letting yourself be pressured, or at least being safe. Don't you think he knows how Charity got pregnant?"

"Charity doesn't have your history," Keith said, his brain catching up to his mouth about a second too late. *Crap.* He couldn't believe he'd blurted that.

So much for finesse. Maybe it had been too long since he'd had a conversation with a woman that didn't start with "How long have you been having these symptoms?" Well, he talked to Charity, but she was more like a— Not letting himself think "sister," he was almost relieved when Treble lit into him.

"What the hell do you know about my 'history,' Doc?"

Having opened Pandora's box himself, he figured he might as well brazen through the aftermath. "Bits and pieces that I've heard in town. Petty theft, sneaking out at night, trying to get into a bar even though the fake ID was ridiculously amateur, not to mention at least half the people there knew exactly who you were and that you were only sixteen. Is it true you got some poor slob ired from the dairy after he made out in a barn with you?" If Harrison had been judgmental with her, he was probably reacting o her track record.

Treble's breath left her in a whoosh. She even leaned forward as if her abdomen hurt. Then she straightened. "You really think I took a leave of absence from a job I love just to drive a state over and deliberately stir up trouble with a pregnant woman and an old man?"

"No." Keith tilted his head back, wondering how a man with precious little family left had ended up embroiled in this particular family drama. "But I do worry that you just can't help yourself."

STARING UPWARD, Treble watched the ceiling fan in the guest bedroom rattle through its repeated orbit. On this slow setting, it didn't do much to cool things down—despite the air-conditioning, she'd felt overheated ever since her little chat with Dr. Caldwell. But on the higher settings, the fan shook so much she had visions of the entire thing crashing down on her.

Was she like the fan, just moving in meaningless circles? As a successful adult, the mistakes of her past should be behind her. But they'd felt as close as ever tonight over dinner. If there'd been a camera in the room, the whole thing could have been aired on Court TV. Did Harrison really have the right to put her life on trial?

The bigger question was, why did she still let it get to her so much?

She tried to imagine a caller with this problem. What would Trouble J say? *If you live your life to please other people, odds are no one will end up happy. Do your best to be comfortable in your own skin without obsessing about what other people think.* That went double for interfering doctors who doled out opinions after less than a day of acquaintance.

Sighing in the dark, she admitted that she wasn't even that angry at Keith. Well, she had been—she glanced at the oversize blue numbers on the digital clock—four hours ago. But he'd been speaking out of loyalty to Harrison and, more importantly, genuine concern for Charity. Treble's sister had been quiet after dinner. *Too quiet,* as they said in old movies.

Harrison had left almost immediately after Keith's departure. Bill had glanced between the two women as though he wanted to say something but couldn't for the life of him figure out what. Then, he'd suggested he clean the dishes so the two sisters could catch up. Treble had lifted a jigsaw puzzle Charity had started onto the coffee table, so her sister could work on it from the couch while Treble sat on the floor. The expression in Charity's blue eyes had been so fragile, so precariously close to tears, that Treble abandoned her plan to talk about dinner, but Charity hadn't responded to any of the other conversational gambits, either.

Living in an apartment complex, Treble had grown used to filtering out footsteps and thumps, so it took her a moment to realize someone was moving around in the house. When light spilled down the hallway, she acted on impulse and got out of bed.

The center of the house was bracketed by the living room and kitchen on one end and the master suite that included Bill and Charity's room and bathroom on the other. In the middle were the dining room, a small bedroom for guests and an identical room that was in early throes of being decorated for a nursery. Treble had been surprised earlier, given Charity's enthusiasm for having her daughter, that the nursery wasn't farther along.

"Well, we've registered for a lot of stuff," Charity had said, "and the baby showers usually come in the last trimester. I'm so excited that you'll be here for the one next week!"

Additionally, Treble had picked up the vibe that maybe Charity had been nervous to commit to the nursery too soon. Just in case.

She blinked, adjusting to the overhead light of the kitchen. As she suspected, her sister sat at the table.

"Hey." Charity looked up from the gallon of ice cream and bowl next to it, her expression sheepish. "Did I wake you?"

"No, I couldn't sleep."

"Me, either. So I thought I'd come have a snack." She gestured with her spoon. "I know ice cream's junk food, but technically, I didn't eat mine after dinner."

Treble sank into one of the empty chairs. "I noticed."

"Want some Butter Butter?"

One of Breckfield's signature flavors, vanilla with peanut butter and butterscotch ripples. The ads claimed Doesn't Get Much Better than Butter Butter. "Thanks, but I don't think so."

Charity sighed. "Yeah, if I had your figure to protect, I'd be wary of hitting the ice cream like this, too. Since I'm the size of a full-grown hippo, I've decided to just give up the ghost."

"Oh, stop. You can't be any bigger than, say, an *adolescent* hippo." Relief washed through her when Charity laughed.

Treble could remember Charity's first day of school. No one in her family had seemed nervous. Their mom had already been through kindergarten angst once, Charity had been dying to get on that school bus every day like her big sister, and Harrison had assumed in that arrogantly Breckfield way that his daughter was so gifted that of *course* she would excel. As it happened, he'd been right. Still, Treble, an experienced and worldly twelve-year-old, was wise enough in the ways of playground bullies and lunchtime seating that she worried on her sister's behalf. She'd looked at the cherubic blonde in her pristine pink jumper and vowed to punch— or possibly shove, if the offender were too young to justifiably hit—anyone who hurt her baby sister. *I just wanted to protect her.*

A lot had changed, but not that. At one point after her mother's death, Treble had experienced a blip of resentment toward the sister Harrison so easily loved, who still had a clearly defined place in the world. But then it had occurred to her that, in a way, Charity was the only piece of Mom she had left.

"Charity, I'm sorry I screwed up tonight."

Her sister put down her spoon. "No. I pushed. I should have known better."

"Than to prompt him into talking about my job or to ask me here in the first place?" Treble swallowed, wishing she hadn't felt compelled to ask the question. She wasn't sure she wanted to hear the answer, especially since she still didn't have a getaway car. *I have got to call Ronnie first thing in the morning.*

"I'm *glad* you're here," Charity said firmly, her tone brooking no further doubt. "I practically coerced you into it, remember?"

"Yeah, but this could be one of those cases of be careful what you wish for."

"Treb. Honestly, I want you here. For my baby's birth, for the showers…for the free manual labor wallpapering the nursery."

"Ah. The truth comes out." Treble grinned, feeling more relaxed than she'd been during the hours of tossing and turning in bed. "I should put that in the freezer for you before it melts. Unless you were going to eat another bowl?"

"Nah, I'd better call it quits. You've inspired me to maintain my adolescent hippo figure."

Standing, Treble reached for the gallon. She paused. "You know I love you, right?"

Charity's eyes shimmered, then spilled over as a few tears rolled down her cheek. "I know."

Wow. That had to be some kind of speed record for going from fine to crying.

"Hormones!"

Treble didn't know if the word was supposed to serve as a reminder for why her sister was so emotional right now, or if Charity were cursing the reason she was so volatile. Either way, Treble decided to be tactful and moved to the refrigerator to give her sister a moment to pull herself together.

Charity caught her off guard by blurting, "Dad loves you, too."

All evidence to the contrary. Treble bit her tongue. Hard.

"He does," Charity insisted.

"Well." Treble spoke slowly, carefully, not turning around. "If he didn't, you couldn't blame him. I was a hellacious handful."

"You were a teenager," Charity countered. "A grieving one, at that. If puberty hormones aren't quite the roller-coaster ride of pregnancy hormones, they're at least darn close. All girls at that age are—"

"Charity, what's the worst trouble you ever got into during high school?" Treble asked over her shoulder.

"I'm a freak of nature, bad example. A square peg." Her cheeks reddened. "I always wanted to be bolder, like you."

"Don't be crazy. You have this great little house and a husband who adores you."

"Yeah, but I had this English teacher I loathed."

"You never loathe anyone," Treble said, sitting next to her sister and swiping a taste of the Butter Butter pooling at the bottom of the bowl. "You're the nice sister."

Charity stuck her button nose in the air. "I can loathe people just as well as anyone! This guy I loathed with the burning fire of a thousand suns."

Treble choked on a laugh.

"Honestly. He was so pretentious, analyzed literature to death, sapping out everything I actually *enjoyed* about it. The thing is, I didn't even agree with most of his interpretations, but I regurgitated what he said on essay tests because I knew it would get me an A. Just once, I wanted to take a stand, tell him he was full of it in front of the whole class. You would have."

"Babe, I'm not a solid role model."

"I don't know about that. You're funny, independent, interesting. You're your own person."

"It can get a little lonely being your own person," Treble admitted quietly.

Charity straightened, her eyes going from dim, as she recalled her past "failings," to the bright intensity of a zealot with a mission. "You're lonely?"

"No. I mean, sometimes, sure, who isn't? But no. Charity! Look at me, I'm content with my life. Very content." Treble realized she was babbling, but couldn't help herself. She had a bad feeling she knew what was coming.

"Bill knows some single guys—"

"Dairy guys. *Not* that there's anything wrong with that, but let's face it, my time in town is limited. I have a job and a house hunt to get back to after this baby's born."

Charity's face fell. "I guess you're right. I know you can't stay…but I'd love it if you could visit more often."

"I will," Treble promised, meaning it.

No matter how difficult dinner had been, Joyous had more going for it than she remembered. The chance to hang out with Charity, the meditative effect of this charming little house, a female mechanic Treble could easily imagine befriending, some of the best barbecue in the Southeast. *And the best-looking town doctor in the Southeast?* Maybe, but Keith Caldwell's sex appeal had no relevance in her life. She might not even see him much for the rest of her visit.

By the time she finally went to bed and dozed off, she still hadn't decided whether never seeing Keith again would be a good thing or a bad one.

Chapter Six

"Morning, Doc Caldwell. Sleep well?"

"Morning, Velma." *And, no.*

Anytime Velma Hoskins encountered someone else before eight in the morning, she asked them if they'd slept well. His receptionist was a firm believer in rest being a key to good health. "I don't drink coffee after noon," Velma would tell anyone who'd listen. "Don't want to interfere with the suggested eight hours, you know. My late mama, God keep her, swore by eight hours every night and frequent napping. She lived to ninety-five." At which age she'd died peacefully, in her sleep.

Keith was all for the medical benefits of getting enough rest, but he sometimes wondered if Mama Hoskins's fanatical devotion to sleep and napping stemmed from having eight children. If he had that many kids running around the house, he'd be counting the hours until afternoon naps and bedtime, too. Nevertheless, maybe he should get to bed early tonight to make up for last night's restlessness. He'd been alternately haunted by the musical sound of Treble's voice when she was having fun and the flat hurt when she'd asked if he thought she was here only to cause trouble.

He cleared his throat, leaning on the desk behind the reception window. "Who do we have coming in today?"

Velma lifted the purple glasses that hung from a chain around her neck. "A couple of routine checkups midmorning, and Maggie Cline called at seven o'clock this morning. I told her we could squeeze her in if she'd get here by eight thirty."

He nodded. "This appointment's for Nathan?"

"Poor little guy has another ear infection."

Actually, probably the same one. Keith didn't think he'd quite managed to get rid of it, as it was proving resistant to antibiotics. With some altering of the original prescription, the right medicine could hopefully knock it out. He wanted to keep *all* the kids who came to see him healthy, but he knew Maggie especially panicked when anything seemed wrong with Nathan.

Loss did that, made you hypersensitive to losing anyone else.

Maggie was a widow whose husband had died in a factory accident the year before Keith moved here. The entire town had rallied around her and her toddler. Because of a generous insurance policy and the money her late husband's company paid after the accident, she was now one of the most wealthy citizens in Joyous. She'd told Keith once that every time she wrote a check, she wished she could return the money and get her husband back. In the past few months, however, she'd mentioned the man less and less.

"I think Maggie is finally finding her footing," he told Velma. "She and Nathan seem more steady every time I see them."

"You just be careful you don't see her and Nathan too often," Velma said, pulling out a handful of manila folders from the patient file drawer.

"Excuse me?"

She jabbed a skinny finger at him. "That girl's sweet on you."

"Maggie? Maggie Cline? I don't think so."

Velma was an astute woman who'd lived in Joyous her entire fifty-eight years, so she didn't miss much. But even insightful town icons had an off day.

She snorted. "Look here, whippersnapper, I'm a woman more than twenty years your senior, and I was married twice. *You're* a clueless male—no offense—who's hardly been on a date since you got here. Which one of us do you think has a better grasp of the situation?"

"Well, when you put it like that," he said sarcastically. It didn't bode well for his authority around here that his only full-time employee called him a whippersnapper. He hoped it didn't catch on with the three part-time nurses.

"I've read about this. Don't remember what it's called, but I know I've read about it. She loved her husband, and he took real good care of her and Nathan. Then Nathan got so sick in the spring, and *you* helped take care of him. It doesn't hurt that you're good-looking as all get-out and she was probably getting to where she's ready to dip her toes back in the dating pool, anyway."

"Transference," Keith supplied. "Is that the term you're looking for?"

"Yeah. Now, personally, I have no objection to you dating, so long as you run off with me eventually." It was a long-standing joke between them. Her voice sobered, full of compassion for Maggie. "But if you don't have any romantic interest in her, you don't want her or that boy to get falsely attached."

As a result of the unexpected conversation with Velma, he found that his smile of greeting for Maggie and Nathan twenty minutes later was nervous. He scanned the young widow's face, but the only emotion he saw was an antsy desire to get her son better.

"Hey, buddy." He lifted Nathan onto the freshly rolled white paper covering the exam table. "Can I take a look in your ear? I lost a shoe and think it might be in there."

Giggling, the towheaded child turned his head so that Keith could flash the otoscope into his left ear.

When the visit was over, Keith escorted them up front. Nathan pawed through Velma's selection of bright round stickers while Keith wrote out a new prescription.

"Thank you," Maggie said. "I don't know what this town would have done if you hadn't come along. Doc Monaghan was fantastic, but we all understood he needed to retire. I know there are other towns close by with capable doctors, but if you're already losing time from work to take the trip or you're like me, with a sick kid you're desperate to have seen…"

Keith doffed an imaginary cowboy hat. "Just doing my job, ma'am."

"*Ahem.*"

He turned to catch his receptionist giving him the evil eye. She hadn't thought he was flirting with Maggie, had she? Had *Maggie* thought he was flirting?

The single mom fluffed the ends of her shoulder-length auburn hair with her fingers, shooting a befuddled glance at Velma before looking back at him. "As grateful as we are to have someone like you on the job, Dr. Caldwell, I hope you still have time to get out and have fun. Like Days of Joy?"

He hadn't been here for last year's fun, but the annual Joyous festival held the first week of July was supposedly a major social happening in these parts. Craft booths that drew both consumers and vendors from a range of counties, fair rides, competitions with final rankings in all age groups at the award ceremony, fireworks, cook-offs and a parade that featured the mayor waving from the back of a white convertible and an appearance by Bonnie the Breckfield cow. In addition to Breckfield, many local businesses sponsored teams, displays, free samples and games. As a result, most of the town was scheduled to close at noon on festival days.

"I'm looking forward to it," Keith said.

"Oh, good." Maggie let out her breath. "Festival's one of my favorite times of year. I'll have several jars of homemade jelly in the canned goods tasting—wish me luck. And, of course, you know about the big dance. Will you be attending?"

"I, ah…" Behind him, Velma's telepathic *I told you so* was deafening. He rubbed an ear. "I really can't say. But if I don't see you there, I hope you have a nice time. Thinking about going with anyone special?" Clumsily done, but it was the gentlest way he could think of to dissuade her before she got out the invitation she appeared to be working toward. Damn, he *was* a clueless male.

Maggie's disappointed gaze dropped to the floor. "I suppose not. After all, I already have a pretty special guy in my life." She shot a wistful glance at her son, took his chubby hand and told Velma and Keith to have a nice day.

On the way out, she looked again at her son, rather sadly, but then smiled and ruffled his hair as he pointed to the plane flying overhead. Keith watched him through the large window that was part of the storefront between Claudette's Beauty Salon to the left and the town's newspaper office on the right—it was hard to say which of those two locations got all the local news first. If she typed as fast as she could curl, cheerfully nosy Claudette could freelance for the *Joyous Journal-Report.* This building, with its trio of businesses, was located on the most trafficked street in town. Across the way was the library. At one end was the Bestest Bakery and Sandwich Shoppe, at the other a feed and supply store frequented by all the farmers and ranchers in the area. While spreads like the Breckfields' were the exception, there were plenty of small farms, parcels of property that had been passed down throughout generations where families supplemented other incomes with fresh produce sales or birthday party pony rides. Keith himself had bought three acres at a good price, even though it was more space than he needed. Right now, he lived at the front of the clearing in a forty-year-old house that boasted no central air—window units only—a gas stove with cranky disregard for pilot lights and unpredictable plumbing. All part of its quirky charm.

The aging two-bedroom was a temporary situation. Eventually he'd get more ambitious with the land and have a house built. *For whom?* Himself? Himself and a wife? Kids? As he'd told Maggie, he really couldn't say.

He cast another look through the window, but Maggie and her

son were no longer on the sidewalk. They'd probably gone around to the back, where the majority of parking was available. He sensed Velma following his gaze. "She didn't think I was disinterested because of Nathan, did she? Because he's a great kid."

"Her dating choices will probably be more limited because she's already a mommy," Velma said noncommittally. "But I hope she and Nathan find the right man."

"I'm not that man."

"'Course not. You and *I* were destined to be together."

He grinned over his shoulder as she retrieved the number of an insurance office from her Rolodex. "I don't know what I did to deserve you."

"I choose to take that as a compliment," she informed him.

Wanting to grab a cup of coffee before his nine o'clock appointment, he left Velma to her work.

When would it be time to find out whether or not he could be anyone's right man? Pushing aside personal relationships had been almost necessary during med school, then his insane hours at a hospital and being the newcomer in town…but he'd settled in now. His mother had made her own fresh start back in Savannah, including a round-faced husband who sold cars and doted on her. Keith was genuinely happy for them, but he didn't know her second husband very well and he'd allowed his demanding hours to become an easy excuse for not visiting often. Though he loved his mom, Savannah would never feel like home to him again. It was part of who he'd been before Gail's drowning, which seemed surreal now, like looking back at someone else's life.

His father's coronary just two months after Gail's death had been like a shot of Novocain to the heart. Keith had become numb, channeling his energy into school. As an intern, he'd mastered the detachment doctors needed in order to survive their profession; inevitably, not all emergency room patients could be saved. Over the past few years, however, he'd realized it wasn't so much detachment as deferral. Rather than risk any more pain, he'd put off feeling anything for anyone. How long could he have existed like that without losing part of himself for good? The lazy pace in Joyous had taken away his excuse for working himself into exhausted oblivion, giving him a better look at what his life had become. Until now, he'd kept people at a distance, but here, he'd needed help integrating in the community, and the resulting friendship with Harrison and Charity had thawed his defenses.

With the icy numbness wearing away, he was more aware of the empty spaces he'd ignored. *Charity's right*…though he had no plans of telling her so. The woman would waste no time lining up dates for every night of July and half of August. He didn't need to pick out rings or anything, just someone nice he could have dinner with. Unbidden, Treble's strong features and sassy smile flashed through his mind. *Anyone but her.*

What he needed was a local girl who would mesh with his calm new life here in Joyous. Treble would be gone soon, causing who-knows-what kind of discord in the meantime. Besides, what possible interest could she have in him after their last encounter? He'd felt drawn to protect Charity and her father, wishing yet again that Harrison would be honest with his family about his heart condition, but Keith hadn't planned to hurt Treble's feelings.

Trying to push aside the picture of her lush mouth and the equally disturbing wounded expression in her eyes last night, Keith refocused. He would start slowly, maybe a cup of coffee with someone who worked nearby or actually setting foot inside Guthrie's and asking someone to dance. Letting himself spend any more time thinking about Treble was the opposite of starting slow—it was the emotional equivalent of throwing himself on the freeway in a sports car with no brakes or air bags.

TREBLE'S THURSDAY and Friday were idyllic, not counting the unwelcome news that she needed a new carburetor. "I'd recommend getting a rebuilt one," Ronnie had said. "Why pay for a new one when this car, despite the magic I plan to work on it, doesn't have many years left in it anyway?" Although the automotive diagnosis was grim, Treble was enjoying her stay more than she'd expected. Bill was easygoing and likable, if not the most exciting man in the world, but Charity made up for that, her pregnancy hormones and occasional moodiness prompting her to say some unpredictable and frequently hilarious things.

Having been cooped up in the house, Charity was thrilled to have company, and they had a lot to catch up on. Charity told her all about their cousin's comically disastrous wedding, Treble shared some of her best nightclub stories, and on Friday, Charity's friend Lola Ann brought sandwiches for all three of them.

"So, you're the radio star?" the brunette asked as she unpacked a white paper bag onto the coffee table. "I've been looking forward to meeting you. You're something of a legend around here." Lola Ann's father worked at the tractor dealership and the family had come here two years after Treble's departure.

"Lola Ann!" Charity glared from her higher perch on the couch.

But Treble was unfazed. "I'll just bet. I gave the local gossips plenty to wag their tongues about." She wasn't surprised Lola Ann had gathered an earful, but it did startle her to know that recent citizen Keith Caldwell had heard so much about her exploits. Even if some of his information was flawed. "Still, you'd think people would have more to talk about by now."

"Nope," Lola Ann said cheerfully, exposing dimples on either side of her grin. "I mean, there's the occasional scandal or good news or noteworthy crop issue, but it's a sleepy town. During the lulls, people fall back on old topics. The fact that Charity and your father are so loved in this town keeps you relevant."

Stepfather. Treble couldn't help the mental correction, though she managed not to say it out loud.

"Can we eat now?" Charity looked annoyed, although personally, Treble found the candid librarian endearing.

Charity's best friend, Penny Paulson, was a woman Treble remembered from their girlhood and Charity's wedding. She taught middle school and, now off for the summer, was currently enjoying a two-week cruise with her husband, a town deputy. They'd scheduled the trip so that she'd be back for the baby shower and well ahead of the due date.

Lola Ann passed around the sandwiches. "Hope turkey is okay with everyone. Mac sliced it while I was waiting, and he baked the sourdough rye fresh this morning."

Treble took a bite and was suitably impressed. The special horseradish dressing on the sandwich cleared the sinuses nicely without being too hot to enjoy. *Mom always said the food tasted better here.* She'd claimed it was the country air.

Treble only remembered bits and pieces of her early childhood in Chattanooga. Her mom had worked at a local tourist attraction, both giving tours and taking shifts in the gift shop. Treble had been left home one Saturday with her father and woke up early from her nap, coming into the living room to find him kissing another woman. She remembered feeling guilt after he left, thinking that if she'd just stayed in her room… Six months later, he'd come back, apologetic, swearing to do better by both of them, but then he'd left in the middle of the night. Treble's mother hadn't said much about it, but Treble suspected he'd taken any cash that was in the house with him. Not long after, Treble's mom had applied for a job with Breckfield, giving tours at the dairy and promising Treble all the ice cream she could eat.

Although Charity and Harrison both knew Treble had planned to track down her father when she left here, neither had ever asked how the reunion went. Which was just as well. There'd been sporadic birthday cards from him growing up, but apparently he'd meant for that to be the extent of their father-daughter relationship. She should have kept it at that.

"Treble? You don't like your sandwich?" Lola Ann was peering at her, her mouth pursed in disappointment.

"Oh, no, the sandwich is wonderful. Truly. I just thought

about something my mom said. She always thought the food here tasted better than anywhere else."

Charity smiled. "I remember. I don't have much of a basis for comparison, not being a big traveler. What do you think, Treb?"

"Well, there are some *great* restaurants in Atlanta—I'll take you if you come visit me—but the food in Joyous can definitely hold its own."

After that, Treble made a concerted effort to keep the chatter going, but the pervasive, nostalgic melancholy lingered after Lola Ann had to leave.

"She seemed nice," Treble commented to her sister. "I mean, it stood to reason that as a friend of yours she would be, but she seemed to actually like me. Whatever stories she's heard didn't scare her off too badly."

Charity laughed, closing her eyes as she rested her head on the back of the couch. "Lola's passion in life is books and she likes larger-than-life people. They remind her of her favorite characters. Besides, she's lived here long enough to know gossip gets embellished with time. No one should be judged based on whispers about what happened ten, twelve or twenty years ago."

"Tell that to—"

"Who?" Charity's eyes popped open. "My dad?"

"I was going to say Dr. Caldwell. Honestly," she amended, "I hadn't planned to say it at all but caught myself too late."

"What do you mean about Keith?"

Treble refused to bring up the lecture he gave her by his truck the other night; it would feel too much like tattling. Besides, he'd genuinely been looking out for Charity, and she could respect that. "Nothing. Just a gut feeling. I'm not sure he likes me much. To be fair, he didn't see me at my best the other night."

"I think he likes you fine. I know dinner was…tense. But before that, you made him laugh. He has a great laugh."

"Oh, yeah."

"Aha!" Charity straightened, looking pleased with herself. "Liked his laugh, did you?"

And a lot of his other attributes. "I was simply agreeing with you," Treble said. "Don't read too much into it."

"Are you sure? Because watching you two work together, there appeared to be some *looks.*"

Drat, she'd thought she'd been sneaky enough not to get caught. "The summer heat has clouded your thinking. Want me to turn the oscillating fan back on?"

"This has nothing to do with heat. At least, not the kind from the sun."

Treble stood, although she didn't really have any clear purpose or destination. "Charity, I'm warning you, drop it. I know you want the good doctor to date, and that's between you and him—or him and whatever woman he ends up dating—but leave me out of it."

Charity arched a pale eyebrow. "You don't threaten a pregnant woman."

Treble had to laugh at her sister's imperious tone. Maybe Keith was on to something with that Napoleon complex theory. "Let's just change the subject, pregnant woman. You guys decided on a name yet for that baby girl of yours?"

"No. There are just too many to choose from, plenty we like but no combination we love yet. We discussed naming her for someone in the family—Mom, maybe—but that didn't fit exactly right, either. There are so many people who've been important to us. Besides, we'd rather she have her own identity and never feel as if she's supposed to be living up to someone else."

Treble, named for a maternal great-grandmother she'd never met, smiled at the gentle fierceness in Charity's voice. "You and Bill are going to make good parents."

"Thank you. As tiring and occasionally alarming as this pregnancy has been, I know deep down *this* is the easy part. It's only going to get harder once she pops out."

Treble grimaced as she walked toward the window. She preferred not to think about the "popping out" details. "You look tired now. Why don't you go lie down, so you're rested enough to visit with Bill when he gets home tonight?" Charity had admitted on the phone that afternoons were hardest but had skipped a nap yesterday, probably feeling obligated to entertain her sister.

"What about you? I made you drive all the way here from Georgia, murdered your car in the process and now I'm just going to make you sit in my living room while I sleep?"

It was a gorgeous day. If it weren't so hot, she would go for a run. "Don't feel bad about the car. Trusty would have died anyway. At least here, there's a mechanic who comes highly recommended and won't gouge the price. And I can keep myself busy. I can brainstorm notes for future shows, do Sudoku or put in a movie. *You're* the one who's watched every DVD in the house three times, not me."

"They occasionally put one of those Sudoku puzzles in the paper. What are they, exactly?"

Treble went and got a book and a pen, happy to show Charity another way to kill time while she was couch-ridden.

Her sister balked at the numbers. "How many math skills do I need for this? Because being pregnant has a way of Swiss-cheesing your brain."

"It's not about math. It's about patterns. Sometimes it helps to glance at the grid without really concentrating and you'll find something you weren't actually looking for. You have to make the numbers line up in exactly the right places so they don't repeat. Here, I'll show you."

Fifteen minutes later, they'd completed a puzzle labeled "moderate" in difficulty, but Charity was actively yawning.

Treble set down her pen. "All right, now I'm going to *insist* you take a nap. And if you're still worried about my having something to do, give me a task. You know I'm looking forward to helping in the nursery. Or maybe I could grab some groceries so it's one less thing Bill has to do when he could be spending time with you?" Sometime between now and next Thursday evening, she needed to go into town anyway; she hadn't yet bought a shower gift.

"You're sure you don't mind running errands?"

"As long as you don't mind me taking your car."

Charity put together a short list, and Treble made sure her cell phone was charged so her sister could get in touch with her.

"I think that's everything," Charity said. "You shouldn't have any trouble refilling my prescription for prenatal vitamins, but have the pharmacist call me if there's a problem. Those are the sandals you're going out in?"

Treble glanced down at the lilac open-toed mules she wore with her short-sleeved, square-necked retro peasant blouse, modernized by the funky print of the sheer fabric, and white shorts. "Yeah. What's wrong with them?"

"Nothing, as long as you can walk without killing yourself." Charity sounded awestruck. "I'd never make it ten steps without toppling over."

They weren't *that* high. Charity should see the six-inch heels. "I've had practice."

"Okay, but if you end up with a broken ankle, we'll be bed rest buddies. Can you grab me my purse?"

It was hanging on the doorknob of the coat closet just inside the house. Treble carried it over to the couch.

"Thanks." Charity dug out her car keys, then startled her sister with a surprisingly accurate and irreverent impression of Harrison Breckfield. "Here are the keys to the car, young lady. I'll expect it back without a scratch and you home by dinner."

Treble laughed. "Brat."

In the garage, Treble found her sister's sensible and economic American-made compact. Probably got exceptional mileage and safety ratings, although secretly, she thought it didn't have a tenth of Trusty's individuality. She climbed inside, and as soon as she'd turned the key in the ignition, classic music rolled from the speakers. Mozart. Or Beethoven, maybe. She wasn't an authority on musicians prior to the nineteen hundreds. Grimacing, she punched radio buttons until she found the station they'd listened to in Keith's truck. A Rolling Stones tune filled the inside of the small four-door. *That's more like it.*

As she backed out of the garage, a shrill beeping started, making her jump.

Simultaneously tapping the brake and glancing back at the dashboard to see where she possibly could have screwed up already, she noticed a flashing red seat-belt symbol. "Give me a second," she told the car. "I was getting to that part."

It kept blinking at her and blaring as if skeptical she'd had any intention of following proper regulations. Yeesh. A car with a censorious attitude. She was calling Ronnie this afternoon for an update on Trusty.

On the other hand, not three minutes down the road, the air-conditioning had fully kicked in, cool currents circling her in a way she hadn't realized possible with the sun shining through the windshield. So there were at least one or two perks to being a rule-abiding conformist. Who knew?

Chapter Seven

For someone who'd sat bumper to bumper in Atlanta traffic, navigating the streets of Joyous was refreshingly simple. Even though a few buildings had changed and the years away had left a few blanks in her memory, there was no real chance of Treble getting lost in town. Traveling on the more winding, rural roads that weren't painstakingly marked might be a different story, but "downtown," four main roads formed a square. All the smaller side streets fed back into it eventually.

The drugstore was exactly where it had always been, although the pizzeria next to it was new. Brand-new, according to the Grand Opening A-frame sign sitting on the sidewalk amid a profusion of colorful potted flowers. After driving the length of the picturesque street, she found an available spot. She parallel parked, relieved when the rusty skill proved sufficient. Though Charity had been kidding with her whole "back by sundown, paint job unscathed" warning, Treble would die of mortification if she got into a fender bender.

In the shade of awnings and roof overhangs, the fresh air and short stroll were pleasant. She'd hit the pharmacy first in case they needed time to fill the prescription. She could always swing by for the pills after running her other few errands. The jovial, mustached man behind the counter, however, assured her he'd have everything ready for her in just a minute.

"Anything for Miss Charity. You say you were her cousin?"

"Half sister," Treble corrected.

"Hmm. Can't rightly say I remember you."

There was a sniff behind Treble, and she turned to find an austere middle-aged woman wearing a navy knit top and a plastic badge that proclaimed her the manager. Even without the name tag, Treble would have known Midge Moore immediately. She'd been a thirtysomething cashier with a pinched expression the last time Treble had seen her. In the interim years, she'd cut her graying hair into a bob that ended exactly at her jawline but otherwise looked exactly the same.

"I remember her," Midge told the pharmacist. "I remember her *perfectly* well. If she makes a move toward the cosmetics aisle, call security!"

The man frowned. "Security? But we—"

"Just page me on the walkie!" Midge stalked off, darting one last suspicious glance at Treble.

I really should apologize for stealing the makeup. Not that Midge had given her much of an opportunity. And acting as though Treble needed to be escorted through the store so that someone could keep an eye on her seemed over-the-top.

Treble faced the perplexed pharmacist. "Don't worry, I promise not to rush the counter and steal all the good drugs."

His eyes widened. "I'll just get you Miss Charity's vitamins so you can go."

Okay. Not a situation where humor was helpful.

Moments later, Treble was back out on the sunny sidewalk, this time feeling like a notorious felon. *Incredibly sexist.* She happened to know one of the men Charity said worked for the sheriff's department used to indulge in weekend cow-tipping, and the current elementary school principal had pulled more than his share of false fire alarms to shorten boring class periods. Then again, maybe misspent youth gave him a foundation for relating to the current pupils.

A wolf whistle directly behind her stopped her in her tracks, and she pivoted. If that were Rich Danner, she— "Bear!"

Technically, the man with the emerald eyes and broad grin on his face was named Teddy, but he'd been six feet tall by his freshman year in high school. The coaching staff tried to recruit him for basketball and, after he'd filled out more, for football. Bear had confided to Treble once during detention that he wasn't much of a team player. He was a decent guy, though, only ever in trouble when he lost his temper on another's behalf. When someone wrote Treble's number and a rather predictable limerick on the wall of the boy's bathroom, Bear had offered to draw and quarter the culprit if he were ever caught.

"Trouble J!" He swept her into a bone-crushing hug that lifted her off the concrete. "I heard you were in town, but had to see it for myself."

Hearing her radio name caught her off guard. "You know about my show?"

He nodded as he set her back down. "Went to a Braves game once in post-season playoffs. Drivin' in, a buddy and I saw your picture on a station billboard. I don't think I ever did convince him that I knew you, but we listened to your show every night I was in town."

She was touched. "You should have called in and said hi!"

The big man in his appliance repair outfit—probably specially made—blushed six shades of red. "Nah, I couldn't do that. Interrupt you at work? Besides, you might not have remembered me."

"Trust me, Bear, I—"

Behind them, a man cleared his throat. They were obviously in his way. She had to admit, Bear was tough to pass on the sidewalk. They both turned to apologize, but her words froze in her throat when she found herself face-to-face with Keith Caldwell.

"Sorry, Doc," Bear said. "I was just renewin' my acquaintance with Trouble here. She's something else."

Keith's gaze went from her eyes to the hot-pink toes peeking out from her mules and back up. "Certainly is."

"Aren't you supposed to be at work?" she asked, flustered by running into him in the middle of the afternoon. She adjusted her tone. "I mean, are you just on a break or are you off to rescue yet another damsel on the side of the road?"

He chuckled, his eyes crinkling slightly at the corners. *Definitely a nice laugh.* "Late lunch. So many patients come in during the noon hour that I wait until things slow down to grab a bite. Thought I'd check out our newest restaurant."

"How was it?" she asked.

Leaning forward, he advised in a low voice, "I'd stick with the barbecue place and the sandwich shop, personally. Unless you consider grease an acceptable food group."

Bear shook his head. "This place has been five different eateries in the last six months, none of them good. I wish they'd scrap the restaurant idea and use the space to sell fishing supplies or hardware. Somethin' useful."

The doctor cocked his head, studying Bear and Treble. "So, the two of you are old friends?"

"Oh, Trouble and I go way back." Bear squeezed her shoulder. "I told her in the ninth grade that if she ever needed someone's kneecaps broken, I was her man."

"I see." Keith took an almost imperceptible step backward.

"Offer still stands, by the way," Bear told Treble conversationally. "What's a decade or two between old friends? Speakin' of which, I guess this'll be the first year we see you at the reunion! Festival days are right around the corner."

She hadn't thought that far ahead. "I don't know." Not everyone from her graduating class held the same place of affection in her heart as Bear.

"Well, you think about it! Meanwhile, I was plannin' to duck into the drugstore before getting back to work. Summer's our busiest time. People get darn cranky about their freezers and window units breaking down in this heat."

Treble nodded. "I'll look for you if I'm at the festival."

Bear flashed a grin. "I ain't hard to spot in a crowd."

His departure left a rather large void. She turned back to the man last seen blaming her for the awkward family dinner and jeopardizing her sister's health.

Keith exhaled. "I should be going, too."

"Yeah. I promised Charity I'd take care of some stuff for her. So…'bye."

He snapped his fingers. "I didn't ask. Did you get any news on your car?"

"Talked to Ronnie yesterday. The prognosis wasn't great, but treatable. She's tracking down a carburetor, hopefully one I can afford. I should have Trusty back next week."

He grinned. "You call your car Trusty?"

"You're mocking me because I named my car?"

"I just find that particular name ironic, considering how we met."

He had a point.

"Have a nice day," he told her.

"You, too."

They both turned, obviously headed in the same direction. *Naturally.* She could just ignore him and keep walking, but she'd feel stupid pretending he wasn't there for the next couple of blocks.

"I parked Charity's car down that way, but if you'd rather, I'll just stop and do some shopping." She punctuated her teasing comment by jerking a thumb to the storefront behind her, not bothering to turn.

Keith's lips quirked into a grin so wicked her knees went weak.

Half-afraid to look, she glanced over her shoulder at the pawnshop window that inexplicably featured an array of handcuffs. Rather than get embarrassed, she just went with it. "Yep, a girl can't have too many pairs of handcuffs. You never know where you might misplace them."

"I could make a crack about that, but my kneecaps and I are terrified of Bear."

She laughed.

He lifted a hand as if to touch her face, but dropped his arm quickly back to his side. "It's nice to see you smile. I figured that after what I said the other night—"

"About how if I didn't watch my mouth I'd be the ruination of my family and put my sister in the hospital? I've forgiven you." More or less. It helped that he'd been trying to look out for the person she'd always been most protective of.

"Really? I'm surprised you're taking it so well."

"Even bad girls have their reasonable moments," she informed him, leaving him to ponder that as she sauntered toward her car.

It took him only a couple of strides to catch up with her. "You need a trained medical professional walking with you," he said. "Catch one of those heels in a sidewalk crack, you're gonna require X-rays."

"You don't like my shoes? They're one of my favorite pairs."

"I *shouldn't* like your shoes. You know what repeated wear of heels like that can do to your knees and feet? But…"

"But?"

His gaze went to her legs, and her body tingled as if he'd actually slid his hands over her thigh. "But," he said softly, meeting her eyes again. There was no need for him to finish the sentence out loud. Words would only be redundant, and she couldn't imagine the mere syllables that would accurately capture the heat in his gaze.

Treble's lips parted. She should say something to end the moment, but she couldn't think when he had that expression on his face. If she didn't stop staring, she really would trip and break something. *Like your heart?* Stupid, out-of-the-blue thought, but at least it got her moving again.

They fell into step. After a few seconds, she convinced herself she'd exaggerated the connection.

"So," Keith began. "This festival? I've never been, but it seems to be a big deal around here."

"Yeah. Have they recruited you for judging? It's normally town 'dignitaries' who officiate over the tastings, livestock prizes, Little Miss Joyous."

"No. Being a newcomer, I doubt I'm eligible for that kind of honor."

Something in his voice surprised her. She tilted her head. "You don't still consider yourself an outsider?" As far as she could tell, he fit in better in six months than she had after years. And not just with the town.

"*Outsider's* too strong. This is my home now, but I'm still proving myself." It took a self-confident man to admit something like that so casually. "Roots in this town go far back."

"*Everything* in this town goes way back," she muttered. Midge Moore's disapproving scowl flashed in her mind.

"They should ask you to judge," he said.

"That your idea of a joke?"

"No, my idea of a joke is the one about the guy who comes into the clinic and says, 'Doctor, it hurts when I move my arm like this, what can I do?'"

She rolled her eyes. The punch line "Don't move your arm like that" was older than she was. "You're hilarious. Really. I should have you on my show sometime."

"That's why you should be one of the judges, because you have your own show. Local girl goes off to become a minor ce-lebrity and comes back to serve as guest judge in the town festival? The *Joyous Journal-Report* could do a whole article."

"You just have this all planned out, huh?" Not used to driving Charity's car, she almost passed it, but stopped when Keith slowed, recognizing the vehicle before she did.

"Well, I work next to the newspaper office. I'm always afraid that if there's a slow news day, they'll canvas the neighborhood looking for story suggestions."

"You yourself pointed out that I'm not remembered fondly," she said, her tone souring despite her noblest intentions. "So I'm sure you'll understand if I don't get asked to participate in the town's most time-honored traditions."

Keith looked down. "About that. I didn't mean to hurl all that stuff at you the other night. And I didn't mean to make it sound as if you're the talk of the town. Those are snippets I've picked up here and there over the past few months because people know I'm a friend of Harrison's."

Somehow, between Keith's joking and admiring her legs, she'd temporarily forgotten that he and her stepfather were close. "It's okay. Most of the talk about me is my own fault." What wasn't her fault, she'd been blamed for anyway.

He paused, then offered her a conciliatory smile. "Guess everyone's past is complicated, right?"

"Including yours?"

"Yeah."

She waited a moment, the silence confirming her hunch that the conversation was over. "See you 'round, Doc," she said, unlocking the car door.

"See you, Trou—Treble."

The rest of her afternoon went smoothly, with no one threatening to sic security guards on her or unintentionally breaking her ribs with enthusiastic hugs. She ran out of time to find Charity a gift, but that earned her an extra day or so to think of ideas. The worst of the day's heat was dissolving into shadows and welcome breezes by the time she steered the car back into the garage.

Charity was awake, seated on the couch and frowning at a Sudoku square when Treble joined her in the living room.

"Hey," Treble said.

"Hey, yourself. I hate you for getting me hooked on this. I messed one up but couldn't figure out where the mistake was and just tore it out of the book."

Treble laughed. "That's happened to me plenty of times. I'm going to get a drink. Want something?"

"Yes, please. Lemonade, if there's any left in there. You have a good time in town?" she said as an afterthought.

Treble paused in the kitchen, recalling the surprise of seeing Keith Caldwell and the much greater surprise of how his smile had made her body flush with pleasure, the unexpected, intense kind that sent tingles up her spine. "You know, I really did." She carried the drinks into the other room. "I can see why you like the doctor so much."

"You saw Keith?" Charity's eyes widened. "You saw Keith and had a really good time. Sounds like there's more to this story I should hear."

Treble rolled her eyes at her sister's excited tone. "Well, we were both in the drugstore, our eyes met and we were overcome. I dragged him off to the condom aisle where I had my way with him. What kind of story were you expecting? We ran into each other on the street, and he was very pleasant. So maybe I was wrong about him not liking me."

Charity sighed. "Your first story was better. I'll bet Keith's really good in…the condom aisle."

"Charity!"

"Sorry. My condition. Sex is off-limits, and my fantasy life is going berserk."

"Drink your iced beverage and cool down, hormone girl." Meanwhile, Treble would do the same. Because if she weren't careful, Keith Caldwell could start making appearances in *her* fantasy life, too.

When and if she decided to end the drought her love life had become, it was not going to include a close friend of her family's or, for that matter, anyone else in Joyous. This town had already been the scene of some of her worst choices and mistakes. While she wouldn't bend over backward to become a demure and respectable citizen, she wasn't looking to repeat history, either. Not even Trouble J was that reckless.

Chapter Eight

Keith watched the first rays of light glisten orange across the embankment, making the trees glow. He forced himself to appreciate the view, even though he'd never again enjoy being out on the water as much as he once had. It would be a little while before the sun hit the lake, which was why he was wearing a thick, long-sleeved T-shirt beneath his life jacket on this last Saturday in June.

"I never realized how peaceful this time of day is," he remarked to Harrison. "That could be because I'm normally *asleep* at this hour."

Harrison chuckled. "Whiner. On a farm, this is practically midday."

"Thank God I didn't grow up on a farm," Keith groused good-naturedly as Harrison handed over the blue plastic tackle box. "What am I looking for in here?"

"The crank bait. Like mine." Harrison held up the lure he'd used, at a safe distance. Keith had treated several emergency fishing wounds and had no desire to be on the receiving end of one.

Truthfully he wasn't much of a fisher, but he'd been trying to get his friend to relax more. Despite the rural setting, Harrison Breckfield was as much a stressed-out workaholic as any Armani-suited CEO in New York, Chicago or Dallas. He was letting a lifetime of being hale and hearty convince him that he was immune to health concerns, but it didn't work that way. Just because he rarely caught a cold or had the stomach flu didn't mean he wasn't a prime candidate for heart failure. While Keith loved some of the local food, the people in Joyous were awfully quick to deep-fry everything from catfish to corn on the cob to Oreo cookies.

So when Harrison proposed going out on the lake to do some bass fishing, Keith had accepted. The man needed more recreation, less salt.

"Do you actually expect to catch anything?" Keith asked, competent enough with rod and reel to cast the line without ending up in the water himself. "Or do you just like being out here?"

Harrison snorted derisively. "Son, I don't need fishing gear to be out on the lake. That's what I have the boat for. I plan to take home some bass. 'Course, that would hold even more appeal if Joan were still with me."

Joan McMillan, Keith knew, was not Harrison's late wife but the longtime housekeeper who had shocked and irritated her employer when she quit two years ago. Now she worked part-time at the town's only retirement home.

"That woman could cook fish like no one's business," Harrison said. "She could cook damn near anything."

Too bad she no longer worked for him. From what Keith had heard about her stubbornly nurturing disposition, he could have enlisted the lady's help to make sure Harrison followed certain dietary regulations. Keith could give him medical advice until he turned blue in the face, but whether or not Harrison chose to take it—or admit to his family the extent of his condition and hand over some of his workload—was beyond Keith's control.

Harrison stared out across the water, talking as much to himself as to Keith. "House is so empty with just me in it. Maybe I should just ask Charity and Bill if they want it, although she seems to love that little place of theirs. And I'm not sure where I'd go after all this time."

Goading him because he knew it would chase away the melancholy, Keith suggested, "You could move into the old folks' home downtown. Probably get some of Joan's cooking that way."

"Old, hell! I ought to shove you right into this lake. I'm in my prime."

"As your friend, I applaud the sentiment. As your doctor, I'll remind you that if you want to keep feeling that way, you have to take care of yourself. You want to be there to watch your grandchild grow up, don't you?"

Harrison looked startled hearing it in those terms. Keith probably shouldn't have been so blunt—it wasn't as though the man were dying—but having lost his own dad to heart failure, Keith rationalized it was better to alarm Harrison a little than risk Charity losing another parent when it could have been prevented.

"Playing hardball, son?"

"I play to win," Keith said with an unrepentant grin.

"I don't know why I put up with you," Harrison grunted. "You're too much like me."

"I'll take that as a compliment, sir."

"Just be careful you don't get to be *too* much like me. You know how Charity's always after you to date?"

"About that. I—"

"She has a point. You don't want to wind up alone in a house that's too big."

"You're not alone. You have friends and family. Two…" Two loving daughters? One? One and a half? "If you're not entirely content with the way your life is turning out, seems to me the proactive thing to do is make some changes. Maybe Treble's visit is the opportunity to do that."

The man's bushy eyebrows rose, angling closer together. "Gutsy move, bringing her up."

"Charity shouldn't have to—she has enough to think about in her condition. And the other night at dinner it looked like you and Treble are too obstinate to work it out yourselves without a nudge." When Keith had first heard that the prodigal stepdaugh-ter was returning, he had worried no good could come of it. He'd come to realize, though, that in his loyalty to the Breckfields, he'd oversimplified the situation.

Despite his initial reservations, Treble's being here might benefit Charity, and it provided an opportunity for Harrison to resolve issues that clearly troubled him. Though their dinner had proven that time around Treble sent Harrison's blood pressure into the red zone, maybe it would be healthier in the long run for Harrison and his stepdaughter to address past conflicts instead of continuing to let them fester.

"You were pretty rough on her the other night," Keith said. Harrison was responsible for the employment of so many people in this town, including his son-in-law, that few people said anything that could be construed as criticism. *He can't fire me.* Besides, the man needed to hear the truth from someone he respected.

"I don't see as how that's any of your business," Harrison retorted.

"But my dating is *your* concern?"

Harrison stared him down, unwilling to bend. "I know you're smart, getting through medical school and all that, but some things you won't understand until you're a parent. That girl— You wouldn't believe the nights she kept me awake, worried about where she was or when she would be home or what the hell I was going to do with her. Nothing worked. I felt like everything she did was to spite me. I won't let her go to some rock concert; she steals my car and then grows up to get a job playing rock music. I take her to the dairy her senior year to give her some part-time hours and try to instill a work ethic, and end up having to fire a man over it. Family man, too. The guy had a wife and new baby at home, and I walked into a barn to find Treble in his arms."

Keith was surprised at how annoying the image of Treble kissing someone was. Someone other than himself, anyway— that mental picture had stolen into his mind more than once.

"She was in error, but shouldn't the adult married male have pushed her away?"

"Why do you think I fired him? Of course he was dead wrong. But he wasn't the first older guy she flirted with, and he was sleep-deprived and making bad decisions already. My point is, she shouldn't have put herself in harm's way, constantly teasing men."

Had Treble ever noticed her stepfather's gruff concern for her well-being, or had she only seen the overlying disapproval?

"Yet here she is now with this sex talk show," Harrison continued, "so she obviously didn't learn her lesson."

"I didn't get the impression that it's a show about sex; callers just sometimes bring up male-female relationships. That's not uncommon, and what passes for scandalous here would barely raise eyebrows in Atlanta."

Harrison grunted, recasting his line. "Surprises me, the way you're defending her. You barely know the girl." Then his eyes narrowed, taking Keith's measure. "Something going on there?"

"What do you mean, 'going on'?" Keith echoed, recognizing it as a lame stall tactic. "Don't be ridiculous. As you said, we just met. I empathized with her, is all, knowing how hard it is to lose a parent and how that can mess you up."

"Charity lost her mama and still managed to make decisions that weren't based on antagonizing and shocking others. *You* lost family and went on to become a doctor." Harrison held up his hand, warding off any further argument. "Why don't we just agree to disagree and enjoy our fishing, son?" In other words, he'd closed the topic and Treble was hereby off-limits.

Funny, that's just what Keith had told himself as he walked back to his office yesterday afternoon. There'd been a moment, when Treble looked into his eyes, when he'd had the insane impulse to kiss her there on the street in front of anyone who cared to watch. *Talk about off-limits.*

She'd been right the other night about healthy adults having certain…needs. He'd ignored his far too long, which didn't mean he was going to go out on the prowl and seduce the first woman who crossed his path. He had self-control, and he had goals. Somewhere out there was a local girl he could laugh with and make plans with, come home to after a long day, a girl who'd understand when his schedule unraveled due to a patient emergency.

Tonight, he'd make his first real step in finding her.

TREBLE'S SHOULDERS were sore, but the sense of satisfaction she felt more than made up for it.

"Looks good," Bill said, standing in the doorway of the nursery. He'd just screwed in the cute switch plate that matched the curtains and wallpaper. The décor was a modified teddy-bear-picnic theme. On a background of the palest pink, there were scenes of four stuffed-animal friends, including an absolutely adorable flop-eared rabbit, who was lying on a blanket and having tea while watching the clouds. Each of the four animals was featured on the curtain, and the teddy bear held the place of honor on the switch plate. "Should we wake Charity up so she can see it?"

They'd started work on the room after an early lunch—Bill had painted the bottom halves of the walls weeks ago, but that still left wallpapering the top and the trim work. Charity had been eager to see the results of their labor but had fallen asleep for an afternoon nap.

"No, let her rest," Treble said. "The baby's room isn't going anywhere."

He grinned. "That's what I thought. Just wanted to get a second opinion in case she fusses about it. I could use a cold beer, how about you?"

"Lead the way." Cold beer followed by a hot shower sounded like heaven.

They crept past his snoring wife into the sun-filled kitchen, golden with the afternoon.

"It's a nice place you guys have here," Treble said as she sat down. Would Bill hear the wistful note in her voice, or was it evident only to her?

He retrieved two bottles from the fridge. "I think so. Maybe when the baby gets older, or if we decide to have more kids, we'll need a bigger place, but right now…it's perfect."

Treble accepted the frosty bottle he handed to her, smiling inwardly at the way he'd removed the cap first. The last few guys she'd dated had been missing the chivalry gene and she forgot that some men possessed it. She sipped her beer, trying to remember when she'd felt so relaxed. If someone had told her a few weeks ago that she could feel as comfortable in her sister's kitchen in Joyous, Tennessee, as she normally did inside her broadcasting booth, she never would have believed them.

"I'm glad Charity talked me into coming here," she said aloud.

"Me, too. She's different when you're here," Bill said. "Braver. She's tried not to show it much, but she's been worried since they diagnosed the previa. I think she feels bolder with you as inspiration."

Treble glanced away. "I'm happy to make myself useful. That first night, my being here seemed…"

Bill shook his head. "As much as I respect Harrison, he can be a hard man. When I proposed to Charity some people made snide remarks about my taking the fast track to the top of the company. But—"

"He makes you work twice as hard as anyone else for half the praise?" she guessed. Bill was below several Breckfield cousins in the chain of command, but she knew her stepfather well enough to know that whatever position Bill held, he'd earned it.

"It's not that bad." Bill swallowed more of his beer, then allowed a wry smile. "Most days, it's not that bad."

"Bill? Treb?" Charity's sleep-slurred voice reached them as she pulled herself into a sitting position, her tousled blond hair just visible over the top of the couch.

Treble stood. "Sleeping Beauty wakes! We have a surprise for you."

"Ooh, I like surprises."

Bill helped his wife to her feet, and Treble followed the couple down the hallway to the nursery.

"Oh. You guys. It's…" Tears welled up in Charity's eyes. "It's just…"

When it became clear that full-on happy sobbing would ensue, Bill pulled her into his arms. Treble took that as her cue to leave, knowing this was a special parenting moment and husband and wife should be alone. Happy to take a shower, Treble scrubbed away bits of wallpaper paste and the primary paint colors they'd used on the trim to brighten the doorway, closet frame and baseboards. By the time Treble toweled off, she'd decided that maybe she could find something to do by herself for the night. She'd been underfoot for every meal since she got here, and since she planned to be here at least a couple weeks more, it might be nice to get out of Bill and Charity's way.

She pulled on a pair of shorts and the black T-shirt she normally layered over a turtleneck when she attended a hockey game, then passed Bill in the hallway as he headed to the back of the house for his chance to clean up.

Charity arched an eyebrow when she saw her sister. "'Puck You'?"

Treble shrugged, running a comb through her long, damp hair. "I go to a lot of Atlanta Thrashers games. Hey, what would you think about my hitting the town tonight? Don't worry, I'd change first."

Charity laughed. "Well, it's Joyous, so there's not much town to hit. You going stir-crazy here?"

"It's not that. I just thought you two might like an evening to do whatever it is boring married couples do." Treble grinned as she heckled her sister.

"Wish we could, but the doctor gave us strict orders."

"I hear conversation can be nice," Treble said sympathetically.

"Talk, talk, talk." Charity made a face. "I miss action."

"And they call *me* the wild child."

"Take my car, stay out all hours. You'll have to be wild enough for the both of us."

Treble smirked. "Haven't I always been?"

THERE WERE essentially three after-hours hot spots in Joyous—with a peripheral fourth in the form of a bowling alley just across the county line. The first was King Cinema, the town's movie theater. There were only two screens, though, so movies sold out quickly and were often behind the times compared to what the rest of the world had already seen. According to Charity, there'd been talk of trying to reopen an old drive-in, but too many parents recalled their own teenage outings; the idea had stalled out indefinitely in town council.

Possibly the seediest place in town was the bar. Technically the name was Duke's, but there were no signs outside that denoted the ramshackle building as such. It was reputed to be a dim, smoky place with décor limited to a single pool table. Treble had tried to glimpse the inside of the building once; from what she'd heard about the owner, he wasn't judgmental enough to care if an ID was valid. But it was a bar for serious drinkers, not troublemaking underage girls, and the no-neck bouncer—a man who would make Bear look slight—had blocked her at the doorway, his phone call to Harrison Breckfield adding insult to injury.

Blinking away memories of the stony ride home, Treble focused on the third social venue and her destination this evening, Guthrie Dance Hall. She'd been there plenty of times. The first thing a person saw upon entry was the wooden dance floor, a stage serving as its backdrop. To the right were picnic tables—long, scarred, unadorned wooden planks affixed to equally unsightly benches. Rustic surroundings notwithstanding, the establishment's cheeseburgers and home fries or chicken-fried steak with gravy could transport a diner straight to nirvana. There was also a ratty foosball game that she assumed would still be there, and a quarter billiards table. Patrons didn't have to be twenty-one to enter the hall, but they were supposed to stay on the right half of the glorified barn. On the left side was a bar with a wide range of beers on tap and a dartboard, where more than one yahoo in a cowboy hat had injured a buddy through drinking and darting.

Judging from the number of vehicles—mostly American-made trucks—crammed into the parking lot, Treble suspected both halves of the hall were equally busy tonight. Classmates from her high school had come to Guthrie after prom, girls in taffeta dresses swirling in a colorful kaleidoscope across the sawdust on the floor. Everything from birthday parties to wedding receptions were held here, publicly inviting comment and participation from the entire town. It wasn't the kind of place where a back room was available for private rental. Not counting the kitchen and restrooms, there was no back room. *What you see is what you get.*

The thought made Treble smile as she got out of her sister's car. Guthrie was one of the few town institutions she'd truly enjoyed while she lived here. She had a dim recollection of Harrison Breckfield taking some of his top staff from the dairy here one night. Maybe they'd been celebrating someone's anniversary of employment or having a small retirement party for someone. She remembered Charity, customarily angelic in her stroller, and herself sitting on one of the benches drinking a chocolate milk shake, the kind that was so gloriously thick that drinking it through a straw was nearly impossible. They'd looked on as Harrison and their mother shared a slow dance on the floor.

It wasn't a stretch to envision that as Charity and Bill's life just a few years from now—Bill out with fellow Breckfield employees, perpetually infatuated with his own wife, the two of them doting parents of a cherubic toddler. The last thing Treble would have expected to feel was jealously knifing through her, but there it was anyway. She wasn't even sure which part she envied.

The smile of unabashed appreciation the guy at the door flashed her went a long way toward restoring her spirits. He handed her change from a ten-dollar bill and made her feel younger than she was when he winked at her. Good-looking kid with the devil twinkling in his eyes, but he couldn't be any older than twenty-four.

"Have fun," he told her, letting his fingers brush hers more than necessary.

She grinned, shaking her head. "I always do."

While country music would never be her favorite style, she couldn't deny the toe-tapping appeal of the song the band was playing. She cut across the edge of the floor, navigating dancers to make her way to the formerly forbidden left side. Looked a lot like the right, with the addition of a few more neon signs and brewery logos.

She took her place beside a redheaded woman ordering a drink from the bartender, idly surveying the crowd as she waited her turn. Awash in déjà vu, she wondered how many of the faces surrounding her belonged to people she actually *knew* and how many merely reminded her of people she'd known once upon a time. Everything about being here was both familiar and foreign.

The redhead's voice was legitimately recognizable, though, catching Treble's attention.

"Ronnie?"

The mechanic turned, looking beautiful but uncomfortable in a skirt and eye shadow. "Hey, Treble. Car troubles driving you to drink?"

Treble laughed. "Something like that. I almost didn't recognize you. You must have way more patience than me to French braid your hair like that."

It was gorgeous, the plaiting bringing out different highlights and her rich color.

"I can't take credit. A friend did it for me. Lola Ann convinced me that wearing my garage cap was not acceptable attire for a girls' night out."

"Lola Ann from the library?" It was a small town; how many Lola Anns could there possibly be?

"That's the one. Lola Ann Whitford. It was my turn to buy a round, so she's freshening up her lipstick."

"She's nice. Met her the other day at my sister's."

Ronnie scanned the crowd. "Are you here with Charity?"

"No, she's on bed rest. I thought she and her husband might appreciate the evening without me underfoot."

"That's right. I forgot about her being on bed rest. Hope she and the baby are doing well. This is going to sound completely insensitive, but I'm a little envious that you were able to come without siblings in tow."

Treble studied the younger woman's frustrated expression. "Your brothers?"

"That's Danny over there, bookkeeper for my dad's garage and technically the only 'son' at Carter and Sons, kicking Joe Stubb's butt at darts." She jerked her thumb at a good-looking auburn-haired man in his mid-thirties whose attention seemed equally divided between the bull's-eye and his kid sister. "And that's Devin."

Seated farther down the bar, a second attractive, jeans-clad man in a plaid shirt scowled at a guy who'd been ogling Ronnie. Treble smothered a laugh. It was the Good Ole Boy Secret Service. She imagined that if any male worked up the courage to make a move on the pretty mechanic, one brother would contact the other through a walkie-talkie. *Hostile approaching. Swarm, swarm!*

"Your brothers spend their Saturday nights stalking you?" she asked, trying to keep her amusement at bay.

"Danny's married, but my niece Ashley goes away to horse-riding camp every summer. This year, Danny's wife volunteered to help there. They get home tomorrow night, so he's currently as free as he is overprotective."

Having once been caught violently off guard by a man's unwanted attentions, Treble thought the way Ronnie's brothers looked out for her was sweet. In a cloying, crazy-making, uncalled-for kind of way. After all, there were dozens of people in the establishment who knew Ronnie and would come to her side if some Neanderthal hassled her.

"Devin," Ronnie continued, "is the total opposite of married. He dumped his last girlfriend for telling him she loved him. Or, technically, because she expected him to say it back. It's been a few weeks, so I was hoping he'd get back in the game, busy himself tonight with single ladies, but he seems content to sit at the bar swapping jokes with his buddies and making sure no man comes within ten feet of me unless it's to ask a question about tire rotation. The truth is, I've gotten used to it, but…"

Treble waited, but Ronnie seemed too distracted to finish the sentence. She was staring past Treble, her green eyes vivid with yearning. Resisting the urge to be obvious and turn to check out whomever Ronnie was checking out, Treble instead said, "Ronnie? I get the impression there's someone you'd like to dance with."

The woman tensed, then shrugged. "Not that he'll ever notice me. Even if he did, the infamous Carter brothers would probably have him calf-roped before he got within ten feet. They both participated in 4-H rodeo when they were younger."

"No rule that says a woman has to *wait* to be noticed," Treble said. "Go make him notice you. It looks like things are getting intense with Danny's dart game."

"Which leaves Devin."

"I could help you sneak away," Treble offered. "I have lots of experience." In her teens, sneaking out had included a tree outside her window. She'd overheard an exasperated Joan, the family housekeeper, admonish Harrison that he should just have the oak cut down. Treble had wondered at the time if her step-father secretly hoped she'd leave one night and not come back, thereby freeing him of his duty to raise his late wife's child.

"You'd do that for me?" Ronnie asked.

"Do you have any moral objections to my flirting with your brother for a few minutes to distract him?"

"None. If he can't get it through his head that I'm a grown woman and not a fourteen-year-old who needs a chaperone, he deserves what—oh, hey, Lola Ann!"

The brunette, shorter than most of the crowd around them, squeezed by a man trying to talk a slim woman into dancing. "Treble! When did you get here?" Lola Ann's bright smile was welcoming.

"Just a few minutes ago. Nice to see you again."

Ronnie leaned forward, her voice conspiratorial. "Treble's going to help me try to get a few minutes of Jason's time."

"Thank goodness," Lola Ann said. "You can't keep carrying a torch for that boy and never talk to him. You don't do some-thing soon, I'm planning to take an ad out in the *Journal-Report* letting him know how you feel."

"Not unless you want your car mysteriously dismantled and sold for scrap metal," Ronnie retorted. "Besides, this isn't just about Jason. My dim-witted brothers need to understand they aren't my wardens. It would serve them right if I asked Jason to coffee over at Bestest Bakery and slipped out of here completely, but I wouldn't abandon you like that on girls' night."

Lola Ann bit her lip. "You can make it up to me later."

"Seriously?" Ronnie blushed at the thought of actually leaving with the aforementioned Jason. Treble had no idea which man in the room he was, but she had a hunch he was cute. "Treble, you'd better go do your thing before I lose my nerve."

"What thing is that?" Lola asked.

"She's going to use her feminine wiles on Devin, and I'll sneak out while he's melting into a little pile of goo."

Lola's Ann expression dimmed a few watts, her dimples disappearing. "Oh."

Ronnie cocked her head. "What? It's foolproof. I mean *look* at her."

Lola Ann did as directed, the last bit of welcome in her expression turning to resignation. "Yeah."

Uh-oh. "Maybe it's not a very good idea," Treble backpedaled. Suddenly she didn't think Ronnie was the only one harboring a crush from afar. "I don't have to—"

"What? You're not backing out on me now, are you?" Ronnie squeezed her hand. "Maybe I can work out some kind of discount on your car repairs?"

Treble couldn't help laughing. "No. While I don't mind flirting with a cute guy for a good cause, flirting for financial gain seems ooky. I appreciate the thought, though."

"Then you'll still help me out?" Ronnie pressed.

"Go ahead, Treb," Lola Ann said listlessly.

"But don't you—"

"It's fine," Lola Ann said, a note of panicked enthusiasm in her voice as her eyes met Treble's. Why didn't she want her friend to know she had a thing for Devin?

"Okay," Treble told them both, turning with a sigh.

Devin was discussing baseball with another man when she approached, monitoring his sister with an occasional glance. His eyes widened with interest as Treble wandered into his field of vision.

"Hi," she said. She turned to the other guy. "Am I interrupting your conversation?"

The man lifted his drink from the bar in a small salute. "Pretty ladies are never interruptions, ma'am."

"Oh, good. Because I was hoping to catch up with Devin here. Ronnie reminded me that we went to school together."

Devin leaned back on his bar stool, smiling lazily. "We were both in the same building during the same hours, but I don't rightly think you can say we were there 'together.' If Ronnie hadn't mentioned me, would you even have known who I was? You only had eyes for Rich Danner, as I recall."

Though she nearly grimaced at the reminder of Rich and her ill-advised feelings for him, she knew Devin was being kind. Half the town had believed she'd been trying to seduce every man she ran across, from high school teachers to married dairy workers. Shaking off the past like dirt from her boots, she summoned a smile. "That was a long time ago, and things change. For the better."

"Yeah, I've grown up a bit since high school," he said, confident in his own appeal. Why shouldn't he be? He was a great-looking guy. Yet the way he smiled at her now didn't have a fraction of the impact as merely standing on the sidewalk next to Keith Caldwell did yesterday.

"You dance as good as you look?" she challenged.

He laughed. "Guess there's one way to find out." Taking her hand, he led her through the throng toward the floor.

The band was playing a fast tune with lots of exuberant fiddle. Treble enjoyed dancing at clubs, but she was a little rusty on classic western footwork. So it was a relief that Devin mostly wanted to spin her in tight circles. She didn't have to worry about following his steps, she merely had to hold on and laugh at the sensation of whirling beneath the multicolored track lighting and hope she didn't throw up.

She meant to check covertly and discover whether or not Ronnie had left the building or was back in her previous corner with Lola Ann, but Treble was too dizzy to focus on the crowd. Her heartbeat was racing and her cheeks felt flushed when the song came to an end. Everyone, including her dance partner, stopped to clap, and she stumbled slightly.

"Easy there," a male voice said near her ear, his hands coming to her hips to steady her.

The scent of Keith's cologne did nothing to slow her pulse. How had it become so familiar in such a short time? His thumb grazed the ribbon of skin bared between her sleeveless white shirt and her jeans. Sensation rioted through her midsection, starting where his flesh met hers, such a small spark to ignite a conflagration of awareness.

She tried to catch her breath as she turned toward him. "Hey."

His lips quirked in greeting, but the expression in his eyes was more complicated than a simple smile. "Hey, yourself. I keep bumping into you in the arms of other men."

"Devin did me the honor of a dance." She fanned herself, smiling at her partner. "You could've warned me you were hell on wheels."

Ronnie's brother flashed a grin. "You looked like you could handle it. Evening, Doc Caldwell," he added with a nod.

"How's it going, Dev? That rash clear up for you?"

"Uh, yeah. The foot cream worked as promised." He shifted his weight. "Thanks for the dance, Treble."

The music had slowed, and now the three of them were standing in the way of couples swaying around them.

"Thank *you*," she said, meaning it. "That was fun."

"You find me later if you want to do it again," he told her. Then he scowled in Keith's direction, his single syllable of farewell as sharp as a bowie knife. "Doc."

Treble waited until the man had merged into the crowd before she tucked her middle finger against her thumb and flicked Keith on the arm. "That was mean."

He rubbed the spot, trying to look indignant. "I'll say."

"I meant *you*. 'How's the rash?'" she mimicked, her hands on her hips.

"I care about his well-being." Keith gave up trying to sound convincing halfway through the sentence, then pinched the bridge of his nose. "You're right. It was immature. It was unprofessional, although technically he asked for the advice at the grocery store and not at the clinic. I just… Watching the two of you spin around, I suddenly felt old and stuffy. As young and self-assured as Dev is, I'm sure he'll bounce back from my momentary lapse of manners."

She arched an eyebrow, gazing in the direction Devin had gone. "He's not *that* young."

"It wouldn't be nice to toy with his affections," Keith said. "He'll be crushed when you leave."

Since she had no interest in anything other than dancing with Devin, she wasn't sure why she felt compelled to play devil's advocate. "You're jumping to the conclusion that he'd get attached. How do you know he even wants something more than a quick fling?"

Keith startled her by brushing her cheek with his fingertips. "Whatever he *thinks* he wants, you'd have a lasting effect."

She froze, surprised by the quiet sincerity that had crept into their bickering. Keith stood motionless, as well, neither coming closer nor dropping his hand. From behind, a teenage boy and his date jostled the town doctor.

The boy drew himself up to his full height, which was still about five inches shorter than Keith. "Dude, dance or get off the floor."

"He has a point," Treble said, glad her chuckle didn't sound as nervous as she inexplicably felt. Now was the perfect time to go, maybe find Lola Ann.

"Absolutely." Keith closed his warm fingers over hers. "We should be dancing."

"What? I—"

He placed her hand on his shoulder, then slid his own to her waist. The nearby whisper of "one, two, three" from a young dancer trying to keep count with a waltz drifted to her. Treble and Keith, however, weren't doing anything so formal. Were her feet even moving? In his embrace, her thoughts had become as formless and fleeting as the atmospheric puffs of smoke from an ancient fog machine. Her blood felt thick and too hot in her veins, and she experienced a completely different kind of dizzy than she had earlier with Devin.

Deciding conversation was beyond her current abilities, she simply let herself dance. The slow, steady pull of the music en-

couraged her to let go of conscious deliberation and fall into in-
stinctive movement. When would she ever again have the chance
to twine her arms around Keith's neck, find out for herself if his
thick hair was silky or coarse across her fingertips? *Silky.* She felt
rather than heard him suck in a breath when her fingers trailed
across the nape of his neck. Had he tugged her closer, or had her
body swayed toward him of its own volition? Sandalwood and
sawdust and the less definable male scent of him swirled together
in a surprisingly heady combination.

Entering the hall tonight, a place where she'd danced away
numerous adolescent nights, had been like stepping through a
door to her past. She recalled once waiting for her date to buy a
soda and overhearing other high school girls discuss how the end
of a date was the most apprehensive moment. "You never know
if there's going to be a kiss," one had said. Treble had thought at
the time that when you were wracked with uncertainty, the best
solution was just to seize the moment. Take matters in your own
hands and end the wondering.

So when Keith's gaze dropped from her eyes to her mouth and
she felt that same fluttering against her ribs she'd experienced
with him yesterday—when, against all reason, it had seemed he
might kiss her—she followed her own long-ago advice. While
the brown demi-boots she wore tonight didn't have a particularly
high heel, she was still plenty tall enough to reach up and touch
her lips to his. Especially since, at the last second, he lowered
his head and met her halfway.

Chapter Nine

An electric current shot through Keith. A tiny, removed fraction of himself couldn't believe he was kissing Treble James. The rest of him just wanted to deepen the kiss and make it last the duration of the night.

His hands were caught in the loose curls of her hair, holding her close as he explored her mouth, learning its taste and dips and curves. She slid her tongue along his, and he wanted to groan with tortured pleasure. But for the second time in the span of one song, other dancers bumped them, jarring Keith back to reality. He jerked his head back, pulling away quickly enough to catch Treble's dazed expression. Even though she'd instigated the kiss, she looked as surprised as he'd been.

He cleared his throat as music gradually replaced the sound of his own heartbeat in his ears. "We should…leave the floor." They were a menace. People couldn't just stop in the middle of a dancing area like that, inviting collisions. *And gossip.*

How many people had witnessed his moment of temporary insanity?

"Sure." Treble's gaze had become guarded, but she met his eyes. "I could use a bottle of water, anyway."

They wound their way through the tangle of bodies, Keith wincing inwardly at all the good-natured hellos he was receiving. He hadn't realized just how many people in Joyous he knew until joining them for a rare night out in the town's most popular Saturday destination. Had he lost his mind? He'd come here tonight wanting to look for the woman Charity, Velma, Harrison and his own intuition told him his life lacked, and instead of asking some nice local girl to dance, he'd ended up making out with Treble.

Okay, it had only been a short kiss, but that mollified neither his inflamed libido nor his misgivings.

"Evening, Doc Caldwell." Jack, the bartender, offered a bemused smile. "Don't usually see you in here."

Keith darted an involuntary glance at Treble, and Jack followed the doctor's gaze, his eyes widening behind wire-rimmed glasses.

"Can I get you and your lady friend a drink?"

Fighting the juvenile urge to disavow any acquaintance whatsoever with Treble, Keith asked for two waters.

"On the house," Jack said, handing them two chilled plastic bottles slippery with condensation.

Treble took hers. "You're a very popular man, Doc. Must have cured a cold or set a broken bone for just about everyone in the county."

"Not really." He twisted the lid off his bottle. "But it sure does feel like it tonight, doesn't it?"

"So, educate me on how this works for people like you. Do we just pretend the kiss never happened?"

He choked, coughing and spluttering but mercifully managing not to spit water on his date. Er, lady friend.

"Because when you dragged me off the dance floor," she continued in the same deceptively mild tone, "I got the impression that maybe I was supposed to apologize or something."

"No." His ego didn't want her to say she was sorry for kissing him.

"Good. Because, if I'm not mistaken, you were thinking about kissing me, too."

Oh, he'd been thinking about it. He'd been thinking about it as he pulled her toward him on the dance floor and noticed the glimmer of her lip gloss—chocolate-flavored, apparently. He'd thought about it yesterday when she grinned up at him during their encounter in town.

"Thinking isn't the same as doing, Treble."

She raked him with a scathing gaze. "Tell me about it."

He blinked, feeling as though the tables had been turned with no warning. "Now you make it sound as though I should apologize. For what, utilizing self-control?" Right up until that second when he'd seen what was coming, thought *hell, yes* and bent into the kiss like a man rushing to his own doom.

Treble shrugged. "We should just agree to disagree. What one person might call restraint, another could call repression. Not reaching for something you want could as easily be cowardice as control."

She was calling him a coward? His temper boiled, at war with the banked but still-heated urge to touch her again. Proving his self-control, he kept his tone civil. "Do you goad your listeners, too?"

Instead of firing a glib response, she thought it over. "Sometimes. When I think I have a good point they need to hear."

He opened his mouth to challenge her, demanding to know if she could *take* advice as easily as she dished it to others. But then he realized he couldn't fault her for speaking her mind, not when he'd done exactly that the other night. He'd hauled her out of Charity's to criticize her behavior, yet she'd forgiven him because what he'd said at least held a nugget of sound advice. Or at least honest intentions.

"You remind me of another outspoken woman I knew once." His words stunned him. He hadn't meant to say anything of the sort, but his sister would have liked Treble. Both women exasperated him while earning his grudging admiration at the same time.

"Is that a flattering comparison?"

His smile felt tight on his face, a mask that might not hold. "Difficult to say."

She glanced around. "I had planned to find Lola Ann Whitford after my dance with Devin. I'd better go do that. Thanks for the water."

Keith would rather have been thanked for the dance—or their brief, searing kiss. He used his few inches of superior height to help her scan the crowd. "Lola Ann's over by the dartboard, with Ronnie."

"Ronnie's still here? Nuts." Treble swished the remaining water around in her bottle somewhat violently.

"Problem with Ronnie?"

"What? Of course not. It's just that I was trying to help her out with something earlier, and I guess it didn't work. I'm really on a roll this evening." She muttered the last bit almost to herself, then recovered. "Take care, Doc."

He nodded, absently curious about the favor Treble had tried to do for the mechanic she'd only met days ago. Watching her angle her hips to thread through the growing number of people in the hall, he thought to himself that Ronnie was lucky. He wouldn't mind having a woman like Treble on his side. Whatever else could be said about the fearlessly irritating woman, she was passionate, loyal and bold.

Because he'd yet to look away from her, he saw Rich Danner approach Treble, staggering slightly. The draft beer in his hand probably wasn't his first. Keith leaned forward as though trying to catch their conversation, which was stupid. Even a few feet closer, he wouldn't have been able to hear them over the din of people chatting and the band belting out a Southern-rock standard.

Still, Keith didn't need the exact words to follow the conversation. Treble's body had tensed almost imperceptibly when the ex-boyfriend reached her side, but in profile, she appeared to maintain her smile as he spoke. She shook her head, gesturing toward the back wall where Ronnie was throwing darts.

Whatever Rich said next erased her smile, and Keith found himself moving forward at the same time Treble did, instinct and an uncharacteristic flare of possessiveness spurring him into motion.

While Keith muscled through the crowd, Treble didn't get very far. Rich had grabbed her shoulder and continued to plead his case. The second time she jerked her arm in an effort to dislodge him, Keith saw red. He lunged and clasped his fingers around Rich's shoulder.

"Let go of her now." Keith's voice was low.

Rich glanced around, his eyes jittery. "What's your problem? I'm just convincing an old flame to dance."

"Let go."

"Sure. Sure, man." The man slid his hand off of Treble. "We were just chatting about old times, Doc. No hard feelings."

Keith didn't trust himself to look at Treble. Would she even appreciate his interference? But her scowling at him was the least of his worries. If she was furious with Rich, it would further fuel Keith's anger with the man. And there was a strict no-fighting rule at Guthrie's.

Reflexively, his fingers tightened on Rich. "Have Jack call you a cab. Go home, and sleep it off."

Rich frowned. "Evening's young."

"Your evening is over."

Rich glanced down at the doctor's hand, looking for a moment as though his own temper was riled. Then he met Keith's eyes. Whatever he saw there penetrated his buzz. "Okay, Doc."

Only then did Keith release him and turn to Treble. Her eyes, unnaturally wide in her pale face, shot through him like twin cannonballs to the gut. She looked shaken. Where was the righteous indignation he'd expected? Frankly, he wouldn't have been surprised if she'd drop-kicked Rich before Keith had a chance to reach them. Yet he hadn't been able to stop himself from coming to her aid.

"You all right, Treb?" It took effort not to snap out the words, switching gears from annoyance with Rich to concern.

"Yeah. Not the first time a guy's asked me to dance and didn't want to take no for an answer." She folded her arms over her chest, the bottle of water peeking up around an elbow, and glared at Rich. "But it had better be the last time you ask."

He nodded, sheepish now. "You know I didn't mean anything by it."

"I don't care." She was standing straighter now, more self-possessed than she had been a moment ago. "Don't ever touch me again."

"You clear on that?" Keith double-checked, only partially satisfied when the man nodded again, then shuffled off posthaste in the direction of the bar.

"Wow," Treble breathed when they were alone. "For a second, I thought you might actually hit him."

Adult skeletons were made up of 206 bones; for a nanosecond, Keith had contemplated breaking all of Rich's. "I'm a physician. Violence is against our creed."

"Right. Well, thank you." The way she avoided his gaze when she said it bothered him. He wanted to see in her eyes that the unpleasant encounter hadn't done any real harm. When she did glance back at him, it was with a dismissive expression. "Would you mind following him? It's for the greater good that we make sure he orders that cab and not another drink."

"Agreed." He almost asked her again if she was okay, but he would have felt like a mothering idiot. It had been a brief moment and was over now. Besides, if she weren't okay, he doubted she'd admit it. They locked gazes for another moment, but then she turned and began walking in the opposite direction.

At the bar, Rich was living up to his promise of calling it a night. He was slumped on a bar stool, cradling a chipped white mug in his hands. The coffee smelled a lot better than he did.

"Taxi's on its way," Rich muttered when he noticed Keith. "But it'll take a while."

Keith nodded. There was one family-owned cab company in Joyous, with two brothers driving old sedans that Ronnie kept in good shape for them. A rural area like this wasn't exactly a hub for public transportation.

"I really am sorry about earlier," the man added, his eyes bleary and his tone defeated.

"I'm not the one you should apologize to." Although he wasn't sure Treble would be interested in hearing anything her ex-boy-friend had to say. The last glare she'd sent him was sharper than anything being thrown at the dartboard.

Rich dragged a hand over his face. "I just miss her so much."

Keith frowned. "I can see why, but that was years ago. Treble's moved on."

"Huh?" His head pitched to the side as he stared up at Keith. "Not Treble. My wife. Ex-wife. I came here tonight because it's too damn lonely at home and I had too damn many beers feeling sorry for myself. Thought Treble could help take my mind off my problems, you know? She was always real good at that."

Keith's finger clenched in an involuntary fist. He didn't know if the man had meant his words in a lewd way or not, but Treble shouldn't be anyone's second choice. And Keith didn't like hearing Rich talk about her, no matter the meaning. "Give up ladies until you're coping better with the divorce. Beer, too, while you're at it."

"Dang, Doc." Rich said something else, but Keith wasn't paying attention. In his peripheral vision, he'd caught Treble heading toward the front door. Her stride was too quick to be casual, and her head was ducked in a way that didn't jibe with her innate boldness. Was she okay?

It's none of your business. She said she was fine. But that wasn't enough to lay to rest the protective instincts that had been aroused. With another glance at Rich, who appeared to be sobering up, Keith followed Treble out the door.

THE NIGHT AIR, though sultry, was considerably cooler than the packed hall. Treble dragged in a lungful of oxygen, trying to stifle the last of the threatening hysteria as she crossed the pavement. She was being an idiot—recognizing that fact was why she'd done an about-face as soon as Keith was distracted and left instead of joining Ronnie and Lola Ann. She'd prefer no one else get a glimpse of her in idiot mode. Rich Danner wouldn't have hurt her. The room had been full, and he'd been wobbly enough that she could have taken him out with a few choice Tae Bo moves. Still, as nostalgic as this evening had made her, there were parts of her teen years she'd rather not relive.

It was Mitchell's hand she remembered on her bare shoulder, not Rich's. The former dairy worker's face had been hard with lust. He hadn't wanted her, he'd merely wanted to prove something. She was surprised and appalled that the memory still had any effect on her. After all, they'd been interrupted before the intent she'd seen in the man's hungry gaze and set jaw could become a reality.

She remembered in slow-motion clarity how *relieved* she'd been to see Harrison Breckfield, emotion prompting the spontaneous "Dad!" she'd never used before or since. But he'd showed no signs of hearing her, too busy drawing his own conclusions about her swollen lips. Then he'd turned to her with an expression that made Mitchell's look kind by comparison.

"He's a married man, Treble, with a new baby at home. Even for you, this is… Get out and go home. Now."

She learned later that he'd fired Mitchell with a hefty severance package. Harrison blamed her for making "a good man lose his job." He probably held her responsible for Mitchell's wife leaving a few months later, but as far as Treble could tell, the woman was well quit of her husband.

"Treble?"

She jumped, her heart in her throat when she faced Keith. She jabbed her car keys in his direction as she spoke, punctuating her sentences. "Don't sneak up on me! You're a doctor. Isn't too much adrenaline at once dangerous?"

"Sorry." He peered at her, a vertical line of concentration forming between his brows. He looked like a guy trying to decipher a sign in a foreign language.

Bad enough that she'd overreacted inside when Rich grabbed her, but now she was making a habit of it. *Pathetic.* "Don't be. I guess I'm just jumpy tonight. I'm two screams away from being one of those blondes in a horror movie who shrieks at her own shadow but goes down into the scary basement anyway."

He laughed. "I'm having trouble picturing that."

"Well, it's a more convincing image when you're eating over-buttered popcorn." She stopped at Charity's car, propping her hip against the hood. "You should be inside, Doc. That's where all the fun is."

He cast a look over his shoulder; the hall was the only building visible in the dark. From the outside, beneath the milky spill of parking lot lights and thousands of stars, it looked smaller somehow. "I'm pacing myself. Tonight was my first time here."

"You're kidding? You've been in Joyous *how* long?"

He shrugged. "Doctors stay busy. And I'm not much of a dancer."

Her mind flashed to the way his body had felt flirting in close distance with hers, his hands splayed over the denim seams of her jeans. "That's not the way I remember it."

"What about you?" he challenged, leaning on the bumper. "Why are you leaving so early?"

She averted her gaze, watching a sizable cricket hop its way across the asphalt. "I've had about all the fun I can stand for tonight."

"You're not letting Rich run you off?"

"Not exactly. He's harmless. Annoying but harmless. He just…dredged up some memories."

Keith didn't say anything, assessing her silently. Treble had never done well with silence. At home, it had meant disapproval.

On-air, it meant she wasn't doing her job. In her own thoughts, it formed a void where self-doubt could rush in.

Hell with it. It wasn't as if half the town didn't already know she and Mitchell had been kissing in that barn. Why not give someone the accurate version? "When I was in high school, after Rich and I broke up and he was kind enough to further my already tainted reputation, one of the guys who worked at the dairy caught me off guard."

Next to her, Keith stiffened, immobile but exuding leashed tension just below the surface. It was like energy being flash-frozen. "How off guard?"

"Not enough to require therapy, but bad enough that Harrison was scandalized when he walked in on us." She kept her tone flippant. "He assumed I'd been playing modern-day Lolita and leading the guy astray. Hard to blame him, really, all things considered."

Keith digested this information. "It wasn't your fault."

"I didn't try very hard to convince him of that. That first second, I was too numb to realize what he thought. Then I was stung and stubborn and… Doesn't matter now."

"Seems like it matters to you."

"You're wrong." Harrison had made up his mind about her a long time ago, and she'd certainly demonstrated over the past decade that she didn't need his presence in her life.

It shouldn't matter what Keith thought, either, but she found herself wondering what he made of her admission. Physicians were trained to analyze situations with scientific detachment, weren't they? Maybe his logical deduction was that a teenage girl who'd run around town with reckless disregard for the rules, earning attention through outrageous flirting, deserved whatever consequences she brought down on herself.

She straightened. "I should go. I didn't tell Charity how late I'd be, and I don't want them to worry."

Keith raised an eyebrow. "You live in Atlanta without having to answer anyone. You really think Charity's going to be concerned about you loose on the wild streets of Joyous at the ominous hour of nine p.m.?"

Okay, put that way, it had definitely been one of her flimsier excuses.

Come to think of it, she didn't have a lot of practice making excuses. Normally she just put herself out there without defending her words or actions knowing people were going to form their own impressions, regardless.

Keith stood, facing her. "I said earlier you reminded me of someone—my older sister, Gail. I used to admire her, the way she seized the day. Full speed ahead and damn the torpedoes."

"Used to?"

"She drowned. It's not something I talk about much." He looked down at his hands, splayed wide across his thighs. "I was with her. Gail was such a strong swimmer, Dad used to call her part mermaid. She challenged me to a race, but an undertow advisory had been posted. When I was younger, I was fascinated by her bravery in bending the rules, even egged her on with dares. But by that summer, I'd realized some of her behavior was just plain self-destructive. I told her not to be an idiot and that I was leaving. I thought maybe she'd come with me, calling me a chicken all the way up the beach, or that the lifeguard would notice her and yell at her to get out of the water, but... Dad died two months later. Heart failure, officially. His heart wasn't healthy enough to withstand the shock and the stress of losing his baby."

"That's awful." Her chest constricted in sympathy. She knew all too well how difficult it was to lose a parent. And coming on the heels of already burying a beloved sibling? Unimaginable.

"Once he passed away, I started blaming Gail. If she hadn't been such a daredevil, if her hobbies had been stuff like stamp-collecting, she would still be here, and so might he. The more I missed her, the less angry I felt. I was able to remember her many good qualities instead of just the one that pissed me off and got her killed.

I started blaming *myself* instead. I beat myself up for not talking her out of a quick swim, for not being able to reach her when it became clear she was struggling. But eventually I realized that no amount of blame could change what had already happened."

Treble had heard all kinds of personal information when people called into her show, but Keith confiding in her was a far more unexpected intimacy. "Why are you telling me this, Doc?"

"I don't know." He shoved his hands in his pockets. "You said it doesn't matter what Harrison thinks of you, but it matters what *you* think. Maybe I wondered whether there are things in your past you're blaming yourself for, things that weren't your fault."

"Well. Thanks for the psychoanalysis, but I didn't think that was your specialty." She'd made it all the way to the driver's side door when her conscience gave her a swift, pointy-toed kick in the ass. "I'm sorry, Keith. That was… You're really not getting me at my best tonight, are you?"

His teeth flashed white in the soft darkness around them. "It wasn't all bad."

Was he thinking of their kiss? Warmth spread through her until she recalled what she'd said to him afterward. "I gave you a hard time for not reaching for what you want when a wiser woman would have applauded you for being a gentleman. I temporarily let myself forget that there are other guys who—"

"No. There's a big difference between reaching for something and trying to take it by force, Treble. You had a point. People afraid of taking any risks at all miss out on a lot of the rewards." He came closer. "In keeping with that theme, are you free for breakfast tomorrow?"

"You're asking me out?" Her breath caught.

Who would have guessed the town doctor had a thing for mouthy women who tottered around in unhealthy shoes and nearly caused bar brawls? Maybe he'd picked up a fever of some kind from one of his patients. Fever was known to cause delusional behavior.

"Not exactly," Keith clarified. "More like I'm asking you in. Harrison and I have this Sunday brunch tradition. The first time, I came to his house to check…well, that's not important. Tomorrow morning I could pick you up on my way. Do you want to join us?"

That sounded as cozy as falling face-first into a beehive. "You, me and Harrison?" The doc was *definitely* delusional.

"We just agreed that sometimes people have to gamble, step out of their comfort zones."

"This isn't one of those times." The words *Harrison and I have this Sunday brunch tradition* were curdling in her stomach like sour milk.

It was one thing for Harrison to have a great relationship with Charity; she was his flesh and blood. Treble had accepted that she and the old man would never be so close. But that Harrison had a more fatherly relationship with even Keith… The day Treble turned twenty-two, she'd returned to her college apartment and found a message from her roommate that Charity had phoned. When Treble called home that night, Harrison answered. As soon as he heard her voice, he'd said, "I'll get your sister for you." He hadn't even wished her happy birthday.

"I know Harrison Breckfield is a friend to you, Doc, but you didn't have to grow up with him." Cringing, she realized Keith's own father had died before watching his son become the compassionate doctor he was now. "I'm not trying to be selfish, but I think it's best for everyone if I don't go."

"A few days ago I would have thought the same thing. I was wrong about you, Treble. Don't you think you and Harrison could be wrong about each other?"

Tears pricked the back of her eyelids, making her feel foolish. "I don't think it's about right or wrong. Some people just… Look, I'll think about what you said. Maybe I can join the two of you for breakfast some other time."

"All right." When she opened the car door, Keith placed his hands over the window, leaning forward to impart a few final words for her to mull over on the ride. "But remember, we rarely have as much time as we expect."

Chapter Ten

"Treble? You do realize that you just agreed Cinnamolicious would be a good name for your niece?"

"Sure, it has a nice ring to it." Treble stared through the lacy kitchen curtains and across the backyard. Belatedly, her sister's words registered, causing Treble to drop a mug into the sinkful of warm suds. "Wait. What the heck kind of name is Cinnamolicious?"

Propped in one chair with her feet up on another, Charity grinned. "A malicious one?"

Treble flicked a handful of water at her. "Next time, *I* get to run into town for groceries and Bill can stay here to groan at your puns."

"At least the groaning means you heard me. Honestly, you looked a million miles away."

Just up the road, actually. Was Keith still at Harrison's, or was brunch over by now? Would the doctor tell the other man he'd invited Treble to join them? She hoped not. Her stepfather would probably view her not showing up as another failure. Which would make him a hypocrite because she'd bet her down payment that Harrison would be relieved not to have her there. She hoped Keith never mentioned it to Charity, either. Treble's sister had never been subtle about her wish to have a whole, happy Rockwellian family. Why let the young woman in her overemotional state get her hopes up about something that had been a spur-of-the-moment invitation Keith himself had probably thought better of within the hour?

With a sigh, Treble allowed herself to think of the other question that had been circling her mind all morning like the wash water swirling down the drain. If Keith's invitation had been for a true breakfast date, just the two of them, would she have accepted?

The jangle of the telephone interrupted her thoughts, and Charity picked up the cordless she kept close to her at all times. "Hello? Hey. What are you doing working on a Sunday?" Charity asked, her voice full of affectionate reprimand.

Harrison, maybe? Lord knows he worked unrelenting hours. Or…Treble's heart rate accelerated, the sun streaming through the glass suddenly hotter than it had felt seconds ago. Perhaps Keith was on the phone.

"Yeah, she's right here," Charity said.

Treble turned with raised eyebrows, not even trying to disguise her eavesdropping. "For me?" she mouthed.

Charity nodded but didn't offer any clues as to who the caller was. Instead, she angled her head suddenly as if she didn't want Treble to know about this part of the conversation. Treble reached for a dish towel so she could dry her hands. Meanwhile, Charity's eyes were growing as wide and round as the frying pan they'd used to make pancakes.

"You're kidding! No, she neglected to mention anything like that."

This didn't sound good. "Charity, is it for me? Give me the phone."

But Charity merely switched hands, moving the cordless farther away from her sister. "You're sure? It's not like—"

"Charity!" When her sister looked up with the world's worst expression of feigned innocence, Treble huffed out an impatient breath. "Did they or did they not call to talk to me?"

Charity's shoulders sagged in defeat. "I guess I should give Treble the phone. What? You're sure you don't want to talk to her now? I thought— Well, okay. Yeah, I can give her the message." With one punch of her index finger, Charity maddeningly tapped the red Talk light, disconnecting the call.

Treble took a seat. "Did you just hijack my phone call?"

"Is there something you maybe neglected to mention about last night's excursion to Guthrie Hall?" Charity asked, her expression completely blank.

Oh, yikes. Treble had actually omitted several details about her evening. For starters, given Charity's overzealous interest in Treble's running into Keith the other day, she could just imagine Charity's reaction to the news that they'd danced last night. And then kissed. And then spent a good ten minutes sitting on the hood of Charity's car exchanging confidences. Treble also hadn't mentioned drunken Rich Danner hitting on her, only to be chased off by the town doctor with murder in his eyes.

"Nothing, ah, comes to mind." Treble was such a patently *bad* liar that she was shocked to this day Harrison hadn't been able to see that she was telling the truth that afternoon with Mitchell. Or would have told the truth if her stepfather had given her half a chance to explain. Instead, he'd merely frozen her out. Again.

Charity pursed her lips. "Well, that was Ronnie on the phone. She said that your car should be ready by midweek. And that she appreciates your help?" There was a pause, as Charity obviously hoped for more information.

If Charity didn't know about Ronnie's crush on this Jason guy, Treble wouldn't be the one to tell her. Relief ebbed through her. "That's all? She just wanted to tell me about Trusty and say thanks?"

"No. There was also the part where she said rather apologetically that she wouldn't have 'dangled you in front of' her brother if she'd known you were involved with Doc Caldwell."

"I'm not *involved* with anyone. You know that. The doctor and I danced only once. I think it might have been a slow dance. Maybe she saw us and drew the wrong conclusion."

"Actually, she seemed to be basing her conclusion on—and

I quote—'that kiss half the women in town were talking about after church.'"

So not only was the gossip grapevine alive and well in Joyous, Tennessee, Treble was once again on the tip of everyone's tongue. The adage must be true—the more things changed, the more they stayed the same.

CHARITY'S CHILDHOOD friend, Penny Paulson, arrived late Wednesday afternoon to help set up everything for the baby shower. Officially, she was the hostess, but given the guest of honor's limited movement, the party would be at Charity and Bill's house.

Treble was in the process of relocating dining room chairs to the living room to provide more seating. "How many women are we expecting?"

Penny, tanned from her cruise, looked up from the cooler of party trays she was unpacking and chortled. "Now, see, once the party starts, you'd have to give me your passy because you said *expecting*."

Since none of Treble's close friends had kids, Mommy slang was foreign to her ear. It took her a minute to realize that *passy* referred to the pacifier she wore around her neck on a shiny green piece of curling ribbon.

Charity, directing from the couch, wore a pacifier on yellow ribbon because it matched the daisy print on her maternity dress. "There will be eight guests."

"Nine total," Penny chirped, "including the glowing mommy-to-be."

Treble waited until the other woman made another trip out to her car before asking, "Remind me, was she always this chipper, or did she just really have a good time on that cruise?"

Charity giggled. "A little of both. Confidentially, she and her husband went through a rocky few months last fall. They've been working on getting their marriage back on track, and the long cruise was part of that. I don't think we could wipe that smile off her face with two rags and a bucket of bleach. But, under normal circumstances, she does have a naturally sunny disposition. We're a lot alike."

They were. Both lifelong friends were bighearted, glass-half-full optimists married to their high school sweethearts, but Penny took cheerful to a whole new level—one Treble hadn't realized could be reached without pharmaceutical help. *Speaking of help.*

"I'll go see if there's anything left in the trunk I can carry for her."

This got another laugh from Charity. "How could there be? Her car isn't *that* big."

So far, Treble and Penny had brought in two coolers of food, a cooler with ice and soft drinks, banners and pink and white balloons that now hung all over the living room and an enormous pink-wrapped gift topped with a silver bow the size of Treble's head.

"What do you think's in the box?" Treble asked as she crossed the living room toward the front of the house.

"It could be the bassinet we registered for, in its unassembled state. Or a big-screen TV."

"I'm sure Bill would vote for the latter," Treble teased. Her brother-in-law planned to grab dinner with a couple of guys from the dairy tonight since his home would be an estrogen extravaganza for the next couple of hours.

She pushed the screen door open and stepped onto the porch. Penny stood by her car, but she wasn't unloading packages. Instead, she was talking to an attractive black woman with close-cropped hair and cheekbones that supermodels would covet.

"Treble, have you met Keisha Lewis? She'll be having her own shower before she knows it!"

Keisha beamed, her hand going to her still-flat belly in the same reflexive gesture Charity made about ten times a day. "I'm four months along with my first. Charity's promised to lie to me and tell me delivery's a piece of cake."

Treble grinned. "Nice to meet you. And congratulations."

Penny hefted the last of her party supplies, and Treble offered to carry Keisha's gift inside.

"It's a Johnny Jump Up," Keisha whispered as they took the porch steps.

More terminology that wasn't part of Treble's everyday life—wasn't "Johnny Jump Up" a drinking song she'd heard in a pub during her month with an Irish charmer?

Keisha was taste-testing Penny's ginger-ale-and-sherbet punch when another car came down the driveway. Treble opened the door to admit two women. The strawberry-blonde with great taste in shoes introduced herself as Heather Lynn Jacob. Not to be confused with her slender companion Heather, a woman who offset her pale lavender sundress with funky sunglasses and the most unruly mop of auburn curls Treble had ever seen. Next came Fawn, a teacher like Penny, but for a much younger grade. Lola Ann walked in as Treble was handing out pacifier necklaces and name tags shaped like diaper pins.

That left only one arrival. At the knock on the door, Treble swallowed, knowing who was on the other side. After Treble's mother had been killed, Joan McMillan had been the most maternal figure in the girls' lives. However, Treble had resented her presence at the time, the warm hugs offered in lieu of her mom's, the scrumptious hot meals designed to help the girls forget their father wouldn't be home in time for dinner. She'd last seen Joan at Charity's wedding when the woman had still worked for Harrison, and while the woman had always been more loving than her stepfather, her disapproval had been equally evident.

Wonder if she's heard the latest rumors, Treble thought as she opened the door. She'd overheard her brother-in-law on the phone last night and, as far as she could tell, Harrison was suggesting Bill not let Treble run amok while she was staying under the Sumner roof. To his credit, Bill hadn't even mentioned the conversation to her. Charity seemed not at all worried about her reputation, although she was annoyed that Treble wouldn't share any details about her night on the town. Charity had expressed skepticism over Treble's official statement: "It was a one-time thing, a quick kiss at the end of a dance that got exaggerated by people who clearly need to get lives."

Joan McMillan, standing on the porch in periwinkle slacks and a white polo shirt with periwinkle embroidering on the collar, looked so much the way Treble remembered that she swore she could smell baking bread and Joan's signature spaghetti sauce.

"You haven't changed a bit," Treble breathed, slightly startled. It was like a memory walking up to you on the street.

The woman's green eyes crinkled at the corners behind her bifocals. "What a polite liar you turned out to be. Not what I expected. On either count."

Not knowing entirely how to take the older woman's words, Treble decided on amusement. Joan had always had a paradoxical expression, a mischievous smile on her matronly features. The truth was, Treble might have really liked the other woman if it hadn't been so tempting to tell Joan all the things she wanted to tell her mother—about who the cutest boys were at school, the classes Treble actually looked forward to, the colleges she wanted to attend. It had been easier to dismiss Joan along with Harrison and the annoying "I know how you must feel" high school guidance counselor than to bond with the housekeeper and feel guilty about it. As an adult with more than a decade of perspective, Treble knew her mother would have *wanted* Treble to have some adult allies, people who cared for the daughters she'd left behind. That knowledge only made Treble feel more awkward over the bad attitude she'd displayed on more than one occasion.

"You going to let me in?" Joan asked gently. "Or should I just hand over the present and get out of here?"

Treble blinked. "I'm sorry. I guess I was—"

"Reliving old memories? It's like that for me, too. I ran into Charity at the grocery store when she was about six months along. She was reaching for the same brand of cookies she always loved as a little girl and it was surreal, the woman she is over-lapping the child I adored."

Treble waved Joan in. "At least one of us was adorable. I probably just gave you gray hairs."

Joan smiled, running a hand through the chin-length hair that had been all-white since Treble was in high school. "Nature took care of that for you, dear. But maybe you helped me get a jump start on the high blood pressure…not that I mind having an excuse to routinely visit Doc Caldwell."

The knowing expression when she said his name made it clear that, yep, she'd heard the latest rumors about Treble.

"It was just a dance," she blurted before she could stop herself.

Joan's laugh trilled over top the conversation of the other women crowded into the living room and kitchen. "I didn't ask, dear. You're a grown woman."

You're a grown woman. She'd said it almost…proudly. Treble swallowed a lump of emotion. She'd told herself dozens of times that it didn't matter what people from her past thought of her; now she knew that was a lie. The understated approval in Joan's voice warmed her soul.

"Thank you."

Pausing just long enough to squeeze Treble's hand, Joan walked into the room to greet Charity. Treble used the moment to compose herself, then turned to hear the rules to Penny's "buzzword" game and how the woman who'd collected the most of her opponent's pacifiers by the end of the shower would take home a door prize.

"Charity shouldn't be eligible," one of the Heathers teased. "She's already getting a pile of loot."

True. The coffee table was completely hidden beneath pastel-colored boxes and gift bags.

"I think we should open presents first," Penny said. "We need to free up the table space for food and games!"

Charity grinned. "Works for me."

Treble was designated note-taker, writing down everyone's contribution so that Charity could write the appropriate thank-you letters. As Charity predicted, the gift from Penny was a bassinet. Joan had hand-knitted an absolutely gorgeous baby blanket. Fawn had put together a breast-feeding supply kit, which gave Treble pause. Other than the prerequisite breasts, she hadn't realized a woman needed supplies. She did her best not to contemplate how some of the more complicated apparatuses worked. There were a couple of outfits so cute that Treble momentarily wanted a baby of her own to dress until she came to her senses and remembered that she could buy tons of clothes for her niece without worrying about how she was going to put the kid through college.

"That one's from me," Treble said when Charity finally got to the plainly wrapped flat box.

The practical part of the gift was a hundred-dollar gift certificate to the town's only store devoted to infants—that way, Charity and Bill could put it toward anything they didn't get or use it for ongoing needs like diapers and crib sheets. The sentimental part was a cherrywood rectangular frame with four square cutouts in various sizes.

"Treble!" Charity pressed a hand to her trembling lips.

"The empty square is for Baby Sumner," Treble said lamely, once again surprising herself with how choked up she felt. Maybe Charity's hormones were contagious?

Inside the frame, there was a baby picture of Treble—she was diaper-clad and crawling away from the camera, laughing over her shoulder—one of Charity, angelic even at a week old, and a black-and-white photo of their mom at six months old. Both girls had been given small cedar boxes of their mother's keepsakes after her funeral, and Treble had found the photo in hers.

Charity sniffed. "So do I waddle over there to give you a hug, or—"

"I'll come to you." Treble stood, then wove her way between the rearranged chairs that crowded the room. As she leaned down to embrace her sister, she whispered, "You gotta stop the water-works, or I'm going to cry, too."

"Nonsense," Charity returned. "You're made of stronger stuff than me."

Really? Because Treble thought it took a certain amount of inner strength to make a relationship last as long as Charity and Bill had and to face the uncertainties of motherhood. Treble hadn't even invested emotionally in a pet. Maybe once she got her own place, she'd get a cat. Better yet, a hamster. Start small.

Penny clapped her hands together, making Treble think two weeks aboard a cruise was definitely too long. The woman seemed to think she was the activities director responsible for keeping them all on schedule. "Okay, ladies, what's say we eat? Charity, you stay there, honey, and I'll fix a plate for you."

Charity nudged Treble. "You'd better get in line. That covered plate Joan brought in was her homemade apple pecan bars. They'll go fast."

Did Charity want a moment to herself? This was quite a crowd for a woman who'd been mostly housebound for the past month. Treble obligingly took a place in line, ending up between the red-headed Heathers.

The one wearing the great lime-green kitten-heel slides laughed self-consciously as she picked up a paper plate. "I need these extra calories like I need a hole in the head."

"Oh, live a little," the other Heather said playfully.

Easy advice to give, Treble noted, when you were built like a stick figure. The observation prompted a self-admonishment not to sound dismissive the next time Alana mentioned her weight. Though her friend back in Atlanta was definitely not fat, the woman had to work harder on her figure than Treble did.

"So, Treble," Keisha asked from the other side of the kitchen table, "do you know most everyone from when you lived here?"

She shook her head. "Just Penny and Joan. Lola Ann moved here after I left, and since Charity and I were so many grades apart, there were a lot of classmates of hers I never had the chance to meet."

Keisha nodded. "My husband and I are fairly new to the area ourselves, but we just love it here."

The Heather with darker hair made a face. "I've lived here my whole life, but my sister and I were homeschooled, so I didn't really start meeting people until I moved out."

"Now she works for the town paper!" Heather Lynn interjected. "I love my job at the local florist, but it must be exciting to be a reporter."

"Oh, you're with the *Joyous Journal-Report?*" Treble asked. "Keith mentioned that's right next to his office."

The immediate silence that followed as speculative gazes turned toward her served as an unspoken *whoops*. Why on earth had she gone and mentioned the doctor? The women had lulled her into a false sense of security by their seeming ignorance of any gossip concerning Treble.

"You mean Doc Caldwell?" A smile flirted at the edges of Heather's lips. "Yeah, passing him on occasional mornings and evenings is one of the perks of working at the paper. I'm not so much a reporter as glorified fact-checker, part-time photographer and horoscope writer."

Treble latched on to the conversational rope, glad the woman had turned the subject back to her job. "Oh, are you an astrologer?"

"No, a single parent. I fill in here and there, occasionally taking an extra duty in exchange for a salary bonus."

"That can't be easy," Treble said, "juggling your job responsibilities and kids." Her stepfather hadn't even had the financial worries most parents would, but other challenges had certainly defined their household.

Heather scooped some pasta salad onto her plate. "I put together a support group for a little while—single parents in Joyous. Me, Becca Gibbons, CJ Sanchez, Maggie Cline, Jason McDeere—"

Heather Lynn sighed dreamily and Keisha fanned herself.

"—But it just didn't last," Heather said. "Because we were already so stretched to spend whatever time we have with our kids that it was difficult to find even more to spend with one another."

"That," Heather Lynn said, "and all the women in the group were lusting after Jason, which could have caused tension eventually."

"True." The other Heather laughed. "He's a babe."

Hmm. Could this Jason possibly be the man whose attention Ronnie wanted last night? Treble tried to catch Lola Ann's gaze, but the brunette kept her eyes averted, giving the ham-and-Swiss finger sandwiches her undivided attention.

"The job *I* want to hear about," Fawn said, "is Treble's. I hear you're practically famous in Atlanta. You must miss being there."

Treble studied the other woman. The skinny blonde was nearly as tall as Treble, but her shoulders hunched slightly as if she was uncomfortable with her height. She wore a black sweater, even though Sunday would be the first of July, and didn't smile much. Few of her smiles so far had actually reached her brown eyes, anyway. *She doesn't like me.* The woman looked vaguely familiar, though Treble couldn't connect her with any specific incident.

"Famous is a stretch, but I like my job," Treble said neutrally.

"You give dating advice, right?" Fawn pressed, dousing her few leaves of spinach salad with buttermilk dressing. "So I guess you date a lot."

Picking up on the faint note of disapproval lurking in the woman's voice, Treble thought it was a shame Harrison abstained from the company of women. Even though she was probably half his age, Fawn seemed like a great match for him.

"Is that true?" Lola Ann piped up, conveniently forgetting the ham long enough to acknowledge Treble's presence. "You give women pointers?"

"Ah…sometimes. I'm not actually an expert—"

"You must know what you're talking about to get your own show," Keisha protested kindly as she returned to the living room with her plate.

There were murmurs of agreement and several simultaneous questions that Treble couldn't answer as quickly as they were asked.

She glanced at the Heather behind her. "I should get out of your way so I'm not holding up the line." But once they were all settled in the living room with their food, the ladies, even Penny, continued to express interest in Treble's job.

"I was going to play this game where we all wrote down a piece of mothering advice on a slip of paper and then have Charity guess who it was from," the hostess said. "Now I'm wondering if we should all write anonymous questions for Treble about relationships and let her answer them."

Oh, no. Trying to sound as polite as possible, Treble demurred, "I wouldn't want to upstage the mother-to-be at her own shower."

Charity sat back, interlocking her hands over her stomach and somehow reminding Treble of Brando in *The Godfather.* "Not at all. You know how happy I was when they gave you your own slot. You should favor us with a small sample of your show, since we only get like four stations out here in the sticks."

Treble wet her lips. "But on my show, the dynamic comes from people calling in. It's not that a listener poses a problem and I solve it for them. I normally ask my audience for their input, too. It's more a...discussion than anything else."

"Still." Lola Ann sounded wistful. "I'll bet you've learned more about relationships than most women ever do. Like how to get a guy who just sees you as his—as a platonic acquaintance, to notice you?"

To Treble, that problem was easier addressed than her trying to see a certain doctor as only a platonic acquaintance. "Well, eye contact is a small but simple start. I think, especially if a woman likes a guy, her tendency is to look away nervously. Meet his gaze head-on. Ask him personal questions, not the type that will motivate him to get a restraining order, but if he's someone you know from work and you only ever discuss job stuff, make it a point to ask him about something else. Or you could tell him about yourself, but asking conveys an interest. It's flattering without being over-the-top."

Penny exhaled audibly, muttering almost to herself. "There's such a thing as having him notice you *too* much."

Keisha, seated closest to the hostess, widened her eyes. "Penny Paulson, don't tell me there's trouble in paradise!"

"Yeah," Lola Ann echoed. "You've been floating around town for the past couple of days like a newlywed."

Penny blushed. "Don't get me wrong, y'all. I'm very happy, and I'm a lucky woman. It's just that…well, most of you know Bert and I went through a bumpy patch. Now that everything's all better, he's trying so hard *not* to take me for granted that we're rarely apart. It was nice on the cruise, doing all that stuff as a twosome, but—"

"He's smothering you?" Keisha guessed. "That's how my husband's been ever since he found out I was pregnant. He's thrilled, but he also acts like I'm so delicate I can't be left alone."

Charity laughed. "Wait until the hormones kick in. Bill was suffocating me—in the sweetest way possible—but after a few really big mood swings, I think he's afraid of me now. That gained me some alone time."

Penny grinned ruefully. "I'd like to find some solution that doesn't involve terrorizing him."

"You could always drop some nice hints that it's not taking you for granted to have separate hobbies," Treble suggested. She *had* picked up lots of ideas and an informed viewpoint from her listeners, but at the same time, she felt like something of a fraud in this living room. Most of these women were in stable, happy relationships. Her helping them was akin to a blind shopping consultant telling customers what outfits looked best on them. "Let him know it would be okay if he and his buddies had poker night at your place. Work Sudoku puzzles or cross-stitch while he watches a game on TV. Buy him a certificate for a round of golf for his birthday. You don't want to push him away now that the two of you are so close, just make it clear that you have interests of your own and encourage him to find some, too."

"I'm impressed," Penny said.

Heather laughed. "Ever think about doing an advice column on personal relationships, Treb? The *Journal-Report* could use some modernizing."

Fawn sat back in her chair, her eyes brooding. Whatever motivation she'd had for bringing up Treble's talk show, it apparently hadn't played out in the way she'd hoped. She forced a smile. "Goodness, Joan, are you suddenly feeling as out of place as I am, being another single gal?"

Joan's answering smile was somehow both tight *and* gracious. "It's a baby shower, Fawn, dear. Traditionally when women gather at these events, relationships and families do come up."

Treble bit her lip, figuring a "you go, girl" wouldn't be appropriate.

As if feeling Treble's gaze on her, Joan turned. "I always knew you were a bright girl. Good to see you're putting it to good use and helping people."

Shifting in her seat, Treble admitted, "It's more about entertainment than bona fide help."

The former Breckfield housekeeper arched a snow-white brow. "Since when is entertaining people *not* helpful in today's stressful world? Well, girls, it was delightful seeing you all, but I volunteered to cover a dinner shift at the home tonight. They're so understaffed there. I hope we raise some cash at the festival."

Treble thought about jokingly suggesting they put together a kissing booth, but the last thing she needed to be introducing as a topic was kissing. Besides, whatever poor souls they rounded up to work the booth might end up having to lock lips with losers like Rich Danner. No, small-stakes bingo was probably a better way to go.

"If there's something I can do to help with the festival," Treble heard herself say, "call me. You have Charity's number?"

Joan paused, her smile slow and achingly maternal. "I do. And you'll be hearing from me."

They hugged, and if it was a little awkward, it was also…nice. Treble regretted not taking the woman up on the comfort she'd offered so many years ago. When Treble got back to Atlanta, she should make it a point to stay in touch with the older woman.

Joan sat on the couch hugging Charity goodbye, too. "I'm sorry to leave before the motherly advice game, although technically speaking, I never had kids of my own. But if I were going to give a new mom advice it would be this—love your child unconditionally. You'll have to discipline them at times and will disagree with them, too, but never act as if love is something that can be revoked as a punishment." Even though she was speaking to Charity, Joan glanced at Treble.

Treble walked the woman to the front door, curious about the vehemence she'd heard in her tone. "Joan, why did you quit working for Harrison after all these years?"

"You know he can be difficult."

An understatement, Treble thought but held her tongue.

"He's a good man, but really seeing what's right in front of him is not one of his strong points." Joan's eyes had taken on an unfocused look, but then she blinked. "I should be going, or I'll be late. Talk to you soon!"

After that, they played a game where everyone supplied random nouns, adjectives, locations and verbs. Penny then used the words to fill in the blanks in a birth scenario.

"If I'm in labor for ninety-nine hours," Charity said, "I'll hurt someone. I didn't mind the part about the doctor being Patrick Dempsey, though."

Heather Lynn, who had contributed that particular actor's name, sighed. "That smile!"

Fawn and Keisha announced that they both had to be going, but everyone else stayed for a few more of Penny's party activities. Finally, Heather stood, saying she'd promised to help with her daughter's troop float for the Days of Joy parade.

The other Heather eyed her. "You look too skinny to have had a kid."

"Thanks, but I wouldn't mind a few more curves. It's hard to feel like a hot mama when I have to shop in the training bra section."

Heather Lynn propped her chin on her fists, her expression dubious. "I felt a lot more like a hot mama before I was a mama. I don't think I'll ever again have the body I had before the boys." She darted an apologetic glance at Charity. "Oops, sorry. I'm not trying to sound negative about being a mommy."

"It's okay," Charity said. "But, for what it's worth, I think you're being too hard on yourself."

"That's what Ray says, too," Heather Lynn admitted. "But *he* hasn't gone up two sizes in the last eighteen months. Sophie, who works with me, said I should get some really hot lingerie to wear in the bedroom and reignite my confidence, but I felt like an overweight centerfold for a low-budget men's magazine."

Treble shook her head. "It's not just about trying to be sexy for him behind closed doors. Find clothes that make *you* feel good. Turn a few heads!" Though she didn't know what Heather had looked like before, she knew the woman wasn't built much differently than Alana after her recent weight loss. The main difference was in how they carried themselves.

"Maybe you're right," Heather Lynn said hopefully. "Maybe I've just made bad fashion choices that are making it worse."

"Did you pick out those?" Treble asked, gesturing toward the woman's cute green shoes.

"Yeah."

"Then you have fantastic fashion sense in there somewhere. Meant to tell you earlier I love those slides."

The woman's eyes were now positively bright with enthusiasm. "Would…would you like to go shopping with me sometime?"

"You bet. No one's ever had to twist my arm to get me in a store."

When it was down to just Treble and Penny cleaning, with the guest of honor resting her head on the couch and surveying her haul, Charity said, "You turned out to be quite the popular lady, Treb. Joan saying she'd call you, Heather Lynn inviting you shopping, the other Heather asking if she could do a short blurb about you in the paper."

"Yeah. Your friends were really nice. Except…" Treble shoved empty plates and crumpled napkins into a black trash bag, searching for the tact that had never been her strong point.

"Except?" Charity prompted.

"I'm not sure Fawn liked me much."

Charity and Penny exchanged glances, then Charity said, "I think her older sister blames you for a breakup back in high school. Not to mention Fawn is close friends with Dinah Perkins."

Treble sighed, feeling tired. "What did I do to Dinah?" *Talk about past sins coming home to roost.*

"Dinah's been determined to get Doc Caldwell out on a date since he moved to town," Penny put in. "She's not happy about you dancing with the doctor at Guthrie's."

"But that was just a dance," Treble protested. "It was practically—" *Nothing?* She found herself saying that about Keith a lot. Running into him in town had been "nothing." That one brief kiss had meant "nothing." So how was it all these nothings were adding up into a niggling, inescapable something? She thought about him every day and steered conversation toward him whenever she thought she could do so without Charity noticing the deliberate maneuvers. Yet now that Treble knew bits and pieces of his past, she was even more curious about how it had shaped him, how, instead of becoming bitter and angry about his loss—twin emotions she remembered all too well—he'd become a person devoted to helping others.

Penny leaned her arms on the kitchen counter, peering around the corner at them. "Just how interested are you in getting involved?"

Treble blushed, even though the reaction made her feel juvenile. "I'm not. Whatever you might have heard, it was just a dance."

Penny's mouth fell open, but then mirth pealed out of her in unguarded laughter. "I meant in the *festival*. You mentioned getting involved with the festival."

"Oh." Treble's fading blush took on new life, her cheeks so hot that her face was probably a radioactive red. "Right. The festival. Is there something you need?" *Please say yes. Please say anything that doesn't have to do with the fool I just made of myself.*

"Actually…" Penny trailed off, her grin feline. "Local PTAs are sponsoring cakewalks and various games on the midway, but I've been put in charge of coming up with an idea to raise money for the middle school library. We need more books, and some of the reference materials are close to being obsolete. I had an idea this week, but need a very special person to volunteer. A gutsy person, comfortable with talking to crowds."

Treble shrugged. "Sounds right up my alley. I'd love to help." Plus, it was for a worthy cause and would give her another avenue for keeping busy while they all awaited the baby's birth.

Penny's smile widened. "Wonderful! Oh, and by any chance, did you happen to bring your bathing suit with you?"

Chapter Eleven

All week, Keith had thought about seeing Treble, then immediately produced reasons why that was a bad idea. Monday morning, Velma had greeted him not by asking how he'd slept the night before but inquiring whether he'd had a good time at Guthrie Dance Hall Saturday. "A friend of my pinochle partner's granddaughter said you were having a *really* good time—danced with a tall brunette, kissed her and left with her."

This revelation had startled Keith. Anyone who'd happened to glance their way at the right moment could have noticed the kiss, but it hadn't occurred to him that people would think he left with Treble. After she drove away, he hadn't had any lingering enthusiasm for his original plan of finding a nice hometown girl who might like to have lunch with him at the sandwich shop or catch a movie sometime at the King Cinema.

"We left separately," he'd told the receptionist, even though it struck him as distantly ridiculous that a thirty-four-year-old man was explaining himself to an employee.

Velma had insisted it made "no never mind" to her. "I just wanted to double-check that this won't interfere with our eventual mad elopement."

Avoiding Treble was driving him mad. Normally he spoke to Bill or Charity about once a week. Now he was avoiding them by association—a fact Bill subtly pointed out when the two men ran into each other Thursday during a busy lunch hour at Adam's Ribs. *Enough.*

So he sat parked in front of the Sumner house on Thursday afternoon, his truck the only vehicle in sight. Was Charity's car in the garage? He hadn't called first, although he assumed Treble was here. For all Keith knew, she'd driven off to Chattanooga to spend the day at the aquarium there. Only one way to find out, he told himself, popping the door open.

As he climbed the stairs, he saw that behind the screen door, the front door was open, suggesting someone was home. Then he saw her, shadowed in the comparatively dim interior. She sat on the couch, her long legs crossed on the cushions, her dark hair spilling loose over the tank top she wore as she stared at a book. From what he could see in profile, she was either nibbling the end of a pen or sucking on a lollipop. He hoped it was the former; he wasn't sure he could get through an intelligent conversation watching her do the latter.

"Knock, knock," he said, loudly enough for his voice to carry through the thin pane of glass lowered on the door in deference to air-conditioning.

Treble's head jerked up, dropping her pen to the carpet. She stood, stretching as she did so, as if she'd been sitting in that position for a while, and Keith drank in her body's lithe movements. Her grace was almost liquid.

He concentrated on not blatantly ogling when she opened the door for him. "Hi."

The hello she offered him in reply was filled with surprise. "I heard a vehicle drive up a few minutes ago, but assumed Bill and Charity were back. They're at the OB's this afternoon."

"I ran into Bill at lunch, and he mentioned her appointment with Dr. Whalen. He also mentioned that you guys were nearly finished with the nursery and that I should come see it."

Treble sat on the edge of a sofa cushion, her elbows resting atop casually parted knees. "So you thought you'd take a look when they weren't here?"

"I wanted to see you," he said simply. "Is this a bad time?"

"No." Her face softened. "And it is nice to see you. Charity mentioned she's used to talking to you pretty regularly, that you make a point to at least call and ask about her pregnancy. Since she hasn't heard from you at all since Saturday night, I was afraid—"

"You thought I was avoiding her because of you." He walked to the couch. "Can I have a seat?"

She nodded, though he detected a new tension in her posture when he joined her.

He kept proper distance, but his body hummed at the proximity nonetheless. This might be the first time he'd seen her barefoot or completely without makeup. Despite her skill with cosmetics and the way her lips had shone when he'd seen her Saturday, seeing her like this had an even greater effect because it felt more intimate.

"You look nice," he said impulsively.

She regarded her cotton tank top and jeans that were worn at the knees and frayed at the hems, clearly skeptical. "Thanks."

Past experience with women suggested that opening with a compliment was a good icebreaker, but maybe not. For one thing, his past experience didn't leave him feeling prepared for someone like Treble. Someone who was audacious by turns but couldn't quite hide the flashes of vulnerability in her eyes. Someone he'd expected to be self-centered, although he'd overheard Ronnie saying something about a "favor" in the sandwich shop and when he'd seen Heather on her way into the newspaper office this morning, she'd made a point of mentioning how smart and helpful Treble was.

"She really made an impression on us at Charity's shower yesterday," the auburn-haired woman said approvingly.

"Yeah, she tends to do that," he'd replied, bemused.

Had Heather mentioned it because she knew he was friends with Charity, or because she'd heard the buzz that he was involved romantically with Treble? Ironic that half the town thought they were carrying on a passionate affair when they sat here now, at opposite sides of the couch like two nervous high school freshmen on a first date.

Treble stood suddenly. "You want anything to drink? Sweet tea, lemonade, ice water? We made cinnamon rolls for breakfast and there are a few left."

"Lemonade would be fine," he told her, following her into the kitchen.

Her hand hovered over the cellophane-wrapped plate as though she couldn't decide whether to take a roll for herself or not. She glanced back at him, her voice low. "I'm sorry I wasn't able to join you for breakfast on Sunday."

"Really?" He found that hard to believe, considering how adamantly she hadn't wanted to be there, yet she didn't seem like someone who would utter insincere words in the name of being polite.

A sassy smile stole across her face. "Well, I vacillate between being sorry and being relieved. Right now, it's sorry."

He grinned back at her, encouraged. "Maybe this Sunday, then."

"Ah...I'm not sure that's a good idea," she said over her shoulder, pulling glasses from the cabinet.

"Guess that 'sorry' was short-lived."

"Well, I get the impression Harrison isn't too pleased with me at the moment. Even less pleased than usual," she added sardonically.

"I'd think he would be proud of you. Bill says you've been a big help to Charity, and half the women I talk to seem to be singing your praises suddenly."

"They are?" She beamed like a premed student who'd aced her MCAT. Then she sobered. "I guess Harrison heard from the other half, the one that saw me with you Saturday."

He laughed. "Oh, you mean our torrid romance? My receptionist asked me about it first thing this week."

"And that doesn't bother you?" She leaned against the refrigerator, crossing her arms as she regarded him. "I had you pegged as someone who would care about his reputation in the community."

"Since when has being favored by a beautiful woman hurt a guy's reputation?" he wanted to know.

Her lips tilted up into a lazy half smile. "Very smooth, Doc."

He dipped his head in modest acknowledgment. "Even if Harrison has heard some twice-removed rumor, he knows me. He can't possibly think we're…" Images of what Keith and Treble could "possibly" be doing suddenly halted his capacity for speech.

She broke through his momentary fantasies with her flat tone. "Right, because he has such a track record of giving people the benefit of the doubt."

Crap, he was moving further from his goal instead of closer to it. Some time since that first dinner, where he'd witnessed how Harrison and Treble brought out each other's negative qualities, it had become irrationally important for him to help mend the rift that wasn't technically any of his business. Maybe Treble's barely concealed hurt had gotten under his skin as much as the glint in her eyes and the shape of her mouth. Or maybe it was penance— Keith had been prepared to dislike her on sight for any difficulty she'd caused his mentor, but he'd conveniently let himself forget there were two sides to every story. Maybe it was simply that after so many years without a father in his life, he thought it was a shame this father-and-daughter pair who obviously shared certain traits, stubbornness chief among them, were estranged.

"I wanted to talk to you about Harrison," he said.

Her eyebrows rose. "Haven't we already had this conversation?"

"When I said I wanted to see you today, it was the absolute truth. But I also wanted to discuss something with you without Charity around. She has enough to worry about with the pregnancy."

The faintly mocking challenge in her expression faded away. "Worry? Is there something wrong with Harrison?"

Keith knew he was wobbling on a fine line here. As Harrison's doctor, he couldn't divulge medical specifics to Treble. "Not wrong, per se. I'm speaking now only as a family friend, nothing more." *Liar.*

"Okay."

"Harrison is used to being the head of a company, the patriarch of his family and, in some ways, this town. I don't think he knows how to slow down without feeling weak. He's still taking out-of-town trips to visit other plants and distributors when he could send someone else—Bill or even another Breckfield employee. He works himself too hard."

She laughed, the short sound bitter. "From what I've seen, he's the picture of relaxation. Sunday brunches? Dinner over here last week?"

"I'm afraid, though, that becoming a grandfather is going to make him feel old and that he'll try too hard to prove he isn't less than he was. It would be great if someone…inside the family could convince him there's more to life than work."

"Then you should talk to someone inside the family," she retorted. "Maybe you didn't notice, but as far as that man is concerned, I'm so *outside,* I practically had to apply for a passport to come here."

He rubbed his temples, wishing he could give her more details about Harrison's cardiac episodes in the past few months. Would that make a difference in her stance? Frustration with Harrison filled him. The man wanted to stay in denial about his health realities, and he was keeping his daughters in the dark to do so. "All right. I said my piece, it's up to you whether or not you want to listen."

She straightened, dropping her arms to her side. "Hey, it's not like I don't hear you. There are just some things I can't change." After a moment, she added, "Not by myself anyway."

A valid point—Harrison had to meet her halfway, and until Keith was certain the old man would bend a little, maybe it was unfair of him to push Treble toward any acts of reconciliation.

"I shouldn't be meddling," he admitted. "I'm not generally a meddler. Keeping a professional distance is one of the things they start preaching as soon as you hit med school."

"Yeah, but from patients, right? That's not the same as inter-acting with friends."

True, but emotional detachment could be difficult to turn on and off with the flick of an internal switch, especially if you'd grown comfortable with the rest of the world being on the other side of an invisible buffer. There were reasons he hadn't had a girlfriend in a long time.

He took a step toward Treble. "And are we friends?"

She regarded him softly. "I—"

The phone shrilled in the kitchen, and they exchanged startled glances.

"Should get that," she finished, tacking a different ending on her sentence. "Hello? This is she." Whatever Treble heard took her by surprise because her face furrowed into perplexed lines he wanted to smooth away with his touch. "Yes, I definitely have experience at that…I suppose I could. I'll talk it over with my sister and call you back tonight. But, tentatively, yes."

Keith smiled inwardly at the thought of her being "tentative" about anything.

She found the magnetic pad and attached pen Charity kept on the refrigerator and jotted down a phone number before hanging up. "Now it's just getting weird. You came over to talk to me, and I've had more calls here today than Charity. When I start getting mail at this address, I'll know it's time to leave."

He chuckled, although the reminder of her eventual depar-ture stabbed his insides like a small fleck of glass in the foot, too small to be seen but plenty sharp to cause discomfort whenever stepped upon.

"Shoot, I came in here ages ago for lemonade and never got around to pouring it." She opened the fridge and pulled out a blue glass pitcher. "That call was from the receptionist at the nursing home. Apparently Joan mentioned me as a possible disc jockey for the big festival dance. The guy they'd planned to use cancelled this morning because his daughter's softball team qualified for some kind of out-of-state tournament."

"So you'll be at the dance?" he asked, truly interested in attending for the first time.

"Maybe." Turning away from him, she poured lemonade into their glasses. "I've already volunteered to help with a booth for the school library, and I want to help Charity out around here as much as I can."

"I'm sure she doesn't just expect you to sit in her living room, waiting to be needed," he said reasonably. "You should come to the dance, even if you don't end up playing DJ."

She sipped her lemonade, watching him over the rim of her glass. "Will you be there?"

"I was undecided," he admitted, "but the idea is growing on me."

Setting her drink down for a moment, she offered him the other one. His fingers brushed hers, and tiny bubbles of heightened sensory awareness fizzed through his veins. For just that moment that they touched, the underlying smell of cinnamon in the kitchen seemed stronger, Treble's smile brighter, the soft sound of her breathing more audible. And then she pulled her hand back, and the world dimmed a little. So what would it be like when she retreated to Atlanta—the sun going dark in the sky?

He shook his head—mentally, at least—such fanciful thoughts unlike him as a man of medicine. "Any word on Trusty?"

Treble passed him, the sway of her hips beckoning him to follow her like the illumination of a lighthouse offering salvation to a storm-drenched sailor. "Actually, that's who called earlier. Ronnie. She said the car's ready to pick up, but by the time she phoned, Bill and Charity had already left. I need someone to drop me off so that I can drive myself back here."

"I can take you," he volunteered. "We could just finish our lemonade, then go."

"You wouldn't mind?" she asked. "If you have the afternoon

off, I'm surprised you didn't have other things you wanted to do with your time."

"Velma will call my pager if there's an emergency," he said, resuming his place on the couch. "I work strange hours sometimes, people phoning late at night because of scares they don't want to drive all the way to the county hospital to have treated. But because I put in some of that evening and weekend time, no one complains when I leave the clinic early every once in a while. Besides, I'm the one who picked you up. Not taking you back to Ronnie's would be like only doing half the job. Isn't follow-through as important as the initial act?"

Treble opened her mouth as if to say something, then lowered her gaze, fidgeting with a slim book that sat on the cushion next to her.

He studied the title, surprised to see the familiar word. "Sudoku? Someone left one in the waiting room right after I first moved here. Now I go through a couple a day." It was part of his routine, like someone else's cup of coffee or morning paper or Sunday crossword.

"Same here." She grinned. "Well, not the waiting room part, but it helps kill downtime at the station."

"Huh." *Go figure.*

"What?"

"Nothing. I just didn't imagine you having a hobby that was so…"

"Logic-based? Quasi-intellectual?"

"Sedate," he said hurriedly, sensing that he'd been on the verge of inadvertently offending her. He scooted closer to her. "Do you do the ones with just numbers, or letters, too?"

She tossed her hair. "Depends on my mood. I like to mix things up. Traditional vertical and horizontal, diagonal variations, irregular grids. You?"

"I'm more of a purist. The alternatives get to be a bit convoluted for me."

"Don't you like a challenge, Doc?"

The teasing gleam in her eyes prompted an answering wickedness in his own tone. "I'm here, aren't I?"

"Yes, you are." Just like that, her gaze shifted from playful to thoughtful, proving once again why time alone with Treble was not for faint-hearted men.

Though Keith wouldn't call her difficult, he couldn't truthfully call her predictable either. Was that why she was so memorable, because he never fully knew what to expect from her but looked forward to each new discovery?

When she spoke, her husky voice was nearly a whisper. "You're staring."

"I'm admiring."

"You shouldn't look at me like that," she said, her tone more beguiling than admonishing.

"Like what? Like I want to kiss you again?" No sense in pretending otherwise. He wasn't enough of an actor to hide the desire in his expression, and saw no point in trying. It had been Treble herself who suggested he practice reaching for what he wanted. And while it might not be logical or even in the best interests of his well-being, he certainly wanted her. He'd tried all week to ignore that basic fact, but all it had done was delay the moment he'd ended up on her doorstep. On this couch, with her bare feet inches away.

Treble wet her lips in a reflexive gesture that heated his blood. Scientifically, he knew about pheromones, testosterone and chemicals like oxytocin. Hormones and standard physiological responses to arousal. But right now, he wasn't an M.D., just a man. All his brain could currently process was that she had tasted like sinful nirvana the last time they'd kissed, and he'd craved her ever since.

He cupped her face with his hands, holding her gently in place. Not because he had any fear that she would turn away—if he thought she wouldn't welcome his kiss, he would never have leaned toward her. Quite the contrary, he didn't want her to initiate their kiss this time. *He* wanted the credit, or the blame, depending on one's viewpoint. Mostly, he just wanted her.

It was a deep, sliding kiss, her tongue meeting his in bold, unabashed strokes. She was tart and sweet and citrusy, paradoxically evocative of cool refreshment even as she stoked an insatiable fever. Their bodies mimicked the explorations of their mouths as they angled in different positions, coming into closer contact. She had one hand palmed against his chest, making him wish his shirt would just dissolve and leave them skin to skin. Her other hand was restless, one moment caressing his shoulder, the next dropping to his thigh as she leaned into him with a small *mmm* of satisfaction. She'd slid her arm up and around his neck so that there was more room for the softness of her body to nestle into his, and her pliant warmth left him taut with need.

Had he ever held a woman who made him feel like this? Had there ever been a woman before Treble? Her mouth melded to his. She was, in this fleeting heartbeat of time, his universe, the intoxicating air he happily breathed. Which was probably why he neither heard the transmission of Bill's old truck, the doors shutting, or even Charity's substantial weight on the creaky porch stairs. Keith remained happily oblivious to those warnings until voices sounded directly outside the screen.

He and Treble sprang apart in the same unison they'd come together, so she must have heard the returning couple, as well. Keith recalled the way he'd been able to see Treble through the screen before she'd realized he was here. Had Bill and Charity glimpsed them making out like a pair of teens who'd sneaked down to the basement for a few minutes of unsupervised groping?

Too bad the small Sumner house didn't have a basement.

He glanced at Treble, their gazes meeting in a fusion of frustration, amusement and chagrin. The door opened and Charity called hello to both of them, but he couldn't tear his gaze from Treble. With her flushed cheeks and rumpled hair, the way her lips were still breathlessly parted, Keith couldn't imagine how anyone past puberty could miss what had been going on here.

Charity confirmed that suspicion when she stopped suddenly, arms akimbo, her eyes widening. Bill stood behind his wife, looking from Keith to Treble, then back again. Although the man was someone Keith considered a friend, right now his protective, steely-eyed expression held a hint of "Boy, I know places in this county where they'd never find the body."

While her husband glowered in silent warning, Charity found her voice. "Nice to see two of my favorite people. And what have *you two* been up to this afternoon?"

Keith swallowed. "Um…Sudoku?"

Bill's eyebrows shot up, his sotto voce question not quite sotto enough as he asked his wife, "Is that dirty?"

Chapter Twelve

Now what? Treble watched Keith cross in front of his pickup, after gallantly opening and closing her door for her. She'd been the one to remember Keith's offer of taking her to pick up the car, and she'd immediately blurted that they were just on their way out. Even though they'd been seated on the couch…and she hadn't even been wearing shoes.

At least my *fib was better than his.* In this case, Treble refused to feel guilty for the deception. If Charity knew the truth, she was likely to launch into a victorious I-told-you-so jig, the female version of an athlete's touchdown dance, and that couldn't be good for the baby.

By the time Treble had escaped to her room to grab shoes, she'd realized she hadn't asked about the OB appointment. Keith beat her to it. When Treble returned, Charity had confirmed that the previa had not resolved itself, as some cases did, and that Dr. Whalen had scheduled a Cesarean at the county hospital for July ninth. Bill had held her hand, offering silent support, as Charity assured them that she wasn't too upset.

"We knew it was looking like we'd have to do a C-section," she'd said, managing to sound more matter-of-fact than she probably felt. "All I need to make me happy is a safe delivery and healthy baby."

It was then that Treble had offered to stay home, and pick up her car tomorrow, but Charity had shaken her blond head.

"No, I think I'll just rest." Her grin had been sly. "You two kids run along."

Embarrassed after all her insistence that Guthrie Hall had been "just a kiss," Treble could barely look at Keith as he started the truck. Wasn't there some saying about two being a coincidence and three forming a pattern? Did the brief seconds where they'd stopped for air make today count as several kisses or one prolonged, rapturous encounter?

She'd think about that later, when watching his hand work the gearshift wasn't making her think about how that same hand had felt tracing her collarbone. There was not a single thing about his appearance or build that could be characterized as *delicate,* but perhaps because of his profession, he had a surprisingly gentle touch. Or, more accurately, a very precise touch. Soft at times, applying heady pressure at others. Damn, what it must feel like for those hands to slide down over a woman's body.

"You can turn those vents toward you," Keith said, indicating the air-conditioning slats in the center of the dashboard. "Or I can turn it up a notch. You look hot."

"Are you being sincere or cocky?" Her temperature had nothing to do with the sun.

He flashed a movie star smile at her. "Little of both."

She chuckled, appreciating his humor even if it was the tiniest bit at her expense. "So, you're telling me *you* don't need those air vents aimed at you?"

"Honey, nothing short of ice water is going to cool me down right now."

She blinked. "Why, Doc Caldwell, I'm shocked at you."

His laugh was deep and masculine, an audible aphrodisiac. "To tell you the truth, I am, too." Whatever else he was, he certainly didn't sound remorseful.

Good thing, too. If he'd been surly or apologetic about what had probably been the best kiss of her life, she might have had to kick him in the shin. "I suppose I've corrupted you."

"You don't know me well enough to make that determination," he said, dropping his voice to a comically mysterious tone. "Wait until you hear my dark secrets…."

For the rest of the ride, he regaled her with an embellished tale of a med school prank. He'd mostly let himself get talked into acting as the lookout for some buddies, but the humor in the story was more in the way he told it than the act itself.

"Could you have been kicked out for that?" she asked.

"Probably not," he admitted. "First-time offenders and all, but there would have been some kind of disciplinary action if we'd been caught. The whole time I was keeping watch for my friends, I was grumbling in my head about how angry I was going to be if they got me in trouble. But when I got back to my apartment—it was about three in the morning by then and I was sleep deprived between working and studying—I had this stupid moment where I almost called Gail to tell her about it. Of course, I immediately realized I couldn't call her, but I knew it was the kind of thing she'd get a kick out of. It was the first time I'd felt close to her since she died. Maybe even the first time I'd felt connected to anyone. I acted put-upon, but those guys did me a favor including me. I wasn't really *that* close a friend for them to trust with their scheme."

Treble leaned her arm against the window, enjoying his profile. "People don't have to know you very well or very long to see you're the kind of person who can be relied on."

"Thank you." He cut his eyes toward her for a single second. "The same seems to be true about you. Pitching in with this festival, suspending your life to be here because Charity was frightened."

"She and the baby will be okay, won't she?" Treble told herself *she* wasn't frightened—Charity would get through this fine—but she wouldn't mind hearing her amateur diagnosis confirmed by a medical professional.

He reached over to squeeze her hand. "Charity's been very careful to play it safe, and Dr. Whalen is fantastic. I've known many pregnant mothers with more severe cases who left the hospital with happy, healthy infants."

She swallowed, nodding her gratitude at his words. Impulsively, she flipped her palm upward, lacing her fingers with his. A mile down the road, she felt oddly shy. When two people were kissing, they were aroused—if they were doing it right—but holding hands was a calmer, more thoughtful intimacy. Though one of the simplest, most innocent touches, something even sixth graders with crushes could indulge in, a person couldn't just say they'd been temporarily caught up in the moment.

Pulling her hand free, she simultaneously reached for the radio dial and asked, "Mind if I turn on some music?"

"Knock yourself out," he said affably.

But she was disgusted with herself for manufacturing an excuse to pull away. So once she'd settled on a station she liked, she found his hand again, cramming her fingers between his.

Keith grinned.

Soon, the Carter and Sons garage came into view, and Keith retrieved his hand to shift into Park. She was relieved to have the contact broken without feeling like a coward for having been the one to break it. An older man with a crooked nose and Ronnie's green eyes met them outside one of the bays.

"Mr. Carter?" Treble asked. "I came by to pick up my hatchback."

He nodded. "Ronnie's got that relic purring like a kitten. Go on inside, and she can go over the invoice with you."

The office was a small multiroom area that had probably been a single room they'd divided with cubicle walls. A large brown air-conditioning window unit kept the place reasonably cool, considering the outside heat index, but chugged along at such a high volume, Treble was surprised Ronnie had been able to hear her during any of their phone conversations about the car.

Ronnie sat behind a small, scarred desk, an amalgam of the two identities Treble had seen up until now—the grease-stained, overall-wearing mechanic and young woman in skirt and makeup at Guthrie Dance Hall. Today, Ronnie wore jeans and a pink T-shirt with a line drawing of a vintage convertible. Her hair spilled in a sunset-colored ponytail through the back of the billed cap sporting the garage's logo.

"Hey, Treb!" Ronnie smirked. "Doc Caldwell."

She's assuming we're a couple. Treble was no longer sure what the hell they were. "Hey, Ronnie. I hear you have my four-wheeled beast tamed into a kitten?"

Fifteen minutes later, keys and payment had been exchanged. Ronnie asked Treble to drive the car around the block and verify that it was running well before she officially took the vehicle home.

"We pride ourselves on customer satisfaction," Ronnie said, once Treble assured her that Trusty was running like new. "Word of mouth is really important for the business."

"Well, I'll try to recommend you to as many people as possible before I leave town," Treble promised.

Ronnie scowled. "Now that you actually have a method of transportation for getting home, how long will you stay?"

"You're stuck with me for at least another week or so. Charity's current due date is July ninth, so I'll probably be here at least a couple of days past that." Part of her hated that she wouldn't be staying long after her niece was born, but a leave of absence only bought so much time. Besides, Charity was surrounded by loved ones here who could help. Treble's main function had been emotional support during an uncertain time. And Treble was glad they'd had this warm, lazy time together before Charity's life was temporarily taken over by bonding with the baby, needing to feed her daughter every four hours and change a diaper every four minutes.

Ronnie's goodbye was cut short as another customer drove onto the lot, his car emitting a high-pitched whistle from the vicinity of the tailpipe. "Sounds like someone is having some exhaust problems. I'll see you at the festival, Treble?"

She nodded, flexing her fingers in a quick wave. "I'll definitely be there."

"Well." Even though he could have dropped her off and left, Keith had stayed while she test-drove Trusty and chatted with Ronnie. Now they both stood awkwardly next to where her car was parked. "I guess I'll let you get back to Bill and Charity."

"Thank you again for bringing me over," she said. "Bill would have, but I hate for Charity to be alone at the house for long this close to her due date."

"No problem. I enjoyed the company. Thank *you* for listening to my med school stories and pretending they were interesting," he said with a grin.

She laughed. "You underestimate yourself. You're fun to talk to."

"Fun." He repeated the word as if tasting it on his tongue like an exotic spice.

He opened her door for her, and she nearly told him "see you at the festival." That became the official town farewell in the days leading up to Sunday's kickoff parade and the six days of activities that followed. Instead, when Treble spoke, what she heard was, "Come over for dinner tomorrow night? If you're free. I know Charity and Bill would be delighted to have you over, and you never did see the nursery."

A slow smile broke across his face. "That's right. I never did, did I?"

"So you'll join us?"

"I will." He brushed his knuckles down the curve of her cheek. "I'll see you tomorrow."

She nodded wordlessly. It wasn't that she couldn't find her voice, she just didn't trust it. She'd already surprised herself by asking him on what some might call a date. Heaven only knew what less restrained invitations she might make if she weren't careful.

SINCE SHE WAS the one responsible for a guest coming to dinner, Treble offered to cook, which worked out nicely since she ended up with a lot of nervous energy to burn. *I blame Charity.* The woman had kept up a running commentary the entire time she'd snapped fresh green beans, which would soon be sautéed with almond slivers.

"Because when you think about it, you hold the record for the most dates Keith's been on since he moved here," the pregnant commentator was saying.

"How do you figure we've been on *any* dates?" Treble asked, despite her best intentions not to engage. Maybe if she ignored her sister and just kept stirring at the stove, the blonde would move on to some other topic.

"Well, you took him to lunch less than an hour after coming to town. And paid, no less. Around here, that's an extremely modern, Cosmo-girl thing to do."

Treble ground her teeth. "It was a thank-you for rescuing me from the middle of nowhere."

"And then you guys had dinner again that night."

Yeah, with the entire family and followed by a lovely chat outside about how she was potentially evil and how Harrison potentially had his head up his own posterior.

"The biggie, of course, was Guthrie Hall."

"We went separately. We left separately." Treble should have imbibed the white wine instead of pouring it into the pot in front of her.

"Right, sure. I know. And anything that happened in between was an 'isolated incident.'"

"Using air quotes like that is a legitimate reason for me to spit in your bowl of risotto." Worse than the air quotes or Charity's smug smile was that—dammit—she had a point. While Treble had to take her sister's word for it that Keith hadn't spent much recreational time with any other single woman, Treble knew that *she* hadn't spent this much time with a man. Coworkers and significant others of friend's didn't count.

What am I doing? Treble didn't try to live her life by following a lot of rules, but contrary to what anyone might think, she didn't go out of her way to create chaos for herself, either. She and Keith were like the numbers in the puzzles she liked to work. Each one had a certain, correct location. If you stuck it in the wrong place, you could throw off everything else. Treble knew where she belonged, not just the geographic area where her job, friends and house-search took place, but the *world* in which she belonged, her personal attitudes and philosophies. Keith was a different sort of person, at home with the fishbowl atmosphere in Joyous, comfortable with interactions and personal interactions that would leave her squirming. Just look at their job descriptions—she frequently worked alone; with the exception of a producer and a few guests, her audience was separated by space and phone lines, and there was a measure of anonymity afforded by her on-air persona. Keith, however, was known so well in town that people noticed when he spent ten seconds kissing a girl in a crowded hall on Saturday night. Sometimes the only thing that separated him from his professional "audience" was a paper gown.

And despite all that, she'd invited him here tonight. *For dinner. He's a friend of the family.* He'd become a friend of hers.

A friend who kissed really, really well.

"Do you honestly have to stir that stuff so much, or are you just manic?" Charity asked irreverently.

Treble shot her a look.

"I figured since you were already planning to spit in mine, I might as well just say whatever," her sister said cheerfully.

"Good risotto takes a lot of stirring." She hoped it would be good. The side dish, which called for two kinds of cheese, olives and sun-dried tomatoes, sounded promising, and she'd been cheered to discover the local grocery store did in fact carry arborio rice.

"You want me to call Bill in here to take over for you while you change?"

"Change?" Treble's voice came out with a squeak she didn't recognize. She cast a glance down over the casual pink-and-white striped blouse she wore untucked over a short denim skirt. "I was planning to wear this. What's wrong with— You're messing with me, aren't you?"

"Sorry. I've gone through all the books and movies in the house. I take my entertainment where I can find it."

"Just so you know, the next time you ask for a favor that involves my trekking here from Atlanta, I'm going to laugh long and hard, then hang up on you."

"Liar," Charity said cheerfully. "Hey, what do you think about Shelby?"

Although Treble wasn't opposed to the non sequitur, she couldn't for the life of her remember meeting a Shelby since she'd come to town. "Which one was Shelby? I'm sure I have an opinion, but I can't put a face with the name."

Charity laughed. "Well, I could show you yesterday's sonogram pictures again if it would help. Bill and I were talking about names last night, and I thought Shelby sounded kind of nice."

"Shelby Sumner. Not bad."

"I really like 'Faith,' but come on…with Charity for a mother? She'd have to have a sister named Hope, and Bill would probably need to legally change his name to Valor or something."

They continued to discuss potential baby names as Treble finished up the risotto dish, green beans and chicken breasts. The timing worked out surprisingly well with everything finished mere minutes before Keith was expected.

"I'll be right back," Treble said, pivoting toward the hallway.

"If you're thinking about changing, I was just kidding earlier. Besides, you don't have time."

"I was not planning to change," Treble called back. But maybe it wouldn't hurt to apply fresh lipstick and make sure the heat in the kitchen hadn't frizzed her hair into some sort of beast from a B horror movie.

As she stood at the mirror in the hall bathroom, running a pick through her hair, Bill appeared just outside the doorway.

"Is Keith here already?"

Her brother-in-law shook his head. "No, but thanks for inviting him. Charity was so quiet on the ride back from Dr. Whalen's yesterday, but she's been chipper as a squirrel in springtime since you told us you'd asked him over. She's been after him to date on occasion and remarked that you could stand to meet a good man, so this is…what do you call those happy coincidences when everything meshes?"

"Serendipity?"

He snapped his fingers. "Exactly."

"Bill. You know I want Charity to be happy, so I'm glad if I did anything to improve her mood. But she's…being realistic, isn't she? Keith Caldwell is great, and I'm sure he'll find a terrific woman." Treble's jaw clenched involuntarily, but she tried to keep her tone as breezy as possible. "He and I are just friends, though. I'll be out of here in about two weeks."

Bill shrugged. "When it comes to stuff like this, I just listen to her. Hell, when we fell in love, she was barely fourteen. Plenty of people told her our relationship wasn't going to last through high school, much less make it to the altar."

"Well, that's different." Her voice softened. "You and Charity are perfect together."

"Exactly," he said again. "My wife has great instincts about love."

"This isn't love," she corrected, but he was already ambling down the hall.

So she repeated it to her reflection just to make her point. What she felt for Keith was nowhere *near* love. They barely knew each other. Yes, she was attracted to Keith and respected him, appreciated his loyalty and dedication, empathized with his past, enjoyed laughing with him and trusted him. She looked forward to being with him, experienced fluttery quivers of excitement when she thought about seeing him tonight, and his kisses made her knees go liquid, along with other parts of her body, but…

Frowning at herself, she tried to remember the point of her mental meanderings. Hadn't she been going somewhere with this?

"Treble? Keith's here," Charity called out in a singsong voice.

Even though she was a nearly thirty-year-old woman and she'd been expecting his arrival, her pulse picked up to a kicky tempo that put a slight spring in her step as she exited the bathroom. As she approached the voices in the kitchen she thought, *oh, right*. Now she remembered her point she'd been trying to make: she was in no danger of falling for Keith. Of course, she'd probably do a better job of convincing others of that if Treble were more sure of it herself.

DINNER WAS A BLAST, as far removed from that first time they'd sat around the table together as late-night talk show hosts were from early-morning news anchors. The easy, spiteful explanation was to note that the chief difference in tonight's meal was Harrison's absence, but Treble resisted the oversimplification. Not only had she and Keith gotten to know each other better since her arrival, her overall attitude had shifted from defensive to admitting that Joyous possessed its own charm.

"The food was incredible," Keith told her with a smile. "If I'd known you could cook like that, I would have encouraged you to enter some of the competitions next week. Especially since you were right, and I *was* asked to judge a few of them."

Charity laughed. "Oh, between the library fund-raising booth, an interview for the *Journal-Report* and being the DJ for next Saturday's dance, I think Treble's already got her hands full, festival-wise. Dr. Whalen cleared me to go for one day if I sit at the Breckfield booth with my feet up, oscillated fans going and sip plenty of water. I'm really looking forward to it!"

Treble pressed her lips together. She hadn't heard much about the Breckfield booth. Since she'd been in Joyous, they hadn't seen much of Harrison, and while Charity might feel comfortable to tease or push in other areas, she'd more or less dropped the subject of her father. And Treble hadn't mentioned Keith's cryptic words to her, about Harrison perhaps not being as healthy as he would have his underlings believe. If his condition was anything serious, hopefully Keith would let Charity know after the baby was born.

Bill reached over to rub his wife's arm. "You look tuckered out."

"I am." She closed her eyes, smiling. "Carry me to bed?"

"Sure thing, sweetheart. Soon as I get that system of pulleys installed in the house."

Without opening her eyes, she swatted her hand in his general direction, making contact only with air. Bill grabbed her fingers and pressed a kiss to their tips.

"I'll take care of the dishes," Treble reminded them. "Bill, you just get your wife to bed."

Charity peered at them from one eye, looking like an impish Cyclops. "Yeah, come on, Bill, honey. I'll teach you how to play Sudoku."

It was good to know that as siblings got older, they matured beyond the childish musical taunt of "Sittin' in a Tree, K-I-S-S-I-N-G," but still retained enough of a bond to find new ways to needle each other.

Despite all the teasing back and forth throughout dinner, Charity really did seem tired, faint purplish shadows appearing under her eyes as the evening progressed. When she stood to tell Keith good-night, she was barely stifling her yawns.

"Want some help with the dishes?" Keith offered once they were alone.

"That would be nice, thanks." Not that she minded tackling the plates and pans by herself, but she didn't want to see him go just yet.

They worked in companionable efficiency, him washing—she laughed when he snapped on a glove, prepared for him to hold out one hand and bark "Scrub brush!"—and her drying. At intervals, she talked about other recipes she enjoyed making and the roommate who'd tried to teach her to cook, and he described a card one of his pediatric patients had made him. Other times, they lapsed into silence and just let the house settle around them. If she'd been alone instead of orbiting in Keith's personal perimeter, would the random creaks, the sudden motor of the refrigerator running over top of the sound of the breeze outside, the rising and falling symphony of insects and bullfrogs seem so cozy?

"It sounds so different here," she said, closing her eyes to isolate her hearing. "I grew up with these same noises every summer, but it's been a long time. Now I'm used to traffic and apartment sounds. There was this one couple that lived in my complex for a few months, I swear they—" She broke off suddenly, deciding that the story that usually got laughs at parties or with coworkers was bad conversational fodder with Keith. It's not that she thought he'd disapprove, it was that she thought she knew how he'd look at her as she described the couple's lusty activities. And if the look in his eyes turned into anything like the expression he'd had this afternoon, she'd be too tempted to give him a live demonstration of what had been going in the apartment next to hers.

"Well, they were noisy," she concluded weakly.

Keith grinned, drawing his own conclusions. "Squeaky mattress springs?"

"Among other things."

"We're done with the dishes," he noted.

"Mmm." Which meant he would be going…unless she asked him to stay. For what? To watch a movie? To make out on the couch? She thought of Bill and Charity just down the hall and how often Charity got up in the middle of the night for all manner of pregnancy-related reasons—water, cravings, heartburn medicine, late-night television when she couldn't sleep after weird dreams or going to the bathroom for the tenth time.

No, it was best if Keith went home.

"Thank you for coming over tonight," she told him. It had been the first time she'd seen him by her own deliberate choice, not through an accident or car failure or anyone else instigating it.

"My pleasure. And not just because the food was so good." He held a hand out to her, intent clear in his eyes. "Walk me outside? The stars are supposed to be incredible tonight."

She laughed out loud, belatedly bringing a hand to her mouth to stifle the sound. "It's been overcast all afternoon and they predicted a cloudy night with scattered showers."

"All right." His grin widened as he closed the gap between them and interlocked his fingers with hers. "Walk me out on the porch so I can kiss you good-night the way I want to without anyone overhearing or walking in on us?"

She smiled up at him. "Okay, you talked me into it."

Chapter Thirteen

Though more than three-quarters of the town had turned out on various curbs, sidewalks and lawns, waiting for the parade to start, Treble spotted Keith in the crowd immediately. His height helped, even though at the moment he was stooped somewhat, talking to a toddler with pigtails whose hands and face were sticky blue from the cotton candy she held. Whatever the kid had said, Keith grinned in return, broadly enough that an indentation deepened next to his cockeyed smile. From the side, he looked like a young Dennis Quaid.

Treble continued watching as Keith tousled the girl's hair and straightened. She knew that his job required a certain proficiency with kids, but he seemed to genuinely enjoy them. *He'll make a good dad.* Whoa.

The thought, so random and futuristic, made her blink.

Whenever she next visited Joyous, would he already be involved with the woman who might one day have his kids? Treble couldn't claim to like that idea, but there were too many men in the world who had children but didn't do right by them— her own biological father included.

So even though the image of Keith kissing another woman the way he'd been kissing *her* every time they'd found themselves alone together since Thursday twisted her guts into painful knots, she hoped he did settle down and have a family. He deserved it.

He'd lost so much of his own family. He explained to her, over an impromptu late picnic lunch from the sandwich shop yesterday, that he and his mother kept in touch but weren't really close. Love didn't always translate into comfortable affection.

"I withdrew after Gail and Dad died," he admitted to Treble at the table they'd shared in a deserted back corner of the town's smallest park, unadorned by new playground equipment or decorative fountains for kids to splash in. "Mom was proud of my scholastic success and becoming a doctor, but I left her in Savannah by herself. When I visited, we didn't know how to talk to each other with ghosts floating around between us. She met this guy who makes her smile, and I'm glad for them. But when I try to stay too long…it's like I suck the joy out of their being together."

Treble had empathized, but encouraged him to give it another try next time he had a long weekend. "After all, I thought this trip home was going to be a disaster of epic proportions."

"And…?" he'd prompted, leaning closer.

She'd met him halfway. "And not so much," she'd murmured against his lips.

"What are you smiling about?" Keith asked.

Treble started. "Did you sprint through the crowd? You were way over there with that cute little girl just a minute ago. How'd I miss your getting here?"

"You were daydreaming. About something good?"

She peered through her lashes. "Ask me when we're alone."

"I like the sound of that."

Unzipping the oversize purse she wore on her shoulder, she pulled out a surprisingly compact video camera.

"What is that for?" Keith wanted to know.

"Charity. Even though she got permission to sit in the booth later this week, she's not supposed to overdo, and with this heat and crowd… It's the first Days of Joy parade she's missed in years, and Bill wants to test out the recorder they got so they can document the baby's first smile and crawling, et cetera. So I'm out here to film for them." She turned the lens toward him, learning the buttons. "Say something brilliant, and I'll record it for posterity."

"No pressure."

"You're a doctor. Don't you guys have to be geniuses whenever the situation calls for it?"

"You seem to have a romanticized image of my career."

"Blame television."

He laughed. "Maybe you should read more books."

Moments later, air horns sounded and members of the high school marching band broke into song, announcing that the parade had officially started. It was only about forty-five minutes long, which amused Treble since she knew some people came out more than an hour in advance to get a good seat. After the parade, Adam's Rib catered a huge barbecue and the rest of the day was spent erecting booths and registering contestants for the competitions that would take place all week.

"Want to grab lunch with me?" Keith asked her.

"I'd love to, but I actually have to find Penny Paulson and get some information about the booth I'll be working on Tuesday and Wednesday." She packed the recorder back in its case. "I promised Charity I'd bring back some barbecue and watch the tape with her so it's sort of like being here."

"All right. I'll look for the middle school booth and see you later this week." When he first leaned toward her, she didn't immediately realize his intent.

As soon as it registered—*duh*—that he meant to kiss her, she took an involuntary step backward. It was a reflexive movement, not premeditated, but she could tell by his stung expression that he wasn't happy about it. "Keith. I...there are so many people around."

He glanced pointedly to his left, then to his right. "Yeah. And most of them are more concerned with getting some of that barbecue than my giving you a quick peck goodbye. I know it's a family audience, I wasn't shooting for anything R-rated."

She fidgeted, seeing two girls she'd gone to high school with who'd been happy to spread rumors about her when Rich dumped her and, in contrast, catching Lola Ann's friendly wave in her peripheral vision. On the curb immediately opposite her across the street, two grizzled men she recognized as working for the dairy chatted with each other. "There are people around," she repeated dully.

Now Keith was the one to take a step back. "You embarrassed to be seen with me? As I recall, you're the one who kissed me at the dance hall."

She was a grown woman, yet after that one kiss at Guthrie, people had practically fallen all over themselves to tattle to Harrison and Charity. While Treble was no longer trying to convince herself there was "nothing" going on with Keith, neither was she eager to foster her sister's hope that this was an actual, lasting relationship. Once Treble was gone, Keith would eventually want a real relationship. Despite whatever jokes he'd made the other day about a beautiful woman only enhancing his reputation, that wasn't quite true. Some of the proper local girls, the ones who knew more than three recipes and would make good mothers, would have definite opinions about him kissing Trouble James. Men who saw her kissing Keith would form smirking opinions, as well. She hadn't been in town long, hadn't known the doctor before this—was she reinforcing whatever odes had been composed to her on bathroom walls?

"Treble, what is this really about?"

"I don't know." Her primary reason for being in Joyous was to help Charity, but it had seemed like a good secondary goal to prove to herself once and for all that other people's opinions didn't matter. So *why* did they suddenly seem to matter so much? As a teenager, her attitude had been "screw 'em," and when people assumed the worst about her, she'd simply lived up to their low opinions. She was more mature and less adversarial now, which was a good thing, she assumed, but that progress had left her without a clear sense of how to carry herself.

Not only wasn't she the same person she'd been twelve years ago, she didn't even feel like the same person she'd been two weeks ago. Getting to know Keith, watching Charity's excitement over becoming a mom, living under the same roof as a happily married couple day in and day out…*it's all clouded your judgment. You're becoming a sap.*

Confusion and irritation sharpened her tone. "Look, you and I both know what we have isn't going anywhere, so I don't particularly want to advertise it. I'm sorry if that wounds your ego."

His eyes narrowed. "Fine. If you'll excuse me, I'm going to get something to eat."

The thought of food turned her stomach, but she held fast to the edges of her composure as she inclined her head. "Enjoy your lunch."

The minute he walked away from her, she wanted to call him back. And *that's* what was wrong. Because even though her statement may have come out bitchy, it was still true. They had no future together, and she was only just starting to realize how much driving away in her newly tuned-up car and no longer seeing Keith Caldwell on a regular basis was going to hurt. Not the quick, sharp sting of a shot, but a lasting, indefinable ache that she didn't think aspirin, ice cream or new shoes would heal.

ON TUESDAY, Keith smiled and shook hands and had his picture taken with various cook-off contestants, but mostly he wished he were back at the clinic. He'd worked a full morning, treating a broken thumb for one of the construction volunteers, a bee sting, a sinus infection, a concussion and a case of dehydration.

"Hey, Doc Caldwell." A woman in a red sundress passed him with a smile, and it took a moment for his brain to catch up to the spark of recognition.

"Afternoon, Heather Lynn." He wondered if he would have

placed Heather Lynn Jacob without seeing her two boys, who'd both been in to see him during the spring. Their mom looked different today, although maybe that was the less harried effect of her not carting around sick kids to the doctor and pharmacy. "You look nice."

Her pleasure at his words blossomed in her pale cheeks, and she smiled shyly. "Why, thank you. Charity's sister, Treble, took me shopping yesterday. She helped me pick this out."

Of course she did. He sighed—hearing the woman's name mentioned didn't exactly further his campaign to keep from thinking about her. Now that he took another look at the gently clinging dress, more a design of the fabric than a revealing cut, he could easily see it appealing to Treble, although he had to admit, she had a good eye for what worked on the florist.

Heather Lynn fluffed her hair. "I didn't think strawberry-blondes were supposed to wear red, in case it clashed or something, but Treble helped me see things differently."

"Yeah. She does that." He glanced down, including Heather Lynn's sons in his smile. "You all have a nice time at the festival today."

Waving, he watched them walk away. Then he glanced up and froze. Standing a few yards away, near a clown twisting balloons into poodles and swans for waiting children, was Treble, staring across the distance with an unreadable expression in her dark eyes.

What should he do? Walking away without acknowledging her would be stupid, petty. They'd already made eye contact, but they hadn't parted on the best of terms. Still, despite his ire with her—that tiny step she'd taken in the opposite direction when he'd tried to kiss her had made him feel publicly rejected—could he fault her logic? He had no idea how to define what was between them, so at least in part, he could understand why she didn't want half the town taking it upon themselves to assign their own definitions. Especially since Treble had grown up here, been labeled the stepdaughter of a town magnate. The surviving daughter of a deceased mother. The troublemaker in her class.

When she continued to meet his gaze, her body language softening, he crossed the space between them.

"Hey." If he reached out and caught a long tendril of her hair in his fingers, would that be too public a display of affection?

"Hi." Her smile was fleeting, regretful. "You still mad?"

"Yeah." He found his own smile. "But I'm not entirely sure why."

"Well, if you need a reason, it's been commonly held that I'm a pain in the butt."

"Being a pain doesn't make you wrong." He took a verbal leap of faith, blurting out the words before he could suppress them. "I'll miss you when you go. If I thought I could get away with it, I'd tamper with Trusty's engine, but everyone would immediately suspect foul play because Ronnie's handiwork has never failed."

"Thank you." Treble's tremulous voice matched her bright eyes.

He lowered his gaze, for the first time noticing her bizarre attire. "Is that a *poncho* you're wearing?" He glanced up to the clear, cloudless azure sky, wondering if she knew something he didn't.

"Uh…yeah." She hitched up the duffel bag that hung by a black strap on her shoulder. He recognized the bag as one he'd carried inside for her that first day they'd met. She'd become such a vivid presence in his life so quickly, it was funny to think that not long ago he hadn't even known her. "I guess it's a rain slicker Bill never uses. He and Charity let me borrow it to throw over my—we never talked about what I'll be doing for Penny's middle school booth, did we?"

"Well, hello, Keith." A honeyed, feminine drawl, thick with generations of Tennessee, interrupted, keeping Keith from asking Treble for more details.

He turned, the friendly public smile he'd been offering earlier back in place, a bit more sincere now that he'd seen Treble. If nothing had truly been resolved between them, at least the worst of the tension had eased, like a bad storm passing on, replacing the howling, destructive winds with only steady rain.

"Hi, Dinah." His smile tightened slightly when he saw the blond receptionist. Not long after he'd moved to town, she'd pursued him aggressively with cobblers and corn bread and baked lasagna. "You know Treble James?"

"Oh, sure," Dinah said, even though she didn't spare a glance for the woman at his side. She kept her gaze fixated on Keith. "How are you doing today?"

"Fine, great. Getting ready to judge some of the handmade quilts that were entered this year and the first-round dessert cook-offs."

Treble touched his arm. "Speaking of which...I'm due at Penny's booth. See you later?"

"Of course." He smiled at her, almost laughing at his own impulse to kiss her goodbye. She certainly wouldn't appreciate the gesture, and it wasn't as if they'd be apart for long. He turned back to Dinah, blinking at how close she was. Maybe it wasn't so much that she'd invaded his personal space as how large her eyes were, still fixed expectantly on him. When he'd been a kid, he and Gail had tossed some sandwich crusts to pigeons at the end of a meal, and suddenly the birds had descended in droves, hopping closer with dark eyes and sharp beaks. Something about the small blonde in front of him struck him as very birdlike.

"I didn't compete in the cook-offs this year," Dinah said. "Usually I enter the fresh bread category. I've always loved the smell of baking bread, find it so comforting. Did you have a favorite comfort food growing up?"

He was half-afraid to answer, fearing that if he said, for instance, chicken soup, he'd find a steaming vat of it on his front porch one day soon. "Dinah, I hate to run, but judge duties call."

In fact, his responsibilities as a festival "official" kept him legitimately busy for the next couple of hours. It was nearly three o'clock when he asked a popcorn vendor if he could point the way toward the middle school library booth.

The older man grinned beneath his bushy white mustache and pointed down the lane. "Go toward the big crafts tent, but take a left at the funnel cakes—if you get to the portable restrooms, you missed the turn. Once you're on the next row, just look for the huge crowd."

As it turned out, "crowd" was not an exaggeration. There was quite an assortment of people, many of whom were hooting and whistling from the back as a guy in a backward ball cap, past age to shave but probably not old enough to buy beer, stood at a duct-taped line on the ground. A small tin pail of baseballs sat in front of him, and a shapely girl waited to his left. Though Keith couldn't see the guy's expression as he turned toward the young woman, he heard his boast that he would win a teddy bear for her.

Then a voice Keith knew well carried out over the crowd, teasing, but with enough playful lilt in her tone to keep it from sounding spiteful. "Honey, if he misses the target, maybe *you* can buy a bucket and win a bear for him. Remember, all proceeds go to a good cause!"

Even though Keith had an idea of what he was going to see when he turned toward the sound of that voice, his body was unprepared for the sight of Treble sitting atop a narrow platform. Her dark hair was dripping in wet ringlets down her back, and the creamy, long-legged body that drove him to distraction bared but for a few brightly striped scraps of—pink? purple?—nylon Lycra. His throat went dry, the blood draining from his head. Every time he'd cupped the nape of her neck or ran his hands down her spine, he'd wanted to explore further. To see for himself the lush curves beneath her clothes. Well, in part, he'd gotten his wish.

He just hadn't expected it to be in front of the greater population of Joyous, Tennessee.

TREBLE WONDERED how long Keith had been standing in the crowd—his perfect stillness distinguishing him from the teenage boys who jostled one another, the moms who fished in their purses for cash and the dads who shifted under the weight of pre-schoolers atop their shoulders—before she noticed him. She met his eyes, and the swell of heat from his gaze practically evaporated the droplets of water that clung to her shoulders and arrowed in slick beads down her collarbone toward her cleavage. Her breath caught. Though she distantly registered the thud of the ball hitting the target, for the first time, she was unprepared for the fall.

The water wasn't cold, just cool enough to be bracing, and she came up, half spluttering, half laughing. All things considered, she preferred this to other volunteer duties. Some poor guy was walking around in what had to be a sweltering-hot Seth the Safety Squirrel costume, handing out brochures on campfire protocol, hiking first aid, and poison ivy and sumac identification.

Treble flipped wet hair out of her face, and called graciously, "Let's hear it for our second winner of the day. Nice throw, buddy."

She'd been surprised that Penny set the throwing line so far back, but the other woman had laughed. "Gotta make 'em work for it, right?" The first guy to dunk her had been spurred on by his ego and the crowd, actually going through two buckets of balls before he accomplished it.

Penny leaned over the counter at the small covered booth adjacent to the tank. "Okay, just a few more takers, then we'll let our mermaid here have a short break."

One of the guys in the audience let out a good-natured boo, another called out his offer to run and fetch her anything she wanted. "Soda, corn dog, the keys to my Chevy?" Laughter rippled around him.

Treble darted a glance to where Keith still stood, to see if he were one of those smiling. Nope. His expression was intense, making her feel so momentarily exposed that she almost looked down to make sure her bikini top wasn't floating on the surface of the water. She tried to push aside her awareness of him long enough to goad passersby into lobbing a few tosses her way. A few took her up on the invitation, but no one else dunked her before Penny declared the booth closed for business until three thirty.

Penny reached the gated side of the booth, towel in hand. It had been hanging on a hook just outside the splash zone, next to the poncho Treble had wriggled out of two hours ago. "You're *such* a good sport for doing this. We really appreciate it."

Treble smiled as she climbed down. "No problem. But if you see my brother-in-law in the crowd wielding a video camera, please tell him taping is against our policy."

"You need anything? Hot chocolate? Well, they probably aren't selling that at a summer festival," Penny said to herself, "but I'm sure we could find you some coffee."

"I'm fine, really. I've only been in twice."

"If you're not cold, would you mind maybe walking around in that bathing suit?" Penny grinned at her. "It would be *excellent* advertising."

Treble's laugh faded when she saw Keith standing past Penny's shoulder. "I'll be back in fifteen minutes, okay, Penny?"

"So this is how you're raising money for more books, huh?" Keith said softly when she reached his side.

She shrugged, pulling the towel around her. "Well, we weren't all invited to taste desserts."

"Did you buy that bathing suit just for this?" he asked. "I heard you were shopping yesterday."

He knew about her road trip to the mall with Heather Lynn? Not that it particularly mattered, but she suspected you couldn't sneeze at one end of town without someone at the opposite end saying, "Bless you."

"No, this is just my bathing suit. Penny asked if I'd happened to bring one with me, and I had. Whenever I travel in the summer, I take it just in case."

"So you didn't specifically get the bikini to help make— sorry—a splash here? That's just what you walk around in at the pool or beach?"

"Yeah." It wasn't really all that revealing, as far as two-piece bathing suits went, she only seemed nearly naked because everyone else was in shorts or skirts and, in a few cases, jeans. "Are you okay?"

"My vision's gone all spotty. Don't you worry about sunburn?"

"It's all right, Doc. I slathered my entire body with sunscreen, promise."

"Little dots in front of my eyes," he said. "And you're doing this again tomorrow?"

"Yeah." She still wasn't sure if he approved, but he didn't sound mad.

His gaze met hers, suddenly more focused and a lot more wicked. "Can I help with the sunscreen?"

Chapter Fourteen

"Come on, come on, come on," Charity chanted, adorably impatient in her red, white and blue maternity shirt. Her earrings were red outlines of large stars. "Why am I the only one ready to go?"

Treble exchanged wry glances with Bill. "She was like this as a kid, too, always antsy for the school bus to come in the morning."

Charity glared. "You'd be excited, too, if the warden gave you a day pass! It truly is Independence Day."

Treble appreciated her sister's enthusiasm—she herself never liked to feel caged—but was glad Dr. Whalen had been playing it safe during Charity's last trimester. In some cases, the OB might not be quite as conservative, but Bill and Charity lived a good drive from the nearest hospital, and no one wanted her sister to take any unnecessary risks. Still, getting permission to sit at a booth today and watch the fireworks over town square tonight had done wonders for Charity's morale.

"Maybe we'll name our daughter Liberty," Charity said as Bill helped her down the stairs.

"Can her middle name be Belle?" he teased as they walked toward the truck.

Treble was helping them carry a blanket and cooler, but would follow in her own car in case they wanted to come home at different times. Flashing back to yesterday evening, when Keith had stolen a soft, hot kiss from her between booths featuring rustic interior decorating pieces and handcrafted Amish dolls, Treble thought about how the night could have ended differently.

She could have sworn, as he nuzzled the side of her neck, he'd murmured that he wanted her. Even if he hadn't put it in words, the sentiment was there. A sentiment she wholeheartedly returned. It had occurred to her that even though she was bunking with her sister, Keith had his own place. Was she brave—or fool-hardy enough—to ask to see it?

Her conjecture had remained exactly that, however, because some guy trying to impress his girlfriend with shenanigans at the rock-climbing demo had managed to break his arm. Keith's medical skills had been needed, and Treble had used the reprieve to go home and let her hormones cool. Only the thought of seeing him again today was already warming her.

"Or July," Charity said as Bill opened the passenger door for her. "July can be a name. Maybe too specific. Summer?"

Treble snorted. "Summer Sumner?"

"Oops." Charity grimaced. "I forgot that, for a minute."

Bill gaped. "You *forgot* our family name?"

"I always thought Autumn was a pretty name," Treble offered.

"For a girl born in the middle of summer?" Charity asked.

Treble shrugged. "Why not? Dare to be different. No rule saying she has to be a conformist right from the womb, is there?"

Charity laughed. "We'll see you at the festival. Drive safe."

Treble gave a jaunty salute. She'd been in the car about ten minutes when her cell phone rang, and she wondered if Charity had forgotten anything back at the house. "Hello?"

"Hi." Keith's voice was as tangible a caress as any touch, and her body reacted accordingly.

"It's nice to hear from you," she said, catching sight of her own moony smile in the rearview mirror.

"Well, we didn't get a chance to say a proper goodbye last night."

"How's that kid doing?" she asked.

"His arm should heal with no problem. His pride was plenty

injured, but his girlfriend fussing over him seemed to help. Or maybe it was just the pain medication kicking in. Look, I know you're driving, so I don't want to keep you. But…any plans after today's aquatic performance?"

"Same as the rest of the town's, I reckon." Had she just said *reckon?* It wasn't a word she recalled ever using on-air. "Watching the fireworks."

"Want to watch them together? You, me, a blanket and a bottle of chardonnay?"

"See, that poor schmo wanting to impress his date could use some pointers from you," she said. "It sounds perfect."

"Great. I'll be the one with the chilled wine and wandering hands."

She laughed, delighted by his flirtatious tone. Lord, had she ever actually thought the doctor was *stuffy?* "I'll be the one with wet hair and willing lips."

BECAUSE SO MANY people wanted to find a good spot for the fireworks or had pre-show dinner plans, the crowd broke earlier Wednesday evening than it had the day before, which suited Treble just fine.

Penny checked her watch. "We'll give it ten more minutes, then close shop. Sound all right?"

"Fine by me." Treble flashed a smile. *I have a hot date tonight.* Keith was meeting her here shortly.

The refrain of a country song trilled from inside Penny's open purse behind the counter, and she bent to answer her cell phone. "Hello. Charity? What's wrong, sweetie?"

Treble's heart lurched to her throat. Oh, God. Had today been too much excitement for her sister? Was something wrong with the baby? *Calm down.* If anything had happened to Charity, wouldn't Bill be the one calling?

"Yeah, she's still here," Penny said. "What—?" There was an

interminable pause as Treble imagined the worst, then Penny nodded. "All right, I'll let her know."

"What is it?" Treble asked, her fingers gripping the edge of her platform seat.

"Charity called from the Breckfield booth she's been helping with today. She and Harrison argued. Apparently, a couple of guys were…" Penny lowered her gaze guiltily. "This is my fault. Some guy made a ribald comment about you that Harrison overheard. I don't think he approves of the way we're raising money for the library."

"Don't worry about it, Pen. His disapproval is nothing new."

"Well, I guess he's coming over here. Why don't we go ahead and shut the booth down?"

"No," Treble said calmly. "This was a two-day stint on my part, and I want to bring in as much revenue as possible." There was another woman who'd work the booth tomorrow and a man who'd volunteered for Friday.

Penny winced as if she'd glimpsed a furious fork of lightning and was cowering in anticipation of the boom and tremble of thunder. She didn't have long to wait.

Harrison Breckfield stalked toward the booth with the stride of a powerful, fit man, though his mottled face gave him an unhealthy appearance.

Treble spoke before he could. "A bucket of balls for five dollars. We're closing soon, so you'll have to hurry if you want to take a shot."

He looked appalled by the suggestion—although maybe she was misreading him; after all, he'd looked pretty appalled already. "Come down from there and put on some clothes."

"Well, I have an outfit in my duffel bag, but I was saving it for the fireworks. It's not really appropriate for the dunking booth."

"You call that appropriate?" He gestured vaguely toward her bathing suit but wouldn't lower his eyes from her face as if just the sight of the bikini would sully him. "Do you know what people are saying about you?"

"I'm not sure," she bit out the words. "What day is it, Wednesday? Today would be Elvis rumors, right?"

"I don't know why I bother trying to talk to you."

She laughed harshly. "*When? When* have you tried to talk to me?" Certainly not after her mom died. Or in any of the condescending lectures over her many failings and outrageous behavior—shouldn't talking involve two-way participation? He hadn't wanted to hear what she had to say. Even during her weeks here in Joyous, their direct interaction had been limited to that one disastrous dinner.

"Harrison."

Both of them turned, surprised at Keith's firm voice. He didn't look happy, but as he was the only one in their little triangle not vibrating with angry emotion, he was pretty calm in comparison.

"I think you should go sit down somewhere, take a few deep breaths," Keith advised.

The older man's eyes narrowed. "I warned you that there were some things you were going to have to stay out of. Charity and I live here, make our home here. I don't appreciate her waltzing in just long enough to make a scene."

Keith glanced around. There was still no crowd at the booth, but other vendors were watching with unabashed curiosity. Those that caught the exact words exchanged would no doubt repeat it for the benefit of others; those who didn't catch what was said would speculate. "Harrison, as far as I can tell, you're the one making the scene."

Her stepfather's already red face now looked positively apoplectic. Treble's heart hurt. She knew that Harrison had been a friend to Keith, and it had never been her desire to cause trouble between them. Maybe he was right that first night they'd met. Maybe she just couldn't help it. Tears pricked her eyes, the hot, salty drops far more unpleasant than the tank of water she'd fallen into a dozen times today.

"All *Treble* is doing," Keith continued, still in that even but unyielding tone, "is helping the library raise money. You support the cause, right?"

"That's not the point!" Harrison whirled on the doctor. "A school counselor warned me once that Treble was desperate for attention, but you'd think she would have outgrown it by now. Tons of people are here today raising money, yet my stepdaughter seems to be the only one half-naked." He turned back to Treble. "I wanted to punch those two roughnecks who were exchanging sleazy comments about you, but how can I protect you if you insist on putting yourself on display?"

Protect her? Treble blinked, surprised that one of the town's most honorable citizens had considered decking anyone on her behalf. As happy as she'd been to see him in the barn that one afternoon, when the intent look in Mitchell Reyes' eyes had genuinely alarmed her, it wasn't protection she'd wanted from her stepfather.

Before she could sort through her thoughts, a female voice interrupted. Joan approached her former employer, taking his arm. "Don't be an old fool. I asked Treble myself to get involved in this year's festival."

"But look at her," the man said, though his anger was faltering now. He seemed more sad than anything else. How ironic to actually have something in common.

"No, Harry." Joan's voice wasn't unkind, but it was stern. Treble had heard exactly that tone many times. "You look at her. She's a grown woman, and you can't keep judging her based on the actions of a sixteen-year-old kid who needed more parental guidance."

"I…" Harrison Breckfield blinked, looking for a moment lost in the streets of his own hometown. Looking very much his age and every bit as miserable as Treble currently felt. "I did the best I could."

Was he talking to her, apologizing in some oblique way? Or merely defending himself to Joan?

As the twosome moved away and people stopped paying attention—or at least, stopped blatantly rubbernecking—Treble shivered.

"Let's get you out of there," Keith said from the other side of the protective cage. He sprung the latch and held his hand out to her.

She slid down into his waiting arms. "I should get my towel. I'm still damp."

Not even bothering to respond, he pulled her against him in a fierce hug. Witnesses no doubt saw their embrace—would remark upon it later—and she found she honestly didn't give a damn.

"You stood up for me," she muttered against his shirt.

He angled back so that he could meet her gaze. "Of course I did." He made it sound unremarkable. Maybe for him it was. After all, he'd ridden to her rescue when she'd been a total stranger, stranded. He'd nearly decked Rich Danner on her behalf even though, as a physician, "violence was against his creed."

For Treble, however, his unflinching defense of her brought fresh tears to her eyes. Her own father hadn't wanted her. Some of the men she'd dated could barely be bothered to remember to call her, much less stand up for her. "Thank you."

"You're welcome." He leaned toward her, then hesitated, his eyes seeking permission that she granted with a nod. Then he kissed her.

And Treble's heart squeezed with something that felt very much like love.

By the time Treble had changed into her blouse and shorts and was situated on a cotton blanket next to Keith, she'd recovered her composure. So she and Harrison had fought—that wasn't news. She wanted to hold on to the glow of Keith and Joan being there for her and forget the rest entirely.

During the last moments of fading light, Keith wrestled with a corkscrew, trying to open the bottle of wine he'd supplied as promised. "I didn't even know they made disposable plastic wineglasses until yesterday," he said.

She hid a laugh, watching him. "They *also* make wine with twist-off caps."

He sent her a wry smile. "Nothing but the best for you."

Despite the number of people present to watch the Fourth of July display, Treble felt nicely isolated with her date for the evening. Everyone was on their own island, the growing dark casting an illusion of privacy even while the steady rush of conversation, the pockets of laughter and the homey aroma of fried chicken over the lighter scent of honeysuckle, provided the feel of community. For a split second, Treble experienced a frisson of déjà vu. This was how she felt sometimes on-air. As if she and her listeners were all in it together, a faceless community of people she couldn't see and didn't always know but who were important to her nonetheless.

Her cell phone jangled, and she flashed Keith a look of apology. "I know it's rude to leave it on during a date—"

"You're talking to a doctor," he said mildly. "I'm not bothered."

"Thanks." She kept it on in case Charity had any news or requests. And it was her sister's voice she heard, shaky, on the other end of the phone.

"Treb? I know we passed each other earlier, but I didn't want to ask in front of Keith. Are you all right? I heard it got ugly."

Treble sighed. If it pained her that Keith had been dragged into an argument on her behalf, it upset her even more that Charity had been involved. Harrison could stalk her down to yell at her if he wanted, but he never should have breathed a word about his displeasure in front of his very pregnant daughter, who'd always preferred the image of him as loving benefactor.

"Don't worry," Treble said. "You know how everything gets exaggerated in this town."

"Yeah."

"Are *you* okay?"

"I've been better, but yes, I'll be fine."

"Enjoy the fireworks, then go home and get some rest."

Charity laughed, sounding more herself. "You're turning into a regular mother hen."

"Good night, brat. Oh, Charity?" Treble cupped her hand around her mouth and turned her head to the side to whisper, "Don't wait up for me tonight."

Once she was off the phone, she accepted a glass of wine. "Keith? I'm sure you know that even a little bit of alcohol can alter a person's reflexes and response times. Maybe I shouldn't drive myself all the way back out to Bill and Charity's tonight."

Keith's eyes were as dark as the night around them. "Do you need a lift?" he asked haltingly, hopefully.

She took a deep breath. "I was thinking…more along the lines of a place to stay?"

Setting down his glass, he leaned in to capture her mouth in a searing kiss she felt down to her toes. As she brushed her tongue against his, a high-pitched whistle erupted overhead in a series of pops and brilliant blazes of white and violet and green filled the sky.

"IT'S NOT MUCH to look at," Keith warned as he parked the car in his driveway, his tone endearing.

"That's all right," Treble assured him breathlessly. Her body still thrummed, not from the tremor of fireworks that had shaken the ground below but from the impact of Keith's periodic kisses throughout the night. She wasn't here to criticize his decorating choices.

He took her hand, guiding her over a sidewalk that was broken in several places. Then they were at his front door, and Keith slid his key in the lock. Treble took a deep breath, part of her still surprised that she was going through with this. She already knew how she would feel driving back to Atlanta, so why compound the inevitable ache?

He left her standing on the welcome mat as he braved the dark room to provide light for them. He'd leaned over a lamp, and the low-wattage bulb threw his chiseled profile into shadowed relief. Her heart flipped over beneath her breast, a somersault that left her giddy and distantly queasy at the same time.

Why compound the ache? The answers were so clear. *One,* because she'd never wanted another man like this. *Two,* because how much worse would that ache be if she didn't at least let them have these few cherished moments before she was gone? She'd regret leaving here without making love to this man, and it wasn't as if abstaining from tonight would make her not miss him later.

"You look sad," he said simply.

"No. Not sad. It's been a wonderful night."

He lifted a brow as he came toward her, neither of them commenting on the evening's inauspicious beginning. All that mattered to Treble now was how it would end.

"I probably should have warned you that the house isn't air-conditioned. At least not very well." His smile turned boyish. "But I was afraid you might change your mind about coming over. Can I get you anything?"

She clasped his hands. "Just you."

Their mouths met in a tangle of pent-up desire they'd both tried fruitlessly to deny. Maybe because they'd wanted this for days or because they were too aware their time left together was easily measured in days, their exploration of each other was bold, purposeful. Perhaps later there'd be time to enjoy each other slowly. Right now, neither had the patience.

A spiral of liquid heat unfurled within Treble, delirious sensations rolling through her as he trailed his kisses from her lips to her throat, into the vee of her blouse. His fingers were just ahead of him, skimming the buttons free of their holes and exposing the lace edging of her bra. Her breasts felt pleasantly heavy, full, ready to be freed to his touch. He pushed aside the front panels of her blouse, and the fabric slipped down over her arms and to the floor.

His own shirt wasn't as effortless to remove, but she made

up for any lack of finesse with her unabashed appreciation of the muscles in his chest. The man was as beautiful as he claimed her to be.

He ran his index finger over the lacy scalloping, tracing a straight line down over the silky cup. "Nice."

Her body tightened in response to the light touch. She hitched her thumb under a bra strap, her tone husky. "It's part of a matched set." Managing a deftness that surprised her, she unbuttoned her shorts and let them fall. Would another woman have been more modest, coy? *Pointless.* He'd seen her in a bikini for the past two days, and coyness wouldn't have darkened his eyes to their current, aroused indigo shade.

Taking her by the hand, he led her into the bedroom. He didn't bother to turn on the light, but illumination spilled in from the living room. She only glimpsed fleeting impressions—quality furniture, walls that needed fresh paint, little personal decoration, but sheets that felt cool and soft against her sensitized skin as he lowered her to the mattress. His fingers had already found the clasp on her front-closure bra, and she arched up toward him as he kissed her breasts, drawing one nipple into his mouth and wringing a cry from the back of her throat. The way he touched her was far more intoxicating and potent than the wine they'd shared earlier.

By the time she pressed one hand against his shoulder and whispered for him to roll back, she'd ceased thinking in words, only in scents and tastes and sensations, free-form and inarticulate. She straddled him, helping him roll the condom down, poised to take him inside her body. He was already in her heart.

She sank down slowly, by excruciating degrees, until he filled her. *"Oh."*

"Treble." He cupped her face, lifting up to kiss her before falling back to the pillow, his hands moving to her hips. He held on to her, stroking her, letting her set the pace.

Riotous, rapturous need coiled deep inside her, tightening

until her movements became less controlled, frantic. Keith rolled with her, braced above her, his eyes locked with hers as pleasure burst within her. She let her eyes close then, forgetting to breathe, offering her body up to his as he continued to move, finding his own pleasure. She pulled him down on her, holding him tightly.

At first his attempted words were little more than pants, but he managed to get out a short sentence. "I'll squash you."

"Impossible. I'm floating." She was weightless, limp with satisfaction. Either she drifted to sleep or her mind simply wandered in perfect relaxation.

Keith stirred long moments later. "Thirsty?"

"Water, yes," she said gratefully. By the time he returned, she'd realized she was also sticky with perspiration. Before the memorable interlude in his bed, she'd spent most of the day outside. "Can I ask you a favor?"

He smiled. "Right about now, you could probably ask me for anything."

"Use of your shower?" She set the water glass down next to the alarm clock on the nightstand. "You could join me."

"That's not a 'favor,' that's you granting wishes."

He warned that the water took a few minutes to get hot, but they managed to stay pleasantly occupied until tufts of steam billowed over the glass door of the shower stall. He reached in to adjust the temperature, then stood back to let her precede him.

"Ladies first."

"Very chivalrous."

"Not particularly. I was admiring your butt." He stood behind her, lifting her hair atop her head with one hand and leaning down to kiss her neck. At the last minute, when she could feel his breath warming her skin, he froze. "You have a *tattoo?*"

It wasn't easily visible, often mingling with dark tendrils even when she wore her hair up. But it was there, below the base of her skull. "It's a treble clef."

He traced the graceful scrolling curves of the symbol as water cascaded down over them. "I can't believe I just made love to a woman with a tattoo."

She stiffened. "Is that a problem?"

"Not remotely. It's just that I was thinking I'd gotten a pretty good look at your body." He slid his hands down over her rib cage as he caught her earlobe between his teeth. "You have any more surprises?"

"None that I can think of…but feel free to take your time looking."

Chapter Fifteen

A jarring sound pulled Treble from the peaceful cocoon of sleep. She awoke in stages of confusion, noting that her surroundings were dark and unfamiliar. The night came back to her in a hazy flood of images and sensual memories. Where was Keith?

"It's just the phone," he said quietly. Now that she had an idea of where to look for him, she saw him silhouetted in the moonlight, tugging on a pair of jeans, his smile rueful. "I told you doctors get calls at strange hours."

She sat up, pulling the sheet around her and watching him head into the lamp-lit living room. The ringing stopped immediately. There was always something ominous about late-night phone calls. Maybe when Keith returned, he'd tell her it was just a wrong number and they could make love again, use the most of their hours togeth—

"Treble?" He hastened back to her, his demeanor so apologetic that she knew bad news was imminent. "It's for you."

Even before she'd said hello into the receiver, Keith busied himself gathering up her discarded clothes. An unpleasant buzzing filled her head, and dread choked her.

"Treble? This is Harrison. Charity's being prepped for the operating room and Bill's with her. They wanted me to find you. We left a voice mail on your cell phone."

It was on, but she must have slept through the ring. Or had

she been in the shower with Keith? Shame tweaked her. It was as if everything he'd ever said about her was true. Charity had needed her, and she'd been...

"Is she okay?" Treble found her voice. "The baby?"

"She woke up bleeding heavily, so Bill rushed her to the hospital. The doctors say she's in pre-term labor. They're going to go ahead and do a C-section. Keith can get you here?"

Squeezing the phone in bloodless fingers, she nodded.

"Treble?"

"Y-yes. We're on the way."

Keith had finished lacing up his sneakers and was carrying her blouse and shorts toward her. He stopped short. "You're shivering. Here, wait."

She didn't turn her head, still staring at the disconnected phone as if it might offer more information, reassurance, but she heard the muted squeak of a drawer sliding open.

"Wear this." He handed her a sweatshirt, which she pulled over her head.

The fabric swallowed her, the fleecy warmth distantly comforting. Her body felt better, but inside she felt untouchably cold.

"Let's get you to the hospital." He helped her stand.

He was good in a crisis, she noted inanely. Right. Of course he was. He was a doctor, he'd seen plenty of crises. Hell, he'd endured several of his own. "Do you think she'll be okay?"

"The baby's nearly full-term," he said calmingly. "Charity's safely at the hospital, where they're all doing what's best for her. By the time we get you there, you'll probably be an aunt."

She tried to visualize Charity, smiling and holding a baby, the only palatable conclusion. During the drive, time stopped meaning anything, passing in slow drip-drops of impatient worry and frustration that they couldn't safely go any faster, then moving in a mindless blur as Treble sat numbly in the passenger seat. Finally, they were there, and Keith was ushering her inside the too-bright maternity ward. It was the middle of the night, technically morning, when the world should be asleep and peaceful, but the activity here was restless. Nurses passing with clipboards and medications, pregnant women breathing whew-whoo-whew in wheelchairs, family members pacing or demanding answers or merely handing each other cups of coffee. Treble registered her surroundings in fits and starts, barely recalling the parking lot but focusing on strange specifics like the yellow cartoon kitty cats one nurse wore on her scrubs.

They found Harrison in a small alcove on an operating floor. He truly looked aged enough to be a grandfather. He didn't get up from the blue padded chair when he saw them approach. "No news yet," he told them. His eyes flicked to Treble's, then away.

How must he view the scene? In her haste to get here, she hadn't even bothered with a bra under the thick sweatshirt. She'd rolled up the sleeves, but the shirt itself fell practically to the hem of her shorts. The outfit doubtless looked ridiculous with her sandals. The distorted reflection in the nearby vending machine reminded her that she hadn't combed her hair after the shower earlier. Tangled strands fell across her face, but she brushed them away impatiently. Given the hour, she couldn't possibly be the only person who'd just rolled out of bed.

But it was unfortunate that she stood in front of her stepfather having just rolled out of Keith's bed. Before Keith had been her lover, he'd been Harrison's friend, and his action probably seemed like a defection to the older man. One she'd caused.

This was a small area—Harrison had chosen to be apart from the larger waiting lounge with its magazines and corner television and numerous chairs—and Treble eschewed the only remaining chairs, which were to her stepfather's left and right. Were she and Keith supposed to sit on either side of the man? Instead, she sagged against Keith, grateful for the arm he wrapped around her.

"Treble!" Bill's voice down the corridor reenergized her, and she straightened, whipping her head around to search his expression. He had circles under his eyes, but the eyes themselves were bright with excitement. "I'm a dad. Harrison, you're a granddad! Brooke Elisabeth Sumner is five pounds, six ounces. Missed being a Fourth of July baby by a few hours, so it's just as well that we didn't go with the name Liberty. She's small but beautiful. Like her mom."

"And Charity?" Treble and Harrison asked in unison.

"She's fine. Tired. They're stitching her up now, but she hung in there. She was real—" Bill's voice broke, and Keith clapped him on the shoulder. They all waited, stranded in myriad emotional reactions to the events of the night. Bill pulled himself together, then looked at Treble and Harrison. "Charity was so worried that maybe she should have stayed home today, like this happened because she went to see fireworks. But the doctor said it could have just as easily happened if she'd stayed home in bed all day. It was just time. Nothing *caused* this."

Treble swallowed, thinking about how Charity had sounded upset on the phone earlier and the chaos that seemed to plague Treble's family when she was around them. "Thank you," she told her brother-in-law. For the first time since the phone rang, she felt a smile blossom on her face. "And congratulations."

SHE'D CONVINCED Keith that he should go home and get at least another hour of sleep—he'd have patients tomorrow that needed him, and after glimpsing her absolutely gorgeous, albeit bald and wrinkly, niece, Treble's admiration for doctors ran deeper than ever.

"You're sure you don't want to ride back with me?" he'd asked.

Even though she knew logically that she wasn't currently needed here—and could come back when Charity and Brooke were awake—she couldn't bring herself to leave just yet. "I want to stay. I know it's stupid sitting out here, but I want to stay for just a while longer."

"I'll take her home," Harrison had said.

When she'd glanced toward him, he'd returned her stare stoically, giving nothing away. Once they were all agreed, Keith pressed a platonic kiss to her forehead and left. The hospital cafeteria started serving breakfast at five, and Bill joined them there, too keyed up to sleep in the uncomfortable chair at his wife's bedside. He hadn't wanted to be away from her long, and by five thirty, Treble was leaving the hospital with her stepfather.

"Thank you for calling me tonight," she said once they were in the car, even though she knew he'd only been acting on Charity's behalf.

"I'm just glad I was able to track you down." His gaze flicked to her. "That didn't…I meant nothing derogatory. I know how much Charity wanted you to be there to see the baby."

She'd avoided the man for years, and it certainly hadn't improved their relationship. Why not finally meet trouble head-on? "It bothers you that I was with Keith?"

"He's a good man. He deserves to be happy."

"Deserves better than me, you mean."

"Dammit, girl. I know I'm a pigheaded old coot—Joan's certainly repeated it ad nauseam, but it doesn't help that you're always looking for a fight! I meant what I said. Keith deserves to be happy. *You* deserve to be happy. I'm not trying to judge—"

She snorted. "You've always seemed more than willing to judge me, even when your view of the situation was skewed. Years ago, at the dairy, just yesterday at the dunking booth."

"I apologize for losing my temper yesterday. Joan read me the riot act. For years, she tried to tell me I wasn't handling the situation with you right, but I thought she was too softhearted. Lately Charity's been taking little jabs, too, and then even Keith who barely kn—" He broke off, realizing that obviously Keith knew her quite well in some respects.

Treble, torn between wanting to defend her burgeoning relationship with the doctor and knowing that relationship didn't actually have a future, merely stared out the window at the thin fingers of light slowly starting to reach across the landscape.

Harrison sighed. "It's a dangerous thing, falling for someone. Not everyone gets the fairy-tale ending, though I like to think Bill and Charity will prove an exception."

"Charity always was exceptional," Treble agreed with a tired smile.

A look of affection passed over his face at the mention of his daughter, but the worry he'd been expressing quickly returned. "I'm sorry I didn't do whatever it was I needed to do differently for you. When Meg died, I felt like part of me was yanked out. The best part."

She could identify with his grief, but it didn't change the fact that she'd needed him. No matter how forgiving she *wanted* to be, years of resentment didn't magically melt away.

"*My* loss was unavoidable," he continued. "Nothing I could have done, no check I could have written, could have changed the outcome of your mother's car crash. But now I know how painful it is to lose someone who has your heart. I'd hate for you or Keith to feel that pain in another week. You've both already had to say goodbye to important people in your lives."

His tone was so melancholy, the loss he'd experienced still evident. Did he regret falling in love with his late wife? Treble could have asked, but she was afraid to hear the answer. Instead, she turned the topic from the past to the future. "You said…if you could have done things differently with me? Do them differently with Brooke. I know how important Breckfield Dairy is to this family and this town, but slow down a little. Look at your priorities and enjoy your granddaughter."

He said nothing for so long that she almost didn't hear his, "Okay." It was slow and rusty, like hinges on a door that hadn't been opened in years.

All in all, fairly impressive for their very first talk.

HAVING NOW ATTENDED his first ever Days of Joy festival, Keith could definitely say the week had been memorable. It was hard to believe that now, it was over. Or would be after to-night's dance.

A portable dance floor that looked like wood but wasn't took up most of the space inside the large, elegant tent. Or maybe *canopy* was a more accurate term, he thought. This made him think more of wedding receptions than the circus, not that he'd attended either in the past few years. To the side of the floor were tables, many with citronella candles in the center. Box fans blew at each entrance, creating a nice breeze, and strands of tiny lights had been woven throughout the interior. The festival dance committee had done a lovely job.

Keith particularly approved of their choice in DJs.

When he'd walked in, Treble had been composing an on-the-spot poem to congratulate a couple on their thirtieth anniversary, then she'd reminded everyone that she took requests. But by the time he reached the table set up with her CDs and equipment, she was no longer addressing the crowd, merely humming with the music, her body swaying. There was a chair behind the table, but she'd chosen to stand.

"Hi," he told her, wondering if she could tell, even from that short word, how much he'd missed her. They'd seen each other in passing since he dropped her off at the hospital in the predawn hours of Thursday morning, but they hadn't had more than five or ten minutes alone. Most of their conversation had been about the new mommy and her beautiful baby, very little had been spared to reference what had happened between Keith and Treble. Absolutely nothing had been said about when she would leave.

She smiled. "Hi, stranger."

"I'm glad you decided to come tonight. With Charity still at the hospital, I thought you might change your mind."

"It was Charity who convinced me to come. That room is tiny, and there's nothing they really need me for. I just like to hold Brooke."

"Dr. Whalen still thinks they'll go home on Monday?"

Treble hesitated, then nodded. When she spoke, her voice was too high, too thin. Full of false cheer. "Then the new family will be back home, and I'll just be underfoot during their bonding time."

A bright edge of panic flared within him, even though he'd known this was coming. "Actually, I'm sure they'd appreciate the help with the new baby."

"Maybe, but my landlord would also appreciate rent. And I'd appreciate the station not giving my job to whatever great new talent has been filling in for me." She wouldn't meet his eyes. "It's time for me to go, Keith."

Keith. It made him think of the way she'd said his name in the shower, her body soapy and sweaty and clinging to his, her voice throaty with sensual bliss. Reluctantly, he blinked the image away.

"Hey, you two!" Joan McMillan joined them, grinning with the energy of a much younger woman. "Treble, you're doing such a great job tonight. I knew you would! You ever want a job livening up radio broadcasts around Joyous, you give Bud Petro a call. Now, can I request something slow and outdated for the golden oldies among the crowd? You'll never believe who agreed to dance with me."

Treble and Keith both followed her sly gaze, and Keith saw Harrison Breckfield, overdressed in a button-down shirt and navy blazer. The man raised one hand, offering them all a nervous wave. With a laugh, Keith bent to kiss Joan's cheek.

The woman beamed. "My, whatever on earth was that for?"

"Because I think you're good for him," Keith said. He knew Harrison had been alone a long time and on some level found that preferable, but even though this was just a dance and nothing more, Keith thought Joan McMillan might be just what the old man's heart needed. Besides—he stole another glance at Treble, who was smiling at her stepfather—one never could tell what would come of a simple dance.

"What about you?" he asked, when Joan had returned to

Harrison's side. "Can you break long enough for a turn around the floor?"

Treble sighed. "I should stay here. But I'm glad to see so many people dancing tonight. Look…"

He did as directed, not sure why she was grinning so broadly at the sight of Lola Ann and Devin Carter walking toward the floor. Keith was more concerned with Dinah Perkins, who'd just edged into his line of vision, along with her friend Fawn.

"Okay, now you *have* to dance with me," he pleaded. "I'm being stalked. Every time I turned around at the festival, Dinah was there, staring at me, asking all kinds of weird questions." She'd been wild-eyed and breathy, reminding him of a college kid he'd seen once who'd accidentally doubled the dosage of her already strong prescription.

Sure enough, here came Dinah and Fawn, although the latter hung back at the last minute so that her friend could talk to Keith.

"You look nice," the blonde began. "The black shirt is great on you."

"Thank you." Then she asked about his favorite color, volunteering that hers was green, and he wondered if there would be a quiz later. Treble, he noted, was no help at all. She'd ducked her head and seemed to be making studious inventory of the available music. It wasn't until Dinah drifted back into the crowd that he realized Treble's shoulders were shaking with silent laughter.

"Let me in on the joke?" he asked.

"It's my fault." She glanced up, her eyes dancing merrily. "The random questions and the way she keeps trying to hold your gaze? I gave some advice at Charity's shower on, um, how to catch a man's attention."

"You told her to stalk me?"

"Of course not. She wasn't even there. I was talking to Lola Ann, but Fawn was there. I think she passed along my suggestions, but something got lost in translation."

"Well, dance with me. Help me show the interested ladies of

Joyous that I'm off the market." The cajoling statement was out of his mouth before he could take it back.

Treble froze.

Damn. He wanted to hold her, not scare her away. But it seemed as though the more he tried to pull her to him, savor the last of their time together, the more she distanced herself with frequently impersonal smiles and little reminders that her home was in Atlanta.

"Off the market?" she repeated neutrally.

If it were up to him, yes. He'd lived in that house for six months and the night he'd spent in it with her was the first time it had truly felt like home. Charity had been right all this time about something missing from his life, only it had been Charity's sister who'd finally helped him see it. He loved laughing with Treble, dancing with her, arguing with her, telling her about his patients, telling her about his past—something he'd never been very comfortable discussing, but she had enough baggage of her own to understand. Whereas so many here saw him as Doc Caldwell, which in a way was as much a persona as her radio personality, she knew Keith.

"For tonight, at least," he evaded, "there's only one woman I'm interested in."

"I can't." She swallowed, making her tone more casual. "I can't be your date tonight. I'm working. You should ask Ronnie to dance. She looks lovely and is standing alone—she'll protect you from Dinah."

Nobody there would have minded if Treble excused herself from behind the DJ table and danced one song with him, and they both knew that. Still, he pressed. "What about after the dance? Could I see you then?"

For a moment, he didn't think she'd meet his gaze, but then she did, looking straight into his eyes. Despite the resolve she projected, he saw the wistful regret, the longing, in those dark depths. "I have packing to do."

"I…should let you get back to work then." Somewhat blindly, he stumbled toward Ronnie, his head and heart reeling. He wound up dancing with the mechanic three times that night, waltzed with Joan and Heather Lynn Jacob once each—Heather Lynn seemed delighted by her husband's scowl, even though the man had said he didn't mind her dancing with the doc—and even let Velma Hoskins show him a few moves. But while he tried his best to be good company for the people of Joyous, his focus was elsewhere.

Watching Harrison and Joan talking in a corner and Rich Danner cradle a mug of coffee in his hands, Keith smiled, a bittersweet moment. Now that Treble had come to town, would Joyous ever be quite the same?

Would he?

The funny thing was, he didn't want to be the same man he'd been before he met Treble James. And he'd tell her that if he thought it would make a difference…or if he thought she'd want to hear it.

Chapter Sixteen

It had been easier this way, Treble thought, leaving from the hospital with its bustle and sterilized rooms instead of saying goodbye at Charity's place, where she'd grown closer to her sister than she'd expected. They'd dutifully loved each other over the years, but she thought they had a better understanding of each other now.

Charity sniffled, propped upright in her hospital bed and looking rumpled but healthy in the robe Bill had brought her from home, Brooke sleeping in her arms. "You really have to go?"

Treble's laugh was a raw scrape against the inside of her throat. "If I don't now, I might never."

Charity met her eyes. "Would that be so bad? Honestly? If you think Brooke's adorable now, just wait until she stops sleeping and crying for fourteen hours out of the day. And instead of buying some house in Atlanta, you could build exactly what you want here. The family owns a ton of land. You're part of the family. Little radio stations out in these parts would probably love to have someone with your exp—"

"Sweetheart," Bill interrupted softly from the cramped chair that had served as his bed since Brooke was born. Treble stayed here during the day so that he could go home and stretch out on an actual bed, but by this time tomorrow, they'd all be back home.

"Was I babbling?" his wife asked.

He smiled. "Why don't you let me take the baby so Treble can give you a hug?"

Though her emotions were running fierce, Treble kept the hug gentle. Charity said the incision still hurt when she laughed or sneezed or moved very fast.

"You are going to make a *great* mother," Treble whispered. "You're intuitive. You've been right about so many things. Brooke is blessed to have a mom like you."

"And an aunt like you. Promise me you'll come visit."

"Cross my heart." Joyous was no longer a town of ghosts. Treble found she could even be in a room with Harrison without all the old phantom hurt and blame and mutual anger flaring to life.

No, the only thing that would haunt her now was the memory of Keith Caldwell. Would it be difficult to avoid him on her much shorter visits to Joyous in the future? If she could go back and do things differently, would she have avoided him on this trip? She hadn't realized it was possible to give your heart so completely to someone in such a relatively short period of time.

Bill looped one solid arm around her shoulders, pulling her into a brief hug that included the baby. "Drive careful."

"I will. You take care of your two girls," she said.

"That's what I'm here for." His easy acceptance of that role—provider, protector, emotional support—reminding her again of Keith. Two good-hearted men who would never intentionally disappoint or abandon.

But there were hundreds of ways to let someone down or hurt them unintentionally, and she needed to get a grip. It was getting to where even the cabinet of medical supplies could remind her of Keith, for crying out loud. *Well, he* is *a doctor.*

"If you wanted to stay just a little longer," Charity said, "Dad was planning to stop by."

"That's okay. He came over to your house early this morning to say goodbye." Before his traditional Sunday brunch with

Keith, she assumed. She hadn't asked. If it hurt this much to *think* his name, she knew she wasn't ready to say it.

In less than half an hour, she was on the road, on her way home. *Home.* Her throat tightened, and she turned up the speaker volume, hoping the CD she'd popped in could blast away her blues. It would be good to be back in her apartment. Her small apartment with no view of the stars amid downtown lights and smog, her lonely apartment where there was no ice cream in the refrigerator for late-night snacking or even a cat for company.

So buy some ice cream. Get a cat. She'd call Alana when she got home, catch up...although her friend was more than likely at Greg's.

Absorbed in her thoughts, Treble didn't notice the pickup truck gaining speed on the road behind her until the horn blared. She jumped, her gaze shooting to her rearview mirror. *Keith?* Her heart pounded, absurdly happy, although she tried to tell herself some of it was the adrenaline of him startling her. She pulled over to the wide, grassy shoulder, her sense of irony prompting a chuckle at the bucolic scenery. This wasn't where they'd first met, but it looked similar enough. She unfastened her seat belt, but hadn't yet climbed out of her car when he slammed his own door and approached at a jog.

Her eyes devoured him. He looked good...but furious. Standing in the wedge of space between her open door and the vehicle itself, he ducked his head toward her, eyes blazing.

"You *left* without saying *goodbye*," he admonished, his tone accusatory and unforgiving. "If Harrison hadn't mentioned he'd seen you this morning, I wouldn't have even caught you in time. You weren't going to tell me?"

She swallowed. "I told you last night. At the dance. I didn't think there was anything else to say—you knew I was leaving."

"Soon!" He straightened, threw his hands up. "I knew you were leaving soon, but I didn't realize you were dashing out of town first thing this morning."

"Well. Then…" She swallowed again. Darn him for chasing her down; she'd tried to spare them this kind of scene. "I suppose it's fortuitous Harrison mentioned I was headed out." Darn *him,* too, for that matter. "Now we have a chance to exchange formal goodbyes."

"I don't want to." Keith's expression was mutinous. Under other circumstances, she would have smiled. Who looked like the rebel now?

"Then why are you here?" she asked tiredly.

"Because we need to talk. I would have driven all the way to Atlanta if I had to, but there's something I need to tell you. I love you, Treble."

Her heart stopped. "Wh-what?" He'd seemed so angry, so contemptuous of the way she was running off, that the last thing she'd expected was a declaration like that.

"You heard me. I love you." He crouched next to her. "You needed to know."

Why? So she could miss him even more? This conversation was a mistake, just something for them to regret later. *Really?* The knowing voice in her head sounded a little like Charity's. *Do you regret making love to him?* No, she didn't. She'd felt too vulnerable to repeat the experience before leaving town, but she wouldn't undo it for anything in the world.

"I love you, too." She was probably a fool for telling him, but better an honest fool than a gutless coward.

He trapped her face in his hands then, kissing her soundly, repeating with his actions what he'd already put into words. She tasted tears and realized she was crying even as she kissed him back.

"Now what?" she asked when they stopped momentarily, their foreheads resting together.

"Now…I look for a job as a doctor in some suburb outside Atlanta," he improvised.

Oh, my God. "You're kidding? You wouldn't seriously do that?" She sat up, shaken to the core that he would even consider uprooting himself for her. "Keith, you haven't known me a full month. You can't *move*."

His gaze was somber. "Life is short. You and I have both unexpectedly lost people we loved. So, I could spend the next few months in Joyous, being miserable without you and writing thoughtful lists with Pro and Con columns, or…I could be with you."

"You make it sound simple."

"Geography's not the hard part. It's all the other pieces of relationships that will get complicated."

"Like the fighting over who gets to sleep on which side of the bed?"

He laughed. "Of course not. *I* get the left side."

She bit her lip. "Keith, people need you here. I'm sure there are thousands of doctors in all the suburbs surrounding metro Atlanta. And you love Joyous."

"I do. But I didn't realize that when I came here, I was looking for something. I found a hint of it when Harrison and Charity befriended me. I got more of it when the people in this town began to slowly make me one of their own. But where I really discovered it—discovered myself—is with you. I want to be with you, Treble."

She wanted that, too, her heart full to bursting even though her head told her they were both crazy. But life was short, precious, and even more precious was finding a person who made you feel like this, saw your flaws and accepted you anyway. Stood up for you, stood beside you, helped you face your fears and demons and become a better person for it.

"Let's be together here," she said impulsively. "In Joyous." Never before had that name seemed so appropriate.

He recoiled, searching her face. "You can't be serious?"

"I've worked so hard to create my own community on-air, a family of sorts, but I already have one." She grinned. "Maybe *this* community could use a little shaking up."

He took her hand, standing and tugged her out of the car and into his arms. "This community would be lucky to have you."

His lips teased hers, coaxing arousal and optimism, the belief that sometimes people *did* get the fairy-tale ending, if they were willing to reach for what they wanted and work hard to keep it.

"Mmm." She sighed against his mouth, feeling it was only fair to warn him between kisses, "I can be difficult, stubborn sometimes…"

He nipped her bottom lip. "Just sometimes?"

"And impatient with small-town propriety. I could cause… trouble for you, even without…meaning—"

He deepened the kiss just long enough to silence her disclaimers. Then, when she'd completely forgotten what she was saying anyway, he pulled away and winked at her. "A little trouble is exactly what was missing from my life."

She grinned. "Well, then I'm your woman."

"That's what I've been trying to tell you." He angled in for another kiss, this one promising to be hot enough to scandalize anyone driving by, but she supposed they'd have to get used to it. Trouble was here to stay.

* * * * *

**Every Life Has More
Than One Chapter**™

Award-winning author Stevi Mittman delivers another hys-
terical mystery, featuring Teddi Bayer, an irrepressible
heroine, and her to-die-for hero, Detective Drew Scoones.
After all, life on Long Island can be murder!

*Turn the page for a sneak peek
at the warm and funny fourth book,
WHOSE NUMBER IS UP, ANYWAY?,
in the Teddi Bayer series,
by STEVI MITTMAN.
On sale August 7*

"Before redecorating a room, I always advise my clients
to empty it of everything but one chair. Then I suggest they
move that chair from place to place, sitting in it, until the
placement feels right. Trust your instincts when deciding
on furniture placement. Your room should "feel right."

—TipsFromTeddi.com

GUT feelings. You know, that gnawing in the pit of your
stomach that warns you that you are about to do the absolute stu-
pidest thing you could do? Something that will ruin life as you
know it?

I've got one now, standing at the butcher counter in King
Kullen, the grocery store in the same strip mall as L.I. Lanes, the
bowling alley cum billiard parlor I'm in the process of redecorating for its "Grand Opening."

I realize being in the wrong supermarket probably doesn't
sound exactly dire to you, but you aren't the one buying your
father a brisket at a store your mother will somehow know isn't
Waldbaum's.

And then, June Bayer isn't your mother.

The woman behind the counter has agreed to go into the
freezer to find a brisket for me, since there aren't any in the
case.
There are packages of pork tenderloin, piles of spare ribs and
rolls of sausage, but no briskets.

Warning Number Two, right? I should be so out of here.

But no, I'm still in the same spot when she comes back out, brisketless, her face ashen. She opens her mouth as if she is going to scream, but only a gurgle comes out.

And then she pinballs out from behind the counter, knocking bottles of Peter Luger Steak Sauce to the floor on her way, now hitting the tower of cans at the end of the prepared foods aisle and sending them sprawling, now making her way down the aisle, careening from side to side as she goes.

Finally, from a distance, I hear her shout, "He's deeeeeeaaaad! Joey's deeeeeaaaad."

My first thought is *You should always trust your gut*.

My second thought is that now, somehow, my mother will know I was in King Kullen. For weeks I will have to hear "What did you expect?" as though whenever you go to King Kullen someone turns up dead. And if the detective investigating the case turns out to be Detective Drew Scoones…well, I'll never hear the end of that from her, either.

She still suspects I murdered the guy who was found dead on my doorstep last Halloween just to get Drew back into my life.

Several people head for the butcher's freezer and I position myself to block them. If there's one thing I've learned from finding people dead—and the guy on my doorstep wasn't the first one—it's that the police get very testy when you mess with their murder scenes.

"You can't go in there until the police get here," I say, stationing myself at the end of the butcher's counter and in front of the Employees Only door, acting as if I'm some sort of authority. "You'll contaminate the evidence if it turns out to be murder."

Shouts and chaos. You'd think I'd know better than to throw the word *murder* around. Cell phones are flipping open and tongues are wagging.

I amend my statement quickly. "Which, of course, it probably isn't. Murder, I mean. People die all the time, and it's not always in hospitals or their own beds, or…" I babble when I'm nervous, and the idea of someone dead on the other side of the freezer door makes me very nervous.

So does the idea of seeing Drew Scoones again. Drew and I have this on-again, off-again sort of thing…that I kind of turned off.

Who knew he'd take it so personally when he tried to get serious and I responded by saying we could talk about *us* tomorrow—and then caught a plane to my parents' condo in Boca the next day? In July. In the middle of a job.

For some crazy reason, he took that to mean that I was avoiding him and the subject of *us*.

That was three months ago. I haven't seen him since.

The manager, who identifies himself and points to his name-plate in case I don't believe him, says he has to go into *his cooler*. "Maybe Joey's not dead," he says. "Maybe he can be saved, and you're letting him die in there. Did you ever think of that?"

In fact, I hadn't. But I had thought that the murderer might try to go back in to make sure his tracks were covered, so I say that I will go in and check.

Which means that the manager and I couple up and go in together while everyone pushes against the doorway to peer in, erasing any chance of finding clean prints on that Employees Only door.

I expect to find carcasses of dead animals hanging from hooks, and maybe Joey hanging from one, too. I think it's going to be very creepy and I steel myself, only to find a rather benign series of shelves with large slabs of meat laid out carefully on them, along with boxes and boxes marked simply Chicken.

Nothing scary here, unless you count the body of a middle-aged man with graying hair sprawled faceup on the floor. His eyes are wide open and unblinking. His shirt is stiff. His pants are stiff. His body is stiff. And his expression, you should forgive the pun—is frozen. Bill-the-manager crosses himself and stands mute while I pronounce the guy dead in a sort of *happy now?* tone.

"We should not be in here," I say, and he nods his head em-phatically and helps me push people out of the doorway just in time to hear the police sirens and see the cop cars pull up outside the big store windows.

Bobbie Lyons, my partner in Teddi Bayer Interior Designs (and also my neighbor, my best friend and my private fashion police), and Mark, our carpenter (and my dogsitter, confidant, and ego booster), rush in from next door. They beat the cops by a half step and shout out my name. People point in my direction.

After all the publicity that followed the unfortunate incident during which I shot my ex-husband, Rio Gallo, and then the subsequent murder of my first client—which I solved, I might add— it seems like the whole world, or at least all of Long Island, knows who I am.

Mark asks if I'm all right. (Did I remember to mention that the man is drop-dead-gorgeous-but-a-decade-too-young-for-me- yet-too-old-for-my-daughter-thank-god?) I don't get a chance to answer him because the police are quickly closing in on the store manager and me.

"The woman—" I begin telling the police. Then I have to pause for the manager to fill in her name, which he does: *Fran*.

I continue. "Right. Fran. Fran went into the freezer to get a brisket. A moment later she came out and screamed that Joey was dead. So I'd say she was the one who discovered the body."

"And you are…?" the cop asks me. It comes out a bit like who do I *think* I am, rather than who am I really?

"An innocent bystander," Bobbie, hair perfect, makeup just right, says, carefully placing her body between the cop and me.

"And she was just leaving," Mark adds. They each take one of my arms.

Fran comes into the inner circle surrounding the cops. In case it isn't obvious from the hairnet and bloodstained white apron with Fran embroidered on it, I explain that she was the butcher who was going for the brisket. Mark and Bobbie take that as a signal that I've done my job and they can now get me out of there. They twist around, with me in the middle, as if we're a Rockettes line, until we are facing away from the butcher counter. They've managed to propel me a few steps toward the exit when disaster—in the form of a Mazda RX7 pulling up at the loading curb—strikes.

Mark's grip on my arm tightens like a vise. "Too late," he says.

Bobbie's expletive is unprintable. "Maybe there's a back door," she suggests, but Mark is right. It's too late.

I've laid my eyes on Detective Scoones. And while my gut is trying to warn me that my heart shouldn't go there, regions farther south are melting at just the sight of him.

"Walk," Bobbie orders me.

And I try to. Really.

Walk, I tell my feet. *Just put one foot in front of the other.*

I can do this because I know, in my heart of hearts, that if Drew Scoones was still interested in me, he'd have gotten in touch with me after I returned from Boca. And he didn't.

Since he's a detective, Drew doesn't have to wear one of those dark blue Nassau County Police uniforms. Instead, he's got on jeans, a tight-fitting T-shirt and a tweedy sports jacket. If you think that sounds good, you should see him. Chiseled features, cleft chin, brown hair that's naturally a little sandy in the front, a smile that…well, that doesn't matter. He isn't smiling now.

He walks up to me, tucks his sunglasses into his breast pocket and looks me over from head to toe.

"Well, if it isn't Miss Cut and Run," he says. "Aren't you supposed to be somewhere in Florida or something?" He looks at Mark accusingly, as if he was covering for me when he told Drew I was gone.

"Detective Scoones?" one of the uniforms says. "The stiff's in the cooler and the woman who found him is over there." He jerks his head in Fran's direction.

Drew continues to stare at me.

You know how when you were young, your mother always told you to wear clean underwear in case you were in an accident? And how, a little farther on, she told you not to go out in hair rollers because you never knew who you might see—or who might see you? And how now your best friend says she wouldn't be caught dead without makeup and suggests you shouldn't either?

Okay, today, *finally,* in my overalls and Converse sneakers, I get it.

I brush my hair out of my eyes. "Well, I'm back," I say. As if he hasn't known my exact whereabouts. The man is a detective, for heaven's sake. "Been back awhile."

Bobbie has watched the exchange and apparently decided she's given Drew all the time he deserves. "And we've got work to do, so…" she says, grabbing my arm and giving Drew a little two-fingered wave goodbye.

As I back up a foot or two, the store manager sees his chance and places himself in front of Drew, trying to get his attention. Maybe what makes Drew such a good detective is his ability to focus.

Only what he's focusing on is me.

"Phone broken? Carrier pigeon died?" he asks me, taking in Fran, the manager, the meat counter and that Employees Only door, all without taking his eyes off me.

Mark tries to break the spell. "We've got work to do there, you've got work to do here, Scoones," Mark says to him, gesturing toward next door. "So it's back to the alley for us."

Drew's lip twitches. "You working the alley now?" he says.

"If you'd like to follow me," Bill-the-manager, clearly exasperated, says to Drew—who doesn't respond. It's as if waiting for my answer is all he has to do.

So, fine. "You knew I was back," I say.

The man has known my whereabouts every hour of the day for as long as I've known him. And my mother's not the only one who won't buy that he "just happened" to answer this particular call. In fact, I'm willing to bet my children's lunch money that he's taken every call within ten miles of my home since the day I got back.

And now he's gotten lucky.

"*You* could have called *me,*" I say.

"You're the one who said *tomorrow* for our talk and then flew the coop, chickie," he says. "I figured the ball was in your court."

"Detective?" the uniform says. "There's something you ought to see in here."

Drew gives me a look that amounts to *in or out?*

He could be talking about the investigation, or about our relationship.

Bobbie tries to steer me away. Mark's fists are balled. Drew waits me out, knowing I won't be able to resist what might be a murder investigation.

Finally he turns and heads for the cooler.

And, like a puppy dog, I follow.

Bobbie grabs the back of my shirt and pulls me to a halt.

"I'm just going to show him something," I say, yanking away.

"Yeah," Bobbie says, pointedly looking at the buttons on my blouse. The two at breast level have popped. "That's what I'm afraid of."

HARLEQUIN®

American R O M A N C E®

TEXAS LEGACIES: THE CARRIGANS

Get to the Heart of a Texas Family

WITH

THE RANCHER NEXT DOOR
by

Cathy Gillen Thacker

She'll Run The Ranch—And Her Life—Her Way!

On her alpaca ranch in Texas, Rebecca encounters
constant interference from Trevor McCabe, the
bossy rancher next door. Rebecca becomes very
friendly with Vince Owen, her other neighbor and
Trevor's archrival from college. Trevor's problem
is convincing Rebecca that he is on her side, and
aware of Vince's ulterior motives. But Trevor has
fallen for her in the process….

On sale July 2007

REQUEST YOUR FREE BOOKS!
2 FREE NOVELS PLUS 2
FREE GIFTS!

Heart, Home & Happiness!

HARLEQUIN®

American ROMANCE®

COMING NEXT MONTH

#1173 MOMMY FOR A MINUTE by Judy Christenberry
Dallas Duets

When Jack Mason came to renovate her apartment with his toddler in tow, Lauren McNabb fell for Ally—and the handsome Jack. But Jack didn't want "The Shark," as she was known in legal circles, around his child. Lauren was beautiful and, after years of being alone, kissing her felt like heaven. But could the workaholic be a mother…and a wife?

#1174 MITCH TAKES A WIFE by Ann Roth
To Wed, or Not To Wed

Fran Bishop, owner of the Oceanside B and B, has always wanted a husband and kids, but meeting men in the sleepy town of Cranberry, Oregon, isn't the easiest thing in the world. When longtime guest Mitch Matthews comes for his annual visit, Fran has no idea that their friendship is about to change—into something more permanent!

#1175 RYAN'S RENOVATION by Marin Thomas
The McKade Brothers

Brooding Ryan McKade had planned to complete his stint with a demolition company, thereby meeting his grandfather's requirement and assuring his inheritance, then be on his way. He sure as heck hadn't planned to fall for the company's secretary. Anna Nowakowski's cheery personality and trusting nature make him want to stay around longer. Except, then he'd have to reveal a few secrets—and would she still want him after he did?

#1176 GEORGIA ON HIS MIND by Ann DeFee

Win Whittaker, a top-level defense attorney from D.C., comes to Magnolia Bluffs, Georgia, on a bet. With only a hundred bucks in his pocket, he has to survive for a month. Which means he needs a job. It so happens that Kenni MacAllister's salon, Permanently Yours, has an opening for a shampoo girl. And that's how it all begins.…

www.eHarlequin.com

HARCNM0707